Praise for *The First Desire*

"Accomplished. . . . Reisman's sumptuous prose, and her canny knowledge of the corrosive ways an average family can come apart, make *The First Desire* a lovely, absorbing companion."

—*Entertainment Weekly* (editor's choice)

"Reisman's hypnotic prose makes her . . . characters live. And her sympathy and wealth of detail make the Cohens' world our own: specific, inescapably flawed, unpredictably meaningful and very, very real."

—*People*

"Only fiction can feel as real as this—and only in the right hands. . . . You needn't be from Buffalo to be swept away by *The First Desire*. You need only be from a family."

—*USA Today*

"A book of rhythms and reveries . . . rich in atmosphere. . . . *The First Desire* is a mystery story, left unsolved because the mystery is identity itself."

—*New York Times Book Review*

"Reisman's first novel is mesmerizing . . . . Reisman demonstrates a rare, poetic understanding of family dynamics . . . [and] writes with beauty and precise imagery . . . . This realism, subtly laced with tenderness and compassion, distinguishes a novel whose addictive embrace continues after the last page has been turned."

—*Publishers Weekly*

"A debut of luminous, distinctive quality . . . . This is a writer quietly taking her own bold course, and to travel with her as she does is a joy."

—*Boston Globe*

trompe l'oeil

trompe l'oeil

NANCY REISMAN

Tin House Books
Portland, Oregon & Brooklyn, New York

This is a work of fiction. Names, characters, businesses, places, and events are either the products of the author's imagination or used in a fictitious manner.

Published by Tin House Books, Portland, Oregon, and Brooklyn, New York

Distributed to the trade by Publishers Group West, 1700 Fourth St., Berkeley, CA 94710, www.pgw.com

Library of Congress Cataloging-in-Publication Data

Reisman, Nancy, 1961-
  Trompe l'oeil : a novel / Nancy Reisman. -- First U.S. edition.
    pages ; cm
  ISBN 978-1-941040-03-4 (softcover)
  1. Dysfunctional families--Fiction. 2. Loss (Psychology)--Fiction. 3. Marital conflict--Fiction. 4. Grief--Fiction. 5. Domestic fiction. I. Title.
  PS3568.E5135T76 2015
  813'.54--dc23
                        2014045523

First US edition 2015
Interior design by Diane Chonette
www.tinhouse.com
Printed in the USA

for Jeanne, Linda, and David
for Rick

& always, for Robert and Rena

PROLOGUE

ROME

Prospettiva
Francesco Borromini (c.1652-53)
PALAZZO SPADA

Rome, the first time: imagine wandering the historic center, the centuries crowding together, tourists in bright scarves speaking languages you can only glean, Vespas cutting fast around the clustered pedestrians. Turn a corner, another, onto a momentarily quiet street: here's one more residential palace, almost tucked away. A doorway, a hall, a courtyard where you'll find a scattering of fruit trees. And in the courtyard, in this city of arched passageways, yet another arched passageway opens before you. This one appears as an alluring question, suggesting elegant spaces beyond, perhaps a dinner table set for eight, a Persian carpet; or a music room, a piano, tall windows. From the courtyard, you approach. Four sets of double columns flank the arch, and repeating rows of blue squares cover the curved ceiling, echoing the floor's square tiles. At the passageway's far end, a statue—a male nude in centurion's headgear—rises in profile, one arm extended forward, one leg extended back, as if he is in motion through that other corridor. A good distance, it seems, from the courtyard's exterior arch. Beside the orange trees, the museum guide—stylish, middle-aged, lipsticked, a woman like many women in Rome—smokes a cigarette and says, *Yes, I will show you.* She gestures toward the passageway. The archway and second hall beckon, but she does not usher you in. Instead the woman hands you her cigarette and enters the passageway as you remain beside the trees. She steps forward, though as she moves, the archway ceiling seems to press down on her, the space itself shrinking, forcing her to stoop. A quick shock, an architectural joke: it's a foreshortened stage, the far end child-sized, the statue a miniature. The woman steps back out and reclaims the cigarette; and now, again, defying you and what you have just seen, the space reasserts itself as the long, high-ceilinged hall, the unfurling space a deft false promise. And—too—a wish?

I

HOUSE I

For the Murphys, there was always the house and the idea of the house, one relatively more stable than the other. From a distance it appeared camouflaged, a silver-gray box perched on stilts; beyond it the sea. To each side, other sea-weathered boxes, variations, one smaller, another with a single peak. The air smelled of salt, seaweed at low tide, smoke from charcoal grills or summer campfires on the next beach. From the deck and the beach below, one could see the Massachusetts coast stretching out and falling away, and in the space beyond, the sea, a vast openness, Massachusetts Bay merging with the Atlantic, the curving arm of Cape Cod reaching far to the southeast and the distant east, leaving the shoreline unprotected from Atlantic swells. A beautiful rough corner of the coast: a spit of land on which the town's early residents would never have built, instead choosing the far side of the harbor, or the inland cliffs. But the longer one lived there, the more permanent the house seemed, even as it rocked in the wind. The storms might slam in directly, but there were long stretches of beach to walk, where small stones mixed with sand, and the sea's blue, the mixed greens and grays, shifted with the light, going violet or sapphire or slate. Out unshuttered front windows, from the weather-beaten deck, from the east- and northeast-facing bedrooms, the sea appeared and reappeared.

Different years, different versions. First, the house had been a ramshackle summer outpost Nora and James had scrimped to buy from James's uncle, a place of ease despite or because of the off-plumb doorjambs and slanted floors and salt-worn wood. Outside stairs led up from the narrow street to the broad wrap-around deck, where in summer they drank cocktails with their friends; a windowed door opened into a large kitchen, drafty or breezy depending on the month. They renovated and win-terized; still, the wind was undeniable, and at night the house swayed lightly, enough so that water in a bowl might register the smallest of tides. Grand ill-tempered swans moved between the shelter of the brook-fed pond to the beach, crossing the narrow bridge of land down the road from the house and into the shallows, startlingly white against the sea.

At first, the Murphys spent summers there. Or Nora and the children did. James drove down for weekends and August vacation time. Theo and Katy were in grade school then, the youngest, Molly, still at home. From one year to the next, the scenes of leisure blurred into each other, as if contiguous with the preceding summers, all other seasons forgotten. Cousins and friends arrived for beach days and barbecues and drinks out on the deck. And then, the year James's promotion came through, they planned a shorter season in Blue Rock, to follow a two-week trip to Italy.

It was a slippery moment in their marriage, a crossroad. They had agreed to move from their small house in Newton to a place with more room, but only that. *Where to* remained vexed. James pushed for the wealthier cloistered suburbs; Nora missed Cambridge, where they'd once lived. In careful tones, they avoided the straining subtext, and when the Newton house sold, they put the furniture in storage, deferred. James had dreamed of travel; Nora had studied art. Rome would give them perspective. And there would be summer in Blue Rock, which from the vantage point of spring always seemed an endless unspooling of days, July a broad yellow plain with no apparent horizon beyond the brimming gold edges of August. For each of them, there was the pull of summer light over the sea, like something remembered from the deepest dream, a vast fluctuating gem that seemed to alter the rooms of the house, the narrow road, and, with luck, briefly, oneself, into their most vivid incarnations.

In June, just after the school year ended, the family flew from Logan Airport.

THE DIVIDE

In the moment of traveling to Rome, James was still a familiar, recognizable James, still visible to Nora as the ardent, playful man who'd once courted her. Still also perceptible the wash of hopeful anticipation from their early days in Cambridge, that first buoyancy; how brightly dappled their lives had seemed, rising, moving further and further from the respective narrow rooms in which they'd lived as children into a lofty expansive space. As if those days, that rising, promised to define all to follow. Even after Theo was born, and despite the late-night hours, cut-up naps, bleary days; he was nonetheless an easy baby, and Irish-fair, blue-eyed, quick to learn. For his first year, they marveled. On weekends, James played hiding games with Theo, stacked blocks to knock down, lifted Theo in flying sweeps. He'd carry a bundled Theo around the neighborhood repeating aloud the names of objects and colors (yellow, bird, truck). Sometimes Nora and James would take Theo to matinees, where he'd easily doze or drink from his bottle and watch the changing images on the screen. On clear weekdays, Nora tucked him into the stroller for visits to coffee shops, or carried him on the local bus to visit her mother in Somerville. If the afternoon was bitter or stormy, Theo would sit in her lap or lie beside her on a blanket for long stretches as she paged through books of art reproductions. She imagined no reason to want any life but her own.

And at first she recognized the emerging shadow as temporary disturbance—the move from Cambridge to Newton, the vicissitudes of another pregnancy—paired with hard losses, her mother's death, her father's decline. Yet the disturbance persisted and deepened, stranding her far from that early expanse. Soon her father, too, was gone. How had this transpired? It seemed she'd been choosing bananas; she'd been laundering sheets. Her mother called, frightened. Snow fell. She drove to a hospital; she iced cupcakes; she dressed Theo in blue pants. But now the cupcakes belonged in the Newton kitchen, and Katy had arrived. Where were her parents? Or for that matter James: she missed James, whose work claimed most of his time. Katy, a baby as beautiful as Theo had been—the eyes more hazel, and the hair a fine dark amber—cried far more often, slept lightly, quickly grew restless. An uncalm baby, a girl who took hours to quiet, responding only to Nora. Eventually Katy settled, happy to be walking, running, a fast-moving girl with strong limbs, impatient with books, impatient with small puzzles and quiet tasks, a girl who loved the multihued beach ball and the tub of blocks and strove to keep up with her brother. A girl of raw energy, as a toddler happiest on the playground or in the backyard snow, as long as Nora remained nearby.

If Nora glanced away, she'd turn back to find soup cans on the pantry floor, a carton of milk spilling over the edge of the table, Katy watching the cascade, or the blue bath beads—a gift forgotten on a low shelf—rolling and smashed in Katy's hands, one in Katy's mouth. *Spit it out. Katy, spit it out. Katy. Now.* And finally *Let's have a cookie instead* and Katy spitting out the shrinking blue globe, her face puckering with the bitter chemical taste, near to sobbing at Nora's frustration. *Sweetheart*, Nora would soothe. And then Katy would hug her hard, in what seemed a silent begging for forgiveness; Theo stood in the doorway watching, a red wooden train car held in midair. *Theo, cookies?* And Nora offered a hand to him as she carried Katy.

They were good children, lovely children—though when exactly had the moment shifted from *almost enough* to something less? She'd said yes and yes again to this life with James, yes to some deferrals—a gallery job? A little studio? James spoke earnestly of his career, what a step up could mean to him, to the family. Might she wait? Perhaps until the fall. Or soon after. How reasonable it had sounded; how quickly she'd agreed. Oblivious, it now seemed, as the status quo altered, the consequences multiplied. During summer in Blue Rock, the sense of possibility returned, though she could not say why. Their Newton neighborhood—lush old-growth trees, smaller well-tended houses—was friendly enough, occupied most of the week by women and younger children, the men commuting to the city or to companies on 128. Days at the park with local kids, Theo and Katy seemed happiest; or down the street at the neighbor Lydia's. Lydia owned a good swing set and a new sandbox, a three- and a five-year-old. She warned her girls, *Don't break your heads*, on the swings, her irreverence drawing Nora in. An appealing chaotic barn-red house in which the kids' toys were perpetually scattered, Lydia's surreal sketches pinned to the refrigerator alongside the girls' finger paintings, her larger paintings lining the halls. Had Lydia been stealthier with time than Nora? More disciplined with art? Maybe. Certainly Lydia had, Nora thought, accrued more knowledge, a worldly savvy—as if she'd traveled abroad alone. During the first months of their friendship, it seemed that little mystified Lydia.

Both of their husbands worked in the city, a realm apart, and for the dozens of small decisions that steered each week, Nora consulted Lydia, and vice versa: with their kids, they spent hours of most days together, their partnership shaping itself around the children's hourly or momentary needs. Sometimes they'd settle in at one house, sometimes the other. You could not hold tightly to your hopes for the day, but with Lydia it did not matter. One could always read stories, and if not read stories, build block towers to push down, or draw animals, or make a parade. If the children would not nap, you made up songs. And while Lydia made up songs, Nora managed to get in the laundry; while Nora led a parade, Lydia started soup. And too they shared occasional distraught mornings, when Lydia would call early and drop her girls at Nora's for an hour or sometimes more. Nora would give them milk in blue cups, settle them with Theo and Katy on comforters spread over the living room floor, and read stories of sentient teapots and kind bears. Later Lydia would arrive, slightly winded, and lie on the comforter and let her daughters climb over her.

There were, too, fleeting despondent moments of Nora's own. The morning, say, when she woke from a dream of her father stopping by her Newton kitchen for coffee, his coat snowy from shoveling—her dream-time pleasure and surprise at his arrival, and the notion that she should have baked (though she could offer toast and jam)—but then one of the kids called, or maybe a door opened, or James spoke. Six AM, and snow in fact falling, but her father was dead again, and James was leaving for work, and her throat seemed to close. She tended to the kids, her throat constricted, and at seven called Lydia. In minutes Lydia arrived with her girls and together they cooked breakfast. Nora did not have to explain the dream, and Lydia did not ask.

More than once Lydia said aloud that she was lonely in her marriage. She said it before her girls started school; she said it when Molly was an infant.

"I leave Dan notes," Lydia said. "That's all we do. Write notes."

"You're exhausted," Nora said, "you're both so busy." And when she said it, Nora thought, and thought again, *Oh, marriage, loneliness, sure*—as if the loneliness were ordinary fatigue, or one day's premenstrual sorrow. You had those moments. You wanted breakfast with your late father, a matinee with your late mother, but you brewed coffee for your friend and built a snow fort. James was busy elsewhere; husbands were busy elsewhere. You got them on the weekends and at parties, home evenings and in your bed, and hoped for the best. It took a certain faith. Or acceptance? When Katy was in nursery school, Theo in elementary, Lydia and her husband filed for divorce. Molly had begun to walk; Nora was coaxing her from a doorway to the kitchen table when Lydia stopped in. Nora poured coffee; she served jam tarts on fluted plates, hid her surprise, as Lydia spooned applesauce for Molly. Sometimes people divorced—why had she not considered this? Where had she imagined Lydia's hard mornings or sad afternoons might lead? Better to suspend the question then: an empty thought bubble.

After the separation, the sad days diminished, and Lydia's sly irreverence returned; when the school year ended, she took a large flat in Cambridge, where her kids stayed most weeks, and she seemed not lonely at all. Once or twice a week, Nora would bring Molly to Cambridge and they'd walk with Lydia in Harvard Square. If Molly seemed content, she and Lydia would try a museum; or they'd stay at Lydia's place and drink coffee while Molly napped on Lydia's bed. Over time Nora began to envision herself there too, say, in a place nearby, a rehabbed Victorian, or a smaller house with a brick-lined garden and a redbrick walk. Or a place identical to Lydia's, where she could live and study for another degree, maybe curatorial, maybe art restoration, and where she could talk to Lydia over breakfast. On ordinary weekdays, Nora would find herself wishing for the morning's infinite expansion, a desire to stay with Lydia in her living room drinking coffee while Molly slept, Theo and Katy and Lydia's girls safe in their schoolrooms, James ensconced in his office downtown. This was where she ought to stop time. Occasionally she'd catch herself touching Lydia's arm or her hair, lightly, as if to say *this*. Delicate happy hours that should not be ruined by thought.

THE MURPHYS I

Still, they were a sparkling couple; at least, that was how they appeared to friends and business colleagues. At times Nora's practicality or James's ability to detach shored them up. She was not the usual corporate wife—a bit more exuberant, as likely to chat with a waitress as with a distinguished guest—but she was young and slender, almost pixie-ish, and laughed easily and spoke more-than-passable French. James had a quick mind, a ready smile, a steady manner that inspired trust and was for the most part genuine. Sandy-haired, long-legged, a soft grit in his voice. They were good dancers, good at parties. They seemed to be in love, and were, in fact, in love, or what they took to be love. They both had mild flirtations—public, innocuous—within their social circle, playing at other pairings. Of course, after Katy there were those moments when Nora would catch herself glancing at the peripheries of her life, at the lives of unmarried friends; and sometimes she met them for walks, and later, with Molly in her stroller, visited Lydia in Cambridge, those casual meetings she might neglect to mention to James. No infidelity, she thought (and then, for a time, stopped thinking). For James there were the office flirtations, the passing attraction to the VP's assistant, lunches with the lively young associate who insisted on buying pints. A now-and-then pick-me-up. Not too often. No one sleeping with anyone else. Just an occasional kiss on the cheek, a momentary glimpse of another life.

MOLLY AND KATY

Often, among the Murphy children, squabbling and peace balanced out. Alliances shifted, Theo alternately sought out Katy and ignored her, the two sometimes vying for Molly, whose own mercurial allegiances no one could predict. And Molly pinched; nothing her parents tried had dissuaded her. It began when she was two. She pinched all of them but most often Katy, though with Katy she could also be wildly affectionate. She'd follow Katy until Katy played hide-and-go-seek with her, or at Blue Rock beach built palaces of sand and pebbles. But every week or two, there would come a moment— sometimes preceded by the emptying of drawers or pulling of books from shelves—when Molly would pinch. And watch the reaction—Katy's or Nora's, or sometimes Theo's—with curiosity, a hint of pleasure. The faintest glee at the mark left behind. She knew that Katy would be punished for pinching back, that certainly Nora and James and Theo would not pinch. Simply shouting at Molly could mean trouble for Katy, despite the provocation. At moments of enervation or exhaustion, Molly would wail until Nora rocked her quiet, all pinching then forgotten.

Some rules Molly would follow, some not. She'd steal and eat candy hidden in Katy's dresser drawer, and then cry and insist on sitting on Katy's lap until Katy forgave her. She charmed adults, including Lydia, whom she never pinched and around whom she rarely cried. She was the most beautiful of the children and the most affectionate. Strangers were drawn to her in ways they had never been drawn to Katy or even to Theo, a dimpled blue-eyed boy.

In those moments when Molly claimed Katy, Katy felt as if she possessed Molly. But there were other moments, when Molly seemed to be in love with Theo or their father first, or when Molly pinched Katy hard enough to bruise and ran from her instead of begging forgiveness. Worse for Katy were the hours Nora devoted wholly to Molly, because Molly was the youngest or because she had charmed Nora. Or pinched her. On weekends, James and Theo would kick a soccer ball or sail, often without inviting Katy; or they would sit in neighboring armchairs and read silently, together and inaccessible. In those moments, Theo pointedly shunned her, but her father? She could not tell if he was obtuse or unkind. In the family constellation, Katy became the odd number, the extra girl (though Molly was last; it should have been Molly). And there were moments promised to Katy, like tiny birthdays—*this afternoon, Katy, we'll go for a bike ride; tomorrow morning, Katy, I'll make you pancakes*—when instead Molly threw a tantrum or charmed everyone away.

By the time she was four, Molly's pinching was as strategic as it was impulsive. True: occasionally Katy did pinch back (and was reprimanded) or hid Molly's dolls, which made Molly frantic; or for hours and without wavering ignored Molly, until Molly began to call Katy's name and search for her—until she might hug Katy, climb onto her lap, and let Katy reclaim her.

At the hotel in Rome, Molly pinched Katy, a small test pinch, hard enough to leave a mark. It was the day they arrived, before they slept. "Brat," Katy said, and then their mother walked in. She noticed the red splotch still fading, and ordered Molly to bed. "You too," she told Katy, but kissed the mark on Katy's arm.

ROME I

The heat did not trouble Nora; for a time it seemed that nothing troubled her. There was at once a sharp clarity to the light and a softness to the days, walking over piazzas and into the shade of cafés and the deeper shadows of the churches. But even the smallest fountain—the little Barcaccia in the Piazza di Spagna—made the kids thirsty, and Nora would promise lemon ices and gelatos and eventually time at the beach. She began carrying bags of oranges, because of their thirst.

In those first days, how easy to occupy only the moment, and what seemed to Nora like a singular self, the illusion of one life, and that life for now in Rome, and with James, with Theo and Katy and Molly, with the Galleria Borghese and the vast park surrounding the villa, the Pincio and the Piazza del Popolo, where James—the playful, attentive James—could watch the kids while she slipped into the churches alone. This was, it seemed, the life she wanted, or one of the lives she wanted, though for months she'd been crossing and recrossing that growing fissure, glimpsing what amounted to a separate existence. And why should she have to choose? Yet all that year, there had been the family life in Newton—if you could reduce family life to one thing—and the life in Cambridge, with Lydia and alone, walking through the museums and along tree-lined streets, as if she were another Nora. And Lydia was a doorway to that Nora. She could not say what being a doorway might mean.

True, in Rome traces of that divide insisted themselves, a separate knowledge hovering in the middle distance, blinking above the Apennines, but she focused instead on marble arches and sculpted friezes and nearby trattorias. And the lightness seemed to be with her here, in the open spaces of the city, with James, with the kids. She was aware, here, that she loved them. In the shadows of the monuments, in the starker sunlight, she loved all of them—love for one finer or more granular, for another steadier or in sharper bursts, but love, certainly. It was the smallness of her life she regretted, the boxed-in days of unbroken domesticity, without space for her own mind. In Rome, for a time, nothing seemed small.

There was, too, a lightness in James, who marveled not only at the city but also at his own presence there. His father had neither walked nor likely dreamed of walking here. But James had *arrived*; this moment balanced on other, earlier arrivals, but he had arrived nonetheless. He knew to look forward—had he always known? To climb steadily without falling. At times a fall appeared imminent, but he persisted; later the moment pixilated and blurred into the grander sweep of success, which seemed a fait accompli. Yet Rome was singular, stunning. As if he had leaped directly from boyhood to the Spanish Steps, or to the grounds of the Galleria Borghese, to find Nora in a blue sundress playing tag with the kids.

He could take a longer view, though he suspected that Nora could not. Perhaps family needs hemmed her in; perhaps she disliked ideas other than her own. But soon enough Molly would be in school. Soon enough (not yet, but soon) they could hire whatever help they needed. Nora would have time to paint. A realtor had sent him lists of gracious homes in stellar districts—any one would have studio space. Once they had lived in Cambridge; they'd fallen in love in Cambridge. Say her attachment was attachment to the past—to their early romance, to her late parents, a short bus ride away. Who could blame her? But you had to look forward. He'd toured a blue-and-white house with several bedrooms, a brick patio, a lush yard. He'd pictured the house often; he could picture it now, as if it were his.

Say the Murphys were happiest, all of them, at the Piazza del Popolo: Nora emerged from the Chiesa di Santa Maria del Popolo to find the others near the central obelisk and fountain, Molly and Theo and Katy not bickering but racing between James and the fountain's lion sculpture, disrupting the photos of other tourists. The vast round piazza seemed a village carnival, full of talk, and tourists crowding to watch a juggler, a round man blowing enormous soap bubbles, a puppeteer with marionettes, and near the Chiesa di Santa Maria di Montesanto a single guitarist playing Bach. It was evening, the air cool. They would buy dinner; she and James would drink wine and lounge on the small balcony off their room after the kids fell asleep next door.

This was not the only moment of collective happiness—though perhaps the state was more simultaneous than collective? The piazza remains irresistible. Like much of Rome, it has unsavory shadows, but when the city is washed in light, so is the mind.

Here beside Ramses's obelisk, water pouring from a stone lion's mouth, no trace, of course, of any of them.

ROME II

If only one walked in Rome every day; if only one ate and slept well; if only one saw enough art. They'd fallen into easy routines: there were meals to consider, entertainments, nothing onerous. Occasionally the kids accompanied Nora into churches—briefly, only briefly, as the girls bored easily, though Theo liked the high intricate domes. That Wednesday, like the other mornings, the Murphys walked the city together. James and Theo studied the cars; they spotted a parked Alfa. Nora stepped into a church with the girls.

Later, the day would come back to her as a broken, shifting puzzle: emerging from the church into the bright air, down stone steps. Telling the girls, *Let's sit,* and the hard stone beneath her. Molly, four, holding Katy's hand. A glimpse of James and Theo, across the street beside the tiny convertible. One of them waved; maybe both of them waved. Lunch? What should they do for lunch? She rummaged in her bag for oranges. And then: *No!* Katy, only seven, yelled *no.* Molly was in the street: a running step, the back of Molly's dress, an instant of space between Molly and a white delivery truck, and then no space.

As if, for Molly, traffic had become invisible. A sick thud, the high screeching brakes, though often Nora's memory is more or less silent—just Katy's *No!* and silence until she heard her son yelling, but of course there were other sounds, her own sounds, the shouting crying truck driver, and James. She and James somehow crossed to Molly's body. She has no memory of crossing, only the image of Molly yards away, crooked and bloody, and then crouching on the stone pavement with James. Everything on the adjacent piazza stopped, everyone stopped, and there was silence even as Nora and James bent over Molly, whose eyes were half-open and distant. They spoke to her, James saying, *Molly hold on*, Nora repeating, *I'm here*, her face close to Molly's, beside them a curious spill of blood. Then shouting in Italian, and medics pushing in, pushing Nora back, and around them a crowd, a ring of people who were not shouting, all silent in the heat, and Katy and Theo, only a few yards away. Nora wanted to grab them and Molly both at once. Katy clutched Molly's sun hat, and Theo, only ten, broke the crowd's silence, yelling in English, *Stop it, stop staring at her.*

Nora wiped her hands on her dress and hurried to Theo, grabbed his hand and placed it in Katy's. For a moment her hands hovered over them while she leaned toward Molly—and then a woman, a stranger, stepped next to Theo and Katy and told Nora *Go*. Go. Black hair pinned up, a hand with a slender gold watch, thin-strapped sandals, coral nails. The truck driver paced and wept. James knelt beside Molly and the medics, and when Nora joined them Molly did not look at her, gazed if anywhere at the shirtsleeve of the medic. Nora kissed Molly's face, didn't she? How vividly she remembers the kiss, but it's possible she's remembering the sensation of a different kiss, earlier, before they left the hotel, or as they left the church and she promised something to eat: the oranges, the almond cookies. There was a moment with the medics and James, James stricken, the ambulance loading up. Theo started shouting again, *Stop*, just *Stop*, and Nora caught a glimpse of Katy's now paste-white face, and of Katy pushing forward, trying to get to Molly. *No.*

"Don't bring them to the hospital," James said.

And what if she had said more firmly, *Let's stay right here*, when she took that moment to look for oranges? But that would depend on how distractible Molly was, if she was listening in the moment or too struck by the brilliant light and the vivid crowds. In her mind Nora could step back to the other side of that moment, to the shadowed entryway and the sudden brightness, but again there was the feeling of the orange against her palm and Katy's shout.

The woman with the gold watch spoke English, and she remained beside them until a police car drove them back to the hotel, Nora between Theo and Katy in the backseat. *Dad will stay with Molly.* It seemed that those words swelled and filled the sedan throughout the ride to the hotel, or as if they were not words but very slow gestures, or as if she had been repeating them, though she had not. They drove with the windows open—there was a slight breeze—and city sounds seeped into the car amid her words. Pedestrians crossed the road as if it were the simplest movement, and the chug and purr of motors punctuated the back-and-forth flow of Italian radio. The police said little and walked them into the hotel. A quiet rippling as they entered the lobby, like another pool of silence spreading, though the lobby was already quiet. Cooler air. At the desk she asked in English for the keys to both rooms, the officer beside her speaking rapid Italian to the desk clerk, who waved over the concierge. There was something wrong with her dress, something wrong with her throat. *Are you thirsty?* she asked Katy and Theo, but Theo shook his head and Katy did not say a word, then or for hours.

The concierge escorted them. *Call me*, he said. His thin angular face and large eyes reminded her of goats. *Please call, signora, if you need something.* In this same room she and James had slept the night before, unaware of anything, had in fact made love. In the morning he'd brought her coffee, and then they'd gathered the kids. She does not remember the lovemaking, only that it happened, and in that room, which was not the room where Molly stayed—though sometimes Molly did stay with them, on bad nights. Shuttered windows opened over a tiled patio, and bougainvillea climbed the side railing, and on the side table they kept a seemingly bottomless carafe of water. A double bed, a painting of a coastal harbor, a painting of women at a café. She told Theo and Katy to take off their sandals, climb up on the bed, *Okay? Just stay there.* She was parched; they too must have been parched, she wanted to pour them all glasses of water. Katy and Theo were frighteningly pale, and her hands were stained with blood and dirt; she could see now the traces her hands had made on their clothes, her own clothes bloody and damp. How unspeakable the day had become. *Just wait*, she said. *Just wait.* She left the bathroom door open and washed her hands. Then she pulled off the bloody clothes, dropped them on the floor. She didn't know what to do with them. Wash them? The blood was Molly's. She must have rolled them up—this sensation later returned to her, of rolling her dress and underthings and wrapping them in a towel. There was blood on her body, on her torso, blood that had soaked through, and it was this that she didn't want the kids to see and that hurried her into the tub. She turned on the faucet. "I'm here," she said. "Right here. Are you on the bed?"

"Yes," Theo said.

"Katy too?" Nora said, and Theo said, "Yes." If she turned just so, she could see their feet in the mirror on the door. She washed quickly, rinsed her hair; the water was at first pink, as if she herself had bled into it, and then clear. She watched the water spin down the drain, watched the reflection of the kids' feet in the mirror. She thought she would be sick, but managed to stave it off, to get herself a towel. "I'm right here," she said, dried herself and slipped on underthings while standing with her back to the doorway. From the closet she grabbed a clean dress and pulled it over her head. Then she poured glasses of water for Theo and Katy. "Can you drink some of this?" she said. They took small sips, and Katy started crying again, and it seemed she was trying to gulp the air. For a time, the three of them stayed on the bed. In turn, the kids went into the bathroom, but kept the door ajar. She set out the almond cookies and oranges, sat on the bed beneath the painting of the café, peeling oranges.

Let's pray. She did say that, on the bed. Though of course they'd just been to a church, at least she, Katy, and Molly had, and she'd crossed herself, some vestigial response from childhood. They'd walked the inner circumference, gazing at paintings and sculptures, a stone sarcophagus she'd hurried the girls past, and then they left, because Molly was so restless she'd pinched Nora's arm. Praying was something they did not often do. On the bed, she and Katy and Theo closed their eyes and held hands, but later, when they knew the praying hadn't worked, she imagined the first of several pacts had begun: her children would not believe in her answers, only in her need to explain. They'd indulge her. About the failed prayers they'd say nothing.

She tried calling the hospital, dialed the number on the card the medic had given her, speaking her bad Italian, and over the line the questions came rapid-fire in an Italian she couldn't make out. *Inglese? Inglese? Please.* She hung up and called the concierge. *Yes,* he said, *this is not a problem, I can help you.*

The concierge appeared carrying a tray of tea and bread and jam, and at first she thought he'd misunderstood, but then he motioned to the telephone, made the call, speaking quickly. His shoes had been shined: his shoes caught the light, and his hands moved fluidly as he spoke. "Signora y Signore Murphy," he said, and then, to Nora, "They do not give me the information, they find someone to speak English for you," and when he handed her back the phone it was a woman, who said Signore Murphy was with his daughter, she was very very sorry, they would want to contact the consulate. Katy and Theo watched Nora's face. "So we will have more information from Mr. Murphy?" she said. And the woman said, "Of course, yes."

"Stay a minute?" Nora asked the concierge. She traveled as far as the next room, the children's room, not looking at Molly's suitcase or at Molly's scattered nightclothes, picking up Theo's and Katy's bags and carrying them back to her own room, where the concierge was coaxing Katy to eat bread and jam.

It was almost evening when James returned to the hotel and found them all on the bed not sleeping, very quiet, and he could not tell from Theo's or Katy's expressions if Nora had told them Molly was gone. They gazed up at him and then seemed to focus behind him briefly, before refocusing on him. The apparent calm was temporary. Theo closed his eyes, and Katy, pale, began sobbing. There was a faint fetid smell— someone had been sick, and someone had tried to clean up— and pieces of orange rind littered the table, beside a tray awash in bread crumbs. He was not wearing his own clothes; he was wearing hospital clothes, and in the hallway outside the room he left a bag containing his things and Molly's. He told them Molly loved them. Katy scooted closer to the center of the bed, and the four of them stayed there. After a while Katy and Theo fell asleep. James didn't know whether or not he wanted to fall asleep, whether or not he was ready for the shock of waking again. For now there was a quiet numbing. He had stepped into the ambulance with his already-dead daughter, pretending she was not, because you needed to have that little stretch of hope, you needed time to adjust. Whether he'd pretended for Nora or himself he didn't know. Someone had to stay lucid, and because someone had to stay lucid he had not screamed or thrown himself on the ground, though the outcome would have been no different, his other children no less traumatized. Maybe they all should have thrown themselves on the ground, he and the family and the piazza full of witnesses, weeping and shaking until the day vanished, or until they themselves lost consciousness and slept on the stone road awaiting some other resolution, say, the erasure of time.

In the ambulance he'd held her hand and stroked her bloody forehead, as though she were still occupying her body. The paramedics again tried to revive her, perhaps out of sympathy for him. In the ambulance he was weeping, though for a time he did not know it; there was only the feeling of illness, what he later understood to be shock, as if he had swallowed a balloon that was now expanding, pressing and cutting off his airway. No recourse. It required effort to breathe and to interact with the Italians, who might judge from his face and voice that he was a man choking.

At the hospital, he'd refused to leave her, refused to stop holding her hand even as they began to take her to the hospital morgue. This he objected to—he could not explain in Italian, he could hardly speak at all, clumsily repeating, *No no, un'altra stanza, per favore*, another room, please, until they let him stay with her in an empty exam room. This he did not tell Nora.

The paperwork he could do. There would always be more paperwork.

"We're here," Nora had said on the phone. "We're at the hotel, we're here," and for a blurry half instant he'd envisioned the usual "we," including Molly, back at the hotel. He'd said,

"It's just me." He had said, had made himself say, "Molly's gone," but it was difficult to breathe, and Nora repeated, "At the hotel, we're here." And *Molly's gone* seemed to him untrue, because Molly was still at the hospital, not entirely gone, but there and dead, and he did not want to leave her alone. That was the worst moment, leaving her at the hospital. The second worst moment.

When he woke up, Katy was holding out a glass of water.

In the morning they moved, all of them, to a pair of adjoining rooms on another floor, the hotel staff transferring their bags, Katy and Theo never reentering the room they'd shared with Molly. One of the maids helped Nora pack Molly's things, most of which smelled of Molly, that still-milky scent she had, the soap fragrance of her clean clothes, her soiled ones stained with fruit and gelato. A few stuffed animals, a small suitcase. The maid's name was Anna. They did not hide the suitcase; it stood in plain view in Nora and James's room. Later, a few pieces of clothing migrated to Katy's suitcase, and one of the animals to Theo's.

Nora knew from the calendar that days passed before they flew out from Rome: blank attenuated hours, a conversation in the hotel lobby with somber-faced police, slow card games at the hotel with Katy and Theo, the murmur of string quartets and symphonies from the radio in her room. James calling from the embassy to say the staff had helped arrange to bring *her* home—meaning Molly, at first not saying Molly's name—his cousin Patrick making arrangements in Boston. To meet the casket, James said, to meet Molly. Nora had insisted Theo and Katy eat—whatever they chose, as long as they ate—though she herself could not and only pretended. She felt bound to James, merged in a way only briefly sustainable, as they shepherded Theo and Katy home, through the city, at the airport, not letting either child out of their sight. It seemed for a time they would never leave the half-life of airports and the long flight to Boston.

Katy had taken to carrying Molly's dolls with her. The stuffed koala was in Theo's bed each morning; on the plane he kept it beside him, half-hidden. Like the children, Nora took Dramamine, a nasty yellow liquid, the taste of it enough to bring on nausea, the too-warm feeling like a premonition. Time became an opaque block. On the flight she would forget and look for Molly, and Katy would forget and look for Molly: you could see Katy glancing about, then suddenly down into her lap, one beat too late.

At Logan Airport, Nora's sister, Meg, appeared in a blue-green summer dress and a woven sun hat, like a slender plant, a thistle—the thought came to her *Meg is a thistle*—but then Meg held her, and Meg's sweet bookish husband Louis took her arm and guided her and James toward the baggage claim, while Meg walked between Katy and Theo, holding their hands. No one spoke, and it seemed at first as if they were miming a family return, as faster-moving travelers streamed around them, rushing into gleeful hugging reunions or onward into taxis. They would go directly to Blue Rock. It was difficult to imagine the present moment. It was difficult to imagine anything else.

After a few moments, in a keen imitation of himself, James inquired about skycaps.

NORA'S PLACES

Her first house: the triple-decker in Somerville. She and Meg and their parents lived on the ground floor, the postage-stamp yard abutting all the other postage-stamp yards; in good weather the yards seemed like a strange harbor, drying sheets and work pants and dresses flapping in the wind or hanging flatly in the treeless light. In front of the house stood one skinny beech near a flower bed where her father tended the string of rosebushes that would blossom scarlet in the heat, just as everything else seemed to be wilting. He'd whistle bits of popular songs—in her mind the whistling and the roses weaving together—and when he finished, he and Nora would eat ice. Fans whirred in windows up and down the street, the neighbors' sounds inseparable from their own. Only a few yards lay between the houses, doors and screens open to infants' cries and family arguments and intimate pleasures. Kids outside called and jeered, lingered on front stoops shooting marbles, or jumped ropes, or blocked off the street to throw baseballs. In winter the shut windows and curtains and snow muted outdoor noise, which carried fewer voices and more work sounds; the chipping of ice and the hard crunch of shovels cutting snow would sometimes drift up onto the porch. The third-floor neighbors thudded up and down the stairs, the Cahill boys yelling, Mrs. Cahill yelling after, "Stop your noise." The Reillys on the second floor were quieter and sadder and more decorous. Nora's mother said the quiet was lucky, though *lucky* sounded troubling. From the Reillys' apartment Nora mainly heard footsteps and water pipes and the murmurs of broadcast baseball games. At Nora's there was at least music: the stack of swing records, her father's whistling, the radio pop, their mother singing while sewing dress alterations. She'd make the girls puppets, impromptu sets for their plays. Most days, the household mood stayed light.

By Nora's high school years they'd moved to a larger flat that Nora preferred. More trees shaded the neighborhood, and around the corner a baker sold shortbread and the Italian loaves Nora would buy for the house on her way home from school. For a time, Meg tumbled into more fervent Catholicism and became tedious—even their mother said so. Meg would bring home small art prints and cards: Madonnas and Annunciations, mostly stylized and generic, a few with the detailed faces of individual women. The sad horrific Crucifixions Meg agreed to keep in a drawer. For a time, the household seemed content, but in Nora's senior year, their mother began to thin, and in colder weather she coughed and slept more—the first intimations of later troubles.

For most of college, Nora lived in a women's dormitory, brick and utilitarian, but her closest friends lived in neighboring rooms, and she spent much of her time in the painting studio and in a lecture hall where faculty projected slides of masterworks to enormous scale. Her second year, she met

James at a friend's engagement party. He studied business; about art, he knew nothing. On their first date, he took her to the Fogg Museum. To Nora and to the paintings she admired, he paid serious attention; behind the security guard's back, he pulled faces. Later they visited other museums—very fine and too solemn, they agreed—and went to unsolemn ball games, and took leisurely walks, stopping for coffee or beer. Not long after graduation, they married and moved into a small Cambridge apartment.

The second Cambridge place, her favorite, was a spacious two-bedroom they rented shortly before Theo's birth: a white-and-yellow kitchen, oak floors, a yard with redbrick pathways, lilacs, a bed of daylilies. By then James had landed in finance, and with his uncle he'd worked out the arrangement to buy the Shore Road house. Fleeting peaceful years, during which she took Theo on walks through Cambridge and saw her parents often. During her second pregnancy, they moved to the house in Newton, a good house, near good schools. Later, when past events sifted and rearranged themselves, Nora would wonder if the move to Newton had been a mistake. As if it had caused not only displacement but also the sharpening of James's ambitions, her mother's death while Katy was an infant, her father's death less than two years later.

Her parents made regular cameo appearances in dreams, stepping through doorways, noticing the weather, crossing into the visible frame of a front porch or a kitchen and again out of view. Yet there was Lydia, the visits back to Cambridge. At times, Blue Rock became Nora's refuge: even when Molly was only weeks old, Nora retreated there, feeding, washing, and diapering Molly; building kites and making picnics for Katy and Theo while Molly napped. Often the beach was empty but for a few people walking, picking up stones, their figures altered by the syrupy yellow, clear white, or lavender light, the evening and early morning reds brimming along the horizons. Now and then she might sense something larger, or something lost and momentarily returned, traveling through the upper atmosphere, or closer, skimming over the tidal ebb.

JAMES

If death separated James from his mother, it was not his mother's death: the early death of his father seemed to break her. He was twelve. For the first month he stayed with the Murphy cousins, while she lay on the sofa at her sister's apartment. His cousin Patrick worked weekends at a country club and helped James get a job as a caddy, pretending James was older.

The Murphy cousins saved him. After he returned to his family's apartment, he visited the cousins every week. With Patrick, he took up running (a ready excuse to go out). His mother resumed her job at Filene's, though it was not full-time, and she remained adrift and forgetful; often he'd find her at home on their sofa, sleeping or listening to the radio, incapable not only of daily chores but also of tenderness, the room filmy with dust. Once a week, Patrick's father came over to see if she'd been paying the bills. *A shame*, Uncle Paul would say. *She's had a rough go of it, your mother.*

A queasy pitching sensation on his boyhood walks home, intimations of dread as he approached the apartment door. His mother could not rouse herself to offer even small gestures of affection. He associated her state with his father's death, yet there were earlier moments, too, before he was twelve, when she was distant and lost-seeming and there was no coaxing her back. She'd been beautiful, his mother, but *Life can be too much for her*, his father would say. The family murmured about miscarriages but she never spoke of them. She'd loved another man before his father, that much he knew. His father—a charismatic talker, happy in crowds—fell into shambling silence in the face of her moods. Until his father's death, James could sometimes still charm her into a smile, an occasional kiss on his brow, but a coolness might descend nonetheless, and after his father died the coolness remained, and only certain mornings in church would she warm and seem at all maternal.

During those boyhood summers in Blue Rock, he never worried about his mother, who seemed content during family visits; after his father's death, she did not return. The house belonged to Uncle Paul then—its foundation solid, its interior walls thin, the rooms furnished with cast-off pieces. Paul and Brenda had lined the bedroom floors with mattresses, so it became an indoor campground on the weekends, full of cousins. The boys slept on the floor of the living room, the bedrooms taken by the parents or the families with babies or the girls.

In his memory: bleached sky, bleached air, bleached dreaming on the slanted oak floor, Patrick kicking in his sleep. In the night, he'd tiptoe over to the narrow windows on the side of the house to watch the sea, or to the unshuttered living room windows, picking his way past sleeping boys. As a teenager he would be the last one up, outside on the concrete patio or down on the beach smoking a cigarette. In the late quiet nights he'd read his uncle's war novels and local histories by flashlight. The place was full of sand: every day his aunt Brenda swept sand. For two weeks each season, gnats from the pond congregated wherever the wind lulled, moving as a cloud into the kitchen, or over the dining table, so small and fine you needed cloth to stop them. His aunt would sometimes turn on the fan and hope, though the gnats persisted until they'd run their course and dropped like seedpods to the floor.

Drafts, always, the house porous. After the season, the families would have one last weekend. Cool, early October. They'd clean the place, shutter and board it up, and turn off the water until spring, emptying glass jars of tea and sugar and flour and oats. They'd cover furniture with sheets and the mattresses with plastic, recheck the roof. On those days he always wanted to linger and would leave the others for a last run on the beach. In the early years, his father, and later Patrick or Uncle Paul, would finally call and call his name, *Jimmy*, and when the irritation became pronounced, *James*. But the irritation was tempered by indulgence, because the family all knew, didn't they? They didn't want to leave this place either. At times a ragged surging seemed as much within James as beyond, a reverberation he could not articulate. He'd run as the autumn sky grew dense, the gray muscled clouds now edged in white, squeezing stretches of blue or breaking them into puzzle pieces, curiously curved, blue patches that became their own temporary alphabet. The sea still held the light and patterning of that alphabet.

Then the wind reshaped the white clouds and the light went gold and faded; the sky flooded with pink and orange, the blue patches more indigo and quickly black. Too fast, the sky was a mottled onyx, starless, the wind pushing more clouds into a single sheet. The chill he might have felt all along was suddenly palpable, a kind of warning, and with it the recognition that yes, against his will the day had left him. He ought to be more sheltered. The day had left behind what seemed a universal loneliness: there would be clouds and wind but no stars; or if there were stars, even brilliant stars, the cold would sharpen. Still, one could listen to the sea—that music did not stop—and beyond the sea he might hear a voice, after a time his own name called, though sometimes the loneliness would wash through him until he felt empty of anything else. This was how years of final weekends ended, with his family calling his name, though often they knew just where he was, and often they would leave him alone until the cars were ready to go. Either a cousin would fetch him, or the landscape would close itself away from him so forcefully and with such ringing despair he'd answer *Here* to the voices and follow their trail to the waiting car. If it was an especially cold day, there'd be a thermos of tea or hot chocolate.

It was more than an hour back to the city, and for the first few minutes no one in the car spoke. Once they'd rounded the harbor—which was still alive, the local restaurants and pubs open, year-round houses lit from within—the shore's hold would loosen, and in those first years his father would say his name again, this time as if ushering James through a door, and begin to talk; later his uncle would turn on the radio and the car would fill with bits of news and football scores about which James might speculate with his cousins. The gray awareness of school would gather weight as the car neared the city, and after his father's death, the leaden substance of his home life would reassert itself in spite of the time at the shore (the sea, the orange clouds), finally eclipsing it as the car reached his street, and he approached the door of the South Boston flat.

ROME

Maddalena penitente
Domenico Fetti (early 17th century)
GALLERIA DORIA PAMPHILJ

Here in Rome, a painting of a woman—young, a girl really—
her eyelids lowered, her face half in light and half in shadow.
She's seated, her right elbow propped on a pale gold book, head
leaning against her right hand. A blue scarf drapes her head and
shoulders, the blues picked up in her white sleeve, gold stitching echoing the book, the book's edges soft, fluidly painted.
In her left hand—rose-copper thumb, rose-copper fingers—a
coffee-colored human skull, the rose copper again picked up
in her cheeks. Look just above and behind her head: her halo
almost melts into air, three-quarters of a copper ring, like the
thin spill of light from an eclipse. She's illuminated from the
right—an unseen window?

Maddalena penitente, yet her state seems like a meditative
grief. In solitude: she pays no attention to the viewer. She is
beautiful, this girl, the artist's model. Say that she did contemplate death while she sat for the painting. Perhaps she allowed

herself to forget Fetti, forget the contents of the book, forget even the symbolic skull—confronted, that day, by more private loss.

FUNERAL DAY

Molly, a girl in a box, a wax doll—starched pink dress, full skirt, long sleeves, high neck, so that to Katy the casket seemed more dress than girl, the face an imitation of Molly's. The casket was propped at the front of the chapel; and when Aunt Meg ushered Katy to a car, it seemed possible that this boxed-up Molly might stay at the chapel. But the casket reappeared, closed, at the cemetery, and you were supposed to believe that Molly was in it, now a girl in a box in the ground.

That day Theo and Katy were nudged and led about like kindergarteners, like babies, in and out of cars, from Blue Rock to the chapel to the cemetery to Rose Murphy's house in Arlington, crowded with sweating adults and tables of food. Pearled-pink and cherry polish on the women's nails; broad link watches circling the men's wrists, cigarettes between their fingers, the talk a viscous cooing. On a message pad decorated with yellow daisies, Katy and Theo played tic-tac-toe and hangman.

Finally the rooms began to clear out, and Aunt Meg patted Katy's shoulder. "Okay, hon?" she said, and "Theo, sweetie?" and let them wait out in the car. Then Uncle Louis drove them to the South Shore, with the windows open and the road breeze coming in, Theo and their father in the front seat, and Aunt Meg and Katy and her mother in the backseat, Katy close against her mother, who smelled of talcum powder and hair spray and sweaty dirt. Once they pulled over so Theo could throw up, and her mother and Meg studied her, as if she might throw up too, though it was her mother who gulped air at the open window. Near Blue Rock you could smell the sea again, and the densest heat lifted. Sun glinted off the harbor and sailboats dotted the bay, too bright, all of it too bright. When they arrived at the house, Katy wanted to run inside, but her mother hesitated on the deck, and then her father nudged them in. They took off their shoes and sat on the couches in their funeral clothes, and Meg lowered the shades, so that the living room seemed a separate, hidden sphere. Katy fell asleep on the sofa, and when she awoke, Theo was sleeping beside her. Her mother had moved to the floor next to the side sofa, where her father sat, bent, their faces tilted down, together, at his knees. One of her mother's hands held one of her father's. The other one twitched. A kind of huffing came from her father. After a few minutes the huffing stopped. Katy waited for it to start again, and when it did not, she tiptoed across the living room and through the kitchen—the table covered by wrapped plates from Rose Murphy and by pastel sympathy cards—then continued in her stocking feet out to the deck and down the stairs to the beach. The exposed midtide sand was studded with small and larger multicolored stones, which bit through stockings but which you could hurl at the sea for hours, if you wanted to: there were thousands of stones you could hurl at the sea.

BLUE ROCK

A few nights after the funeral Nora and James finally slept together alone, sharing neither a room nor a bed with Katy or Theo or both. A cooling night, the sea breeze carrying the scent of salt and kelp and smoke from a campfire on the beach, black air interrupted only by the night-light in the corner. Half-naked and weeping, they fell into avid, drowning sex, the grief emerging as a raging insistence; as if each might obliterate or immerse the self in the other, alternately banishing the self and shoring it up with the other's body, avidity somehow evidence that they were alive and also willing to vanish, and in this flux might bring her back as they once brought her. They were thin, both of them, their skin warm in the chill air, his movements abrupt and ungentle. Even as Nora made love to James her muscles seized, and in her belly an animal sickness blurred into the pleasure: it seemed if she kept moving she might move past the pain into a mindless release, or a kind of coma. The tension seemed at once unbearable and insufficient, and the only way beyond was to drive further and further into it, into James, around James. Both of them weeping unaware until they climaxed and the weeping did not subside. They woke again around three and he entered her again and for a while they drifted, dozed with him inside her. For a few nights it was like this, the mixed-up striving for solidity, oblivion, a welling violence streaked with tenderness, and during the day, a blankness.

For two weeks, they stayed at the house on Shore Road. Daylight sleepwalkers, awakening without thought, thought remaining absent beyond basic routine. For Nora the initial relief in arriving and the safe haven of the house leveled out. She could speak to Theo and Katy and James, but she could not read or answer the telephone; occasionally she observed herself taking it off the hook. She did not call Lydia; elsewhere there had been a friend named Lydia, but Nora was not elsewhere, and here her mind had become a razed field. The days stretched, her body increasingly detached from herself, as if it were a hollow stem or a blade of autumn beachgrass, without will except in her efforts to conceal a recurring breathlessness. There was the steadying presence of the sea, which seemed to both acknowledge and contain all that roiled within her, so she could move through the day without her mind.

One thing made sense to Nora: to stay in Blue Rock. Even though they had planned to live closer to the city, even though James's daily commute would leach hours. She'd seen a snapshot of a house James had toured in Wellesley, a large suburban house in a very small photograph. The house could disappear in her hand.

✣

August. The Murphys so closely resembled a vacationing family that at a glance you would have suspected nothing. Even with a second look—because the scene was orderly, their clothes clean. You'd have had to pay more attention to the body language; you'd have had to look into the faces. Theo and Katy moved in tandem then, staying within arm's reach of each other. A few steps separated their bedrooms; each evening their parents wished them good night and left doors open, but soon Katy or Theo would move to the other's room, and together they snuck downstairs and slept on the living room sofas. Together they'd slip into Molly's room, Theo opening the closet, Katy the drawers. They'd listen at the wall abutting their parents' bedroom, at the windows, beside the bed. And together they'd rush out, hurry down the stairs and through the kitchen to the windswept deck, then lock away the moment.

Each morning, James ran; late day he'd drink beer from the bottle—one before and one during dinner, although he could have downed a six. If he'd been alone, or just with Nora, he would have. For a few morning hours he'd feel clearer, but by 2:00 PM his agitation would spike. Soon he began to run before dinner as well, the running and beer his linchpins to the day. At odd moments between, some version of Rome replayed itself: here was the sharp green convertible, there Nora and Katy and Molly, emerging from the church across the street. *There they are*, he'd say, and Theo would wave, he himself would wave. Catch Molly's eye, catch Katy's, though not Nora's: Nora was riffling through her bag. In Blue Rock, he found himself assessing each of them in turn. Often Nora's crushed expression mirrored his own, though once or twice a strange flintiness had come into her face when they were alone, as if she too were assessing, swimming back and forth between self-recrimination and their silent, mutual accusations (you *failed* her; you *beckoned*). Was waving beckoning—had he beckoned? Had Theo? (What could one expect of a ten-year-old? A seven-year-old?) So impetuous, Molly—at times she'd broken away from all of them. But more than once as the scene replayed, Nora's distraction seemed criminal; more than once, the notion *Katy let go* popped up before he could quash it. He needed a roadblock, a mental detour. For now, he took the wooden stairs to the gravel drive and the tidal flats, away from the kids, away from Nora. He counted his steps as the beach seemed to slide backward underfoot, paced until the counting sufficiently diffused his agitation and he could return to the house.

There in Blue Rock, hadn't he always felt most himself? Yet most raw; he'd have more control, wouldn't he, when he returned to work? He'd told the office he'd be settling a family matter before starting the new position; he still had banked vacation days. In conversations with the chief financial officer, his sentences had seemed magically coherent, his tone surprisingly bright, as if the pre-Italy James were speaking through him.

Nothing like the private family conversations, which were fragmented and attenuated and slow, often spanning days. Without preface he'd asked Theo what happened *at the end*, meaning the end of the ball game they'd watched two days earlier. In the attenuation there seemed a tacit suggestion that they were all still waiting for Molly to reappear. And although he braced himself for his mind's traumatic replay of Rome, he did not anticipate the way the color of the sky that day echoed in a Blue Rock sky, or a neighbor's morning glories evoked the vine pattern of the hospital administrator's dress, or the way bending bars of light and late purple shadows at the hotel reappeared through the living room window. The most prosaic objects—a sugar cube on a plate, an empty soda bottle—held a flaring sadness.

It was happening to all of them. At dinner, Katy and Theo would chew absently, side by side, apparently observing the reflected light on the bay, the darkening sky, the objects on the table. Nora's hands kept moving: she'd pass platters and move the salt and arrange the burger and the corn on her plate, picking them up and setting them down, performing but not eating a thing. "Nora," Meg would say. She'd look directly into Nora's face, pick up her own burger, and bite it, her gaze fixed on Nora until Nora did the same.

ROME

La Maddalena
Michelangelo Merisi da Caravaggio (1594-95)
GALLERIA DORIA PAMPHILJ

This time, the woman is crestfallen. She's seated on a low chair, almost as if kneeling, the hem of her green brocade dress spilling onto the floor. A study in green and dark amber: her long hair coppery, robe deep amber, her skin fair, her face and neck, bare upper shoulder and chest pale, tinted with amber undertones. Almost red, her hands, as if they're too warm, or cold. Her head tips toward her left shoulder, face downward, eyes cast down, nearly closed. The trim on her bodice, her sleeves, an exaggerated white. Here too the illumination is aslant, but sharp, dramatic— a spotlight from the angle of the viewer. A triangle of light slices the wall above her head, though most of the room remains in shadow. A red sash circles her waist, and on the floor beside her, an amphora of pale amber liquid stands beside scattered jewelry: a string of pearls, pearl earring, gold bracelet, gold chain. Her elbows and forearms rest on her lap, one hand pressed against the other, as if to cradle an invisible infant or a lover's head.

She herself is fairer-skinned and older than the Fetti Magdalen, her head uncovered, hair a copper fire mostly in shadow, her clothes those of a Renaissance strumpet. A distinctive face, painted with realist fidelity; her gaze also seems inward, away from the viewer, the painter. But the dramatic light, the angle, this costuming—the painting's bold theatricality—reveals exhaustion, a wilder sorrow. Also shame? No shred of privacy, not even the privacy of shadow. If she could escape the harsh light, the judging view, might the shame dissolve into more tender melancholy? Beyond the frame and any view—even yours—she might rest.

NEW SCHOOL

It was like walking off a plank, the sensation from a pirate's tale in which you'd been kidnapped, your hands bound, your mouth gagged, the sky a mocking cartoon blue painted out to an empty horizon. Red-orange mustaches, black eye patches, black bandanas on the pirates, the masts of their cartoon ships flying skull-and-crossbones flags, sometimes giant and pristine, sometimes half-burned and pocked with holes through which you could see only that mocking sky and lines of smoke in the distance where the rescue ships have sunk. Maybe your mother was on one of those ships, or on shore, or on an unsunk ship too far away to find you: certainly your father was farther out at sea, searching the wrong region for your kidnappers. Fins cut the otherwise glassy cartoon water. Nothing like the actual sea off Blue Rock.

No difference, that day, between stepping *in* and stepping *off* into a free fall. School buses lined up along the side of the school, each snout almost touching the squared back of the next bus, so they formed a thick yellow chain. Kids poured off the buses, laughing girls, gaggles of boys, strangers. Her mother kissed her cheek, readying to drive away, and Katy's throat tightened. She willed herself to leave the car, blinked at the building's flat brick exterior, the windows like dozens of unlidded eyes. She had to work to breathe, even though Theo was with her. Her mother waved. "Okay," Theo said. He walked her up the school's front steps, holding her hand, as if she were a little kid, as if she were Molly.

She'd been inside before, once, the previous day: her mother had brought them, *For a dry run*, she'd said, the building empty except for teachers and secretaries, Nora a hummingbird flitting from place to place in the waxy-smelling school, pointing out the bathrooms, making Katy return to the front entrance, then find her second-grade classroom, find the bathroom. The sort of thing you'd never admit, mortifying, except that it took great concentration to find these routes, given the identical wooden classroom doors with identical unsmudged windows, hallways splitting off into additional hallways. Wings, her mother said. It was as if, between school years, Katy had become retarded.

"You know where you're going?" Theo said. First day: they were at the front entrance. Theo had that sour look as if he might throw up. She would vanish one way, Theo another—to the fifth-grade wing, which Katy had not learned to find.

"I'm okay," Katy said. "See you later." Other kids streamed around them, and she let go of his hand and pretended he was still there as she joined the stream heading along the route she'd taken twice the day before. When she found the classroom, she chose an empty seat a few rows back, along the wall. A miniature island.

The teacher was a middle-aged lady in a blue-and-green pantsuit and a round poof of brown hair and candy-pink lipstick, like a fruit tree with the trunk obscured by leaves. Roll call. "Kathleen

Murphy? Kathleen?" Katy raised her hand but not high enough, not at first, and had to repeat "Here." She managed to say, "It's Katy," before the teacher moved on to the next name.

Say whatever you want, her mother had told her. *Say what you need to say.* She meant about Molly. About the summer and Molly and maybe, or maybe not, about how everything since had been vacuumed flat.

If they ask about summer vacation, Theo had said, *tell them you rode bikes and swam.* But no one asked. The older kids had lockers; her grade still had cubbies and a coatroom, so you could put your lunch away, or your notebooks for other subjects. She traveled class to class and collected textbooks, so that by lunch there was a small stack to take home and cover in brown paper. In the cafeteria, she found the line to buy milk and a seat at a table off to the left, where she could eat her sandwich and chips and fruit from home and nobody would bother her.

Maybe she had become retarded; that could happen, couldn't it, even if you didn't start off that way? Because the previous spring she'd talked all the time. Last year, she'd talked from the first day of class; she'd already known everyone.

She had not called or written to any of her Newton friends. She'd said she would write postcards from Italy and the first day in Rome she did, but her father didn't mail them and then Molly was dead. She'd wanted to send them out anyway: in Newton, Molly wasn't dead. No one in Newton had seen the white truck, or Molly on the street, or the hotel room where Theo got sick and their mother rinsed off blood. That was Italy. But Katy still could picture Molly in the kitchen in Newton, wearing pink pajamas, eating buttery toast.

The plank, all week. It took a few days to recognize the other kids in her class. There were safe spots: her cubby, the end stall in the Pepto-Bismol-pink girls' bathroom, the cafeteria seat at the far end of the third table. Fractions in math, which she'd already learned. Her homeroom teacher, the tree-like Mrs. Graham, didn't shout, even when Katy's attention wandered. "Katy? Kathleen?" It happened most late in the day, but also some mornings, when the invisible rope she clung to slipped and moved in one direction, while she seemed to move in another. The chalk squeaked and the rustling of other kids in their seats sounded like rising birds; a girl near her named Cynthia leaned in to whisper to another girl. A spitball hit the floor. Her index finger collided with hardened gum stuck under her desk; her shoes pinched her feet. From the playing fields outside the window, boys yelled *Here*, and then a murmuring background voice again became sensical, Mrs. Graham saying, "Katy? Do I have your attention?"

She didn't lose track of Mrs. Graham's voice, but the sounds stuck the way Italian had, strings of vowels and consonants she heard but did not interpret. The words stretched and puckered. She copied what Mrs. Graham wrote on the board, but sometimes missed a piece. A page number. The third week of school, her mother visited her classroom at the end of the day and spoke with Mrs. Graham and copied down all the assignments Katy had already copied. "She needs to be given written instructions," her mother said, as if Katy weren't in the room. "Most of the instructions," Mrs. Graham told her, "are written down. She only needs the right page."

"We just moved here year-round," her mother said.

"She'll adjust." Mrs. Graham smiled, but now Katy was marked.

It would happen in other places. Outside. Around other kids. On the bus. She tuned in halfway, missing the first parts of stories, the beginnings of bus fights or jokes. "What?" she'd say to Theo—when he was around—and in whispers he'd explain.

Theo never misread the instructions, never misheard the others. He was cautious: these were year-round kids from the harbor town streets and the bluff. For passing instants his face would go blank before settling into ordinary watchfulness, like a television skipping through the empty, electric-snow channels, but he didn't lose information. Teachers liked him, they had always liked him—he was handsome, well-mannered—but he wasn't a pet. It didn't take long for him to make friends. A few, even in the first weeks, normal boys who seemed lively and unconfused. Sometimes when he joined them, Katy would panic, but all September he was patient with her, explaining, sticking by her in new places (as if she were Molly or in fact retarded). At home, he brought his reading into her room while she finished homework; then he'd return to his room, where he'd sleep. She did not follow him, nor did they sleep in the living room again. He stayed in her room longest—long enough to need a blanket—the night after Molly's nursery school refused to refund a deposit; through the walls they could hear their father shouting, *She's dead—you want to have that conversation?* their mother shouting, *Shut up.*

Some mornings upon waking Katy had to remind herself that Molly was dead, and in that way Rome kept repeating, and Molly kept running into the street.

By October, Theo's old impatience returned. He wouldn't hold Katy's hand in public, though sometimes he'd walk close to her, nudging her, letting her know he was there. She couldn't blame him, really. She'd drift, sometimes just giving up, letting herself slide, and then discover she was alone in a deep dirt pit. Everyone called down clever suggestions of how to climb out but no one lifted her to solid ground. Perhaps she'd have to live there, part-time, always it seemed, everyone nodding in quiet recognition and pitying consolation. *Yes, too bad she isn't like the others,* a shrugging acceptance that she was defective but meant no harm. The way, in Newton, her classmates had talked about Candace Green, a plain girl with skinny white legs and narrow, slightly out-turned feet, a girl who didn't say much, and sometimes was the butt of mild jokes, though not the worst jokes, the worst reserved for even more objectionable kids. Candace Green. Maybe Katy was now Candace Green, only unskinny, and as the weeks progressed, and she comforted herself with cookies and chips, further and further from skinny.

It was better in gym, when she ran or played soccer. By mid-fall her concentration improved; she could follow the through lines of Mrs. Graham's lessons. Still, every success felt provisional, Katy herself tainted—permanently? Nothing seemed more permanent than now.

Afternoons when she did homework, her mother would sometimes sit next to her and smooth her hair and read, as if Katy were a small cat. But when Nora turned her face or crossed the room, Katy could see how brittle she was; and in neighborhood conversations she was strangely cheerful, smiling and chatting with the other women as if she'd parachuted into the world she'd always wanted.

Outside the house, no one spoke about Molly.

HOUSE II

From the wraparound deck, you entered through the kitch-
en: white walls and long side windows, a broad oak kitchen
table, the white peninsula of the breakfast counter separating
the work space from the table. Painted cabinets lined the far
left wall, above old laminate counters. A chunky white electric
stove, a decades-old refrigerator, its edges curved, the manu-
facturer's name embossed in chrome script. A stainless-steel
kitchen sink along the entry-side wall, a window just above—
sometimes lined with tomatoes—from which Nora gazed at
the house across the narrow road and the brook-fed pond, and
later blew smoke from rationed cigarettes. Sand, always, on the
kitchen floor (oak planks beneath the table; linoleum near the
stove), uncontrollable in summer, a warm soft grit the family
swept twice a day. Two parallel doorways led from the kitchen
to a broad living room big enough for two sofas and several
chairs, windows on three sides facing the bay and the east- and
westward stretches of beach—on sunny days swaths of blue.
Below and beyond the windows and the back deck, a concrete
patio abutted a seawall of concrete and stone. In fair weather,
the blue wooden shutters stayed open, held by steel hooks, and

in storms they were bolted shut, the light and the views of the sea cut off. Other touches here and there: a small alcove beneath the stairs, for a time a toddler's playhouse, for a time a one-desk office.

The clouds of gnats infiltrated the kitchen in May— prompting Nora to hang mosquito netting for a few days before the gnats died and fell into shoes and coffee cups. On the second floor, four bedrooms, modest, the largest at the far end of the hall, with its own tiled bath. What had once been a single large room James and Nora had divided into two, one mid-hallway, one at the near end, beside the bathroom at the top of the stairs. These also faced the bay. For a time, the mid-hallway room was Molly's and pink; soon after Rome, painted white and emptied. A fourth bedroom—Theo's favorite—opened at the top of the stairs along the street side facing the pond, a side window catching the eastern shoreline.

The night view from the deck: a vast sky clotted with stars.

AFTER I

If it had been her own father, her beloved late father, appearing
across the street, Nora too would have run: for her, too, there
would have been nothing but his face, his wave. Imagine making the leap toward him, recognizing him but not the objects
around him, apprehending the man but not the moving traffic. Only in your mind is there clear space between you and
your father; only the mind can make a truck vanish. She did
not mention this to James. Yet had she told Lydia this, Lydia
would have nodded—yes, love, minds, trucks. Just as, for hazy
liminal moments, flying dreams can leave us verging on ascent.
But Nora had not called Lydia, or answered Lydia's phone messages; nor had she sent Lydia the engraved memorial card for
Molly (unsent cards waited stacked in a box, death repeated
in tasteful script). Even when she'd settled Theo and Katy into
school routines, she did not write to Lydia. Because after Rome
you do not get other doorways. Because another Nora might
exist—this seemed clear now—only if the children were safe;
if Molly still existed, if Theo and Katy had lost nothing. It
did not surprise her that both Lydia and Molly showed up in
dreams, sometimes together, or that they crossed into dreams

about Nora's mother. It seemed that they might all occupy the same unreachable place.

Of course in waking life, the actual Lydia could appear. One October afternoon, she arrived, her presence made palpable by the downshifting of a motor outside the house, a blue VW, quick steps up the stairs. A sunny day, Theo and Katy still at school. Through the kitchen window, Nora saw Lydia's hair falling loose over a dark suede jacket, then a sheaf of yellow chrysanthemums. She did not want to open the door. She waited, but Lydia was knocking, Lydia had seen her.

"Nora."

It seemed the light was too bright, dizzying. She opened the door to wind and Lydia, Lydia rushing forward as Nora backed away.

"Nora?"

An odd heat flooded Nora: she propped herself with the curved back of a wooden chair.

Lydia stopped. She slid the sheaf of flowers across the table, took the chair closest to the door. "Will you talk to me?" An herbal scent, the familiar Lydia. "I'm so sorry."

Nora shook her head, refusing what, exactly? In May, they had talked in a familiar kitchen. Here was another familiar kitchen. Two still points, it seemed, over the chasm of months, ocean, Rome. One might gesture at the chasm; one might peer down, identify shapes.

"Nora. Come on."

Between them, the table, the chrysanthemums, the muted wind, which seemed to blow pointillist light through the windows and plain kitchen air, onto the flowers, the bowl of apples. She wavered. Perhaps the blowing light might tip her over. Imagine an armful of grass falling onto the table. Imagine it falling to the floor. Lydia repeated her name. Nora had been looking for oranges; she had been distracted. In Rome there had been no Lydia; there, Lydia had been absent. But if oranges were elements of distraction, Lydia was a deeper element. A layer upon which the oranges might float.

And now Lydia watched Nora from the far side of the table, the Lydia who'd found her way to Cambridge with her two girls intact. If one's kids were intact, one might move. One might then be Lydia; one might accompany Lydia, or visit her.

"Theo and Katy are in school," Nora said. "Adjusting."

"Of course," Lydia said.

It was difficult to suspend certain knowledge. Lydia too, had taken care of Molly, and of Katy and Theo. Loved them. At least, in the Blue Rock kitchen Lydia did not weep or assault Nora with her own grief. Offered no false comforts: chrysanthemums were only themselves. Nora had been distracted, and was now more so. She had Theo; she had Katy. Certain desires could lead to ruin, though how to identify which ones? You could not say ruin began with oranges, only that oranges were present. What was her desire for Lydia? *Let's sit.* She had said that in Rome. A flimsy command, hardly words at all. There had been hand-holding, hand-waving. Why recount any of it? You had to accept the ruin: here, this is yours. On the far side of ruin, Lydia wore a fringed jacket. She belonged there. Nora did not.

"I don't know how to do this," Nora said. She seemed to be speaking underwater; or perhaps the light had thickened. "Talking," she said.

"Do you want tea?" Lydia said. "What do you need?"

The kettle stood in the sink; Nora had been filling the kettle. "Oh," Nora said. Could she drink tea? This was something she did. It seemed irrelevant.

"I'll rest," Nora said. "Maybe I'll just rest." She heard herself tell Lydia, "Today's not the best day."

❦

A space Nora had once associated with Molly remained as an empty quadrant of air, or a kind of silence housing all things Molly or attached to Molly's death, and therefore ever-deepening. Distraction, yes: regularly, the day's anchors would slip, Nora would slip with them into that space, and then rediscover her kitchen minutes later. As if she were driving a long distance and, coming upon a tollbooth, realized she'd made no notice of the last fifty miles. What had happened in those miles? There must have been road signs, exits. On the radio a broadcast of some kind. Or, in the kitchen, Katy or Theo, asking a question, or handing her a plate, and the dishwasher now emptied.

So, the territory took shape: solid ground would accumulate after Molly, but that blank air would remain, and Nora would continue to disappear into it and reappear in a different moment. Italy, when it surfaced, was always overlit, the piazzas swimming. Time please for lunch. The hotel. Time to return to the hotel with the family, with Molly, as they had for days without thought. Perhaps this was how they'd gone wrong: delaying lunch.

✤

And James. With the routines of the office, he could skate over the accumulating weekdays. But the grief would open up in him at night: his bad nights seemed all the same repeating night. Once or twice a week, in the early hours, Nora would find him struggling in sleep, overwrought, his breathing labored, his face damp. "What?" He'd be shaking his hands, flapping them around. "Jimmy," she'd say. His hands. "Jimmy," she'd repeat. "Bad dream."

He'd become alert then; for him, the bedroom would define itself as bedroom, Nora as Nora, his dream already becoming a dark cumulous layering pushed into the distance, and his heart racing. And his hands? He'd curl and flex his fingers.

She might be stroking his face. Some nights she'd give him glasses of water. Some nights they'd make love, and his panic would melt into that.

WINTER

Beyond the windows the sea turned from greenish gray to slate gray to solid onyx. Katy trailed Nora from kitchen to living room to laundry room and back, often on pretext of helping. When Nora finally stationed herself in one spot to read the news or mix biscuit dough, Katy would settle nearby. This pattern repeated over weeks, months, the distance between Katy and Theo having widened, Nora having found steady routine. Say that for Katy, the house became saturated with Nora, or what she could find of Nora. Say its imprint on her as *home* originated now: after Italy, in the variations of winter light, the months indoors with her mother. Perhaps this was the germ of Theo's slow retreat into a different life: he took refuge on the blue living room sofa, from which vantage point he could glance up from his books to the kitchen, the stairs leading down to the laundry room. Separate but still within view. Nora appeared to be Nora. Katy appeared to be Katy; Theo, Theo. And yet. At moments the house might seem to be a constructed set, solid furniture apparently hollow and insubstantial; this perception floated from one of them to the next, occasionally resting with James. At moments their bodies seemed equally hollow; at others, completely in charge. In all weather they ran and walked on the beach. They kicked soccer balls against the interior seawall (Theo) or threw stones (Katy), ran, or swam at the local pool until exhausted.

Short days, the coast bound in slush, wet snow, thin panes of ice, pelting rain. Other days snow swept across the coast. The cloud cover seemed permanent, varying between a featureless gray sheet and ridged, surging dark storm clouds. The longing for spring blurred into other longings: James longed for the very house in which he lived, but a past, summer-tinted version. Surely it could not help to look back. Subversive, how such longing came upon him, say, in the early mornings when the roads were barely salted, as the moving red trails of taillights glowed through the blue-black predawn, or after work, when dusk had already passed and the sky along the South Shore was a blanket of chalky indigo. Always, it seemed, he was driving in darkness, and in the wash of traffic he imagined he could hear the surf. There were occasional clear days, clear frigid nights. He longed for cool nights in spring and summer, and autumn, when the days might still be brilliant, the bay a fat sapphire melting at the edges—longed for autumn as if the recent one had failed to arrive. He could not say what this meant.

Occasionally at work, too: in the office elevator while punching buttons, an unbidden image might appear. He'd mentally review a risk analysis, sift numbers, wait through the floor stops, and then he'd tumble from the analysis to the deck under a slant of orange light, a slant of yellow light, cirrus clouds sweeping east. Salt. The old October feeling of walking away while one's name is being called.

COCKTAILS

"How long do you think you can stand still?" James said. "Everything around you is moving." Though in fact certain things, many things, stood in place. The blue sofa, the kettle on the stove. And it depended, didn't it, on how you defined motion? Often Nora seemed to go somewhere; she seemed to return. She waved an arm in the direction of the lamp.

"What?" James said.

If each day she too commuted, to Boston or nearer—if each day she too arrived at an office, a school, a gallery, gave over to that particular clock—and later each day returned to the same address, would she have discovered a different kind of motion (say, his) and sooner? Or was the fact of being Nora, rather than James, or James rather than Nora, the key? For months they'd received invitations formal and casual, for company dinners at restaurants, company soirees in private homes; for months they'd politely (Nora) or more effusively (James) declined. Nora could imagine herself on a small olive-shaped boat crossing the pool of a martini glass, but not at a cocktail party itself.

"An olive-shaped boat?" James said. The James who courted her might have laughed, but their courtship itself was a tiny receding boat. His tone had become corrective.

And he would persist. Because he was James. Because as a boy he'd learned to travel to another place in his mind, as if there were two chambers linked by a corridor, with doors he'd learned how to close. Since then the number of chambers had increased, hadn't it? In the time she'd known him.

"Sooner or later," he said, "you have to return to the world."

Assuming a cocktail party was the world, Nora thought, and for a moment there was the flickering sensation of another room—a blue glass lamp, a white teacup, profuse leaves beyond a window filtering the light through square panes—she recognized as Lydia's in Cambridge, that wafer of time before Italy. But now Nora's mind also had hallways and doors.

Returning to the world without Molly: in some way Nora remained the holdout, lingering beyond the starched order of business and school days. Still waiting. Knowing better, yet watching for signs. She could see in Theo and Katy the grain of disbelief that Italy had ever occurred, the momentary slip into dream logic. Often, before Italy, they had found Molly in surprising corners of the Blue Rock house. Once again, the house was immediate and real, Rome unreal. You waited for a sign until you forgot that you were waiting, now and then remembering *yes still waiting*, if more secretively. Eventually the waiting diminished. This had been the case after her parents' deaths, yet once or twice a year she'd still inadvertently dip into a blurry, suspended disbelief.

Eventually, she told James yes. She bought new dresses, new pumps, new lipstick, made an appointment at the hairdresser's, as if she were still the sprightly Nora. She hired a good-natured, slightly hippie-ish teenager to babysit, a girl Theo and Katy both claimed to like. Yet the nights Nora and James went out, Theo would not wish them good-bye, and Katy would refuse to sleep anywhere but the couch.

Receptions at upscale restaurants; cocktail parties in lavish homes. James's colleagues were not unkind, but they didn't seem quite *solid* to Nora, as if perhaps they were made of lacquered sponge foam (but who was she to demand ballast?). She wore little black dresses and pearls. The women clustered and dispersed, weaving around and through the clusters of men, chatting about vacation spots and Junior League events, the men tossing statistics as they speculated about ball teams and venues, mall sites, business zones. There were the expected sexual jokes, mild in mixed company—allusions to prowess and voluptuous girls, innuendos tossed at the wives—the women's cheerful remonstrations, James laughing (her James, his laugh) with the others. Nora stepped back and pretended to sip her drink, watching the proceedings over the top of her glass the way Katy might, or Molly, gazing back and forth between an effervescing drink and the party crowd.

She found herself pretending to like whimsical photos of cats.

At the Lowrys', olives sank into cocktails. Nora drank a martini, and that night accepted a cigarette, though she hadn't smoked around company people before. It was soothing, the martini; after the martini she too was smiling (*she'd done this before, she could do this*), and that appeared to be all anyone expected now, all James expected. He nursed his drink and complimented the women and elicited men's opinions of the Bruins' bench. They were happy talkers, the Lowrys and the Lowrys' seventy-five guests. Nora was drawn instead to the furniture: the living room sofa was upholstered in black fabric covered with small white and red tulips, green leaves and curving stems framing the profusion of flowers. It occurred to her that she had seen the fabric somewhere else. Where? Or was it simply the pattern, reminiscent of Morris, an echo of a month she'd once spent paging through catalogs and drawing vines and leaves in a little sketchbook? An Arts and Crafts exhibit somewhere? She wanted to take off her shoes. She wanted to curl into a corner of the sofa and smoke a cigarette, or two cigarettes, and have another martini.

"What is it?" Claire Lowry, leaning in.

"Wonderful fabric," Nora said. "So intricate."

Claire Lowry smiled and lightly touched Nora's hand. "Can we get you another drink?" She scanned the room for her waiter. "Tell George, dear, what you'd like."

So a second martini appeared. She was not drunk, though she perceived a pocket of space between her body and the room. The Lowrys' anniversary cake, a white baroque tower ringed with sugar roses, apparently belonged to an alternate universe, something Alice-like, transforming while you switched from martinis to champagne. Alluring, sweet, belying the frantic scrambling and concussive days, and she found herself slipping behind a kind of scrim in the mind, as if only a silhouette Nora remained at the party. She asked the waiter George where she might find another cigarette.

On the drive home James's face settled into contentment, lips slightly upturned. He patted her arm before they pulled onto the highway, the streetlights sliding past the window, the air tinted deep greenish blue. The radio broadcast a harmonized jingle for a car dealership, the Bruins' play-by-play. In Blue Rock, the sky was soft black, layered clouds revealing stars only toward the northwest, the moon hidden, the wind picking up, and when she stepped out of the car, all sounds seemed to give way to the slap of waves against the seawall and their sloshing ebb, and the gusting wind in which she felt encased. She followed James up the wooden stairs to the deck and through the door into the dark kitchen; as soon as she was inside, the wind fell away, the waves now a murmur conversing with the murmur of TV. For an instant James became the silhouette, receding as he approached the bright living room and the television and now-speaking babysitter. Then he stepped out of view. Nora stood in the kitchen without turning on the light, and the feeling of the scrim returned to her, and she imagined smoking the extra cigarette she'd tucked in her coat pocket; imagined the room's shadow and the murmurs covering her. Diving into the moment the way seals dive into the sea, resurfacing elsewhere. But the TV murmuring stopped, and Nora left her pumps off at the door, the cold floorboards startling her back.

REPRODUCTIONS

The Magdalen with Two Flames (c.1638-43)
METROPOLITAN MUSEUM OF ART

The Magdalen with the Smoking Flame (c.1640)
LOS ANGELES COUNTY MUSEUM OF ART

The Repentent Magdalen (c.1635-40)
NATIONAL GALLERY OF ART

Georges de la Tour

Maybe La Tour was right: one view of her is not enough. Repeatedly, he painted her, always in candlelight. A young woman, her long dark hair falling over her shoulder and down her back, into shadow. She is beautiful; she is always beautiful, and always alone, seated beside a table, sideways to the viewer, always partly hidden. She wears a white blouse, a red skirt. Near her again and again in varied arrangement: a book, a skull too large to be a child's, a single candle. In *The Magdalen with Two Flames*, an ornate mirror reflects and doubles the candlelight; in other views, a cross lies on the table.

The Magdalen with Two Flames is perhaps the most elegant: she sits straight-backed, her white blouse covering her shoulders (though her pale neck and upper chest are visible), the skirt covering her legs to the floor. In her lap, the skull, on which her hands lie folded together. Her head is turned away— her gaze, like ours, apparently drawn to the flame reflected in the tabletop mirror.

La Tour's most tender version: *The Magdalen with the Smoking Flame.* Here her posture—like the Fetti Magdalen's—suggests her private grief. The right side of her face is revealed in candlelight, her gaze directed at the flame. The blouse here is off the shoulder, her skin pale, her dark hair falling and falling into shadow. Light glazes her left forearm and her left hand, on which she rests her chin and cheek. It's that hand against her cheek, and the details of her face—the dark iris touched by light, the curve of her lip (red enough to echo the ruby skirt) that reveal her vulnerability. Bare feet, bare calves; a ball of light spills onto her left knee. In her lap, the skull gapes toward you, although her right hand rests on its crown, gently, almost comfortingly. In her solitude, a delicate melancholy; a sudden sound, or a shift in light, would break the mood. If she knows we are hovering in the shadows beyond, she's managed to claim privacy—as if only our invisibility keeps the moment aloft.

Shadow almost fills the final *Repentant Magdalen*, the candle's flame obscured, silhouetting a skull on top of the book. The woman has moved to the right of the table and now she's in profile, leaning on her right hand, her left hand resting on the skull. She contemplates a second skull set in a frame not unlike a mirror's. The shadows seem to mute even the darkness of her hair, and only her upper body is visible. Light settles on her blouse, on the billow of sleeve around her planted right elbow, so that her arm and the sleeve form the shape of a tulip bulb, or of a lowered trumpet horn. Her mouth is covered by her hand and the falling shadows. A palpable gravity; a palpable tenderness. She has receded even farther from the viewing eye and, in the story, from the world; and so you move closer, peering through the shadow. The paradox of capturing privacy: perhaps La Tour wished to shield her entirely, yet could not resist the image.

Wait long enough and your eyes might adjust to the darkness.

SARA

As if Nora herself were an egg, or a water balloon; as if her body were rigged for disaster, her family grew rabidly solicitous. Had James—or anyone—treated her this way during past pregnancies? Maybe her father, maybe with Theo? It seemed not: if she remembered correctly, if memory had not blunted and discolored, James had been fearless. Unworried, at least about the pregnancy itself, and Nora's capacity to carry, confident of the beautiful normalcy of new cells and the beautiful normalcy of their development. As if by not imagining what might go awry, one dodged the possibility. Or as if his certainty also reflected a belief in Nora herself, that her intelligence and good character—whatever he loved in her—would ensure healthy gestation. And Nora? She must have had faith in his faith.

A hopeful season, yet a house of cards, the family's anxiety skewed in a new direction. At least domestic tasks lightened, as Theo and Katy dutifully attended to chores, and James caught up on repairs, cooked weekend suppers. But there were extreme, near-comical moments, say when she poured herself tea from an ordinary teapot, and James insisted on pouring instead, as if *tea* might overwhelm her.

So perhaps the mode of Molly's death had begun to blur, suspicion shifting to Nora's body itself; the failure to keep one child safe shadowing the task of properly carrying another. Or perhaps the reappearance of June, and the echo of departure for Rome and the first anniversary of Molly's death, had them all silently spinning. James and Katy and Theo would swarm around her, then vanish into their separate retreats, occasionally eyeing her from doorways and the peripheries of magazines. When Katy climbed the stairs to her room, she was reluctant; in an hour she'd return and again follow Nora.

For the first months of the pregnancy, Nora felt, if anything, solid and capable, but later she wanted more sleep, and her distraction deepened. The chores she began, she sometimes left unfinished. Perhaps, she thought, her family's well-meaning mistrust had undermined her. In the last months, she often found herself alone in their company, in a private elsewhere sometimes shared and frequently disturbed by this forming kicking child who would leave her body in its own good time.

They would not have said—no one would have said—they were trying to replace Molly. A moving forward, another child, the family reshaped, though of course the imprint of a third child—the echoing third girl—remained. In their minds, say the baby became not-Molly, a blank space beside that imprint, an easy elision. And if the child was a boy? Even a quiet, shy boy—how quickly Molly/not-Molly might be swept aside for a new paradigm.

And for all that, the baby herself, once in the world, seemed the weight of a handkerchief, the weight of a spoon. You could imagine her levitating from the crib, even from your arms, guided by sound; her eyes still a milky gray-blue, gradually focusing. A sleepy, almost gossamer presence; a wisp, taking up the merest space, a corner of the space that had been Molly's. Sara, a name that sounded weightless, blending into Nora, toward whose voice she would bend.

And once Sara was born, how quickly the dynamic changed: how quickly Nora returned to being an ordinary Nora, no longer suspect, no longer a curiosity, as all of them focused on the baby. And although Nora felt in ways returned to a familiar shared life, it also seemed as if she had come ashore farther east, as if the pregnancy and the glare of family scrutiny had subtly and permanently set her apart. The bleary first months were a kind of plateau, a flat expanse of present tense, of managing days and nights, the recent past having dropped behind a curtain. But there were still lost moments when Nora would be brought back suddenly by Sara's cry and wonder if it was the first cry or the sixth; occasional frantic dreams from which she would wake to find Sara sleeping or just waking, and Katy stretched out on the nursery floor.

During the late evenings, after Katy and Theo had gone to bed, James would carry Sara to the living room and hold her sleeping against him as he read a report. He tracked their separate breathing, at times imagined a tether between them preventing her from floating off. In those hours, the sense-memory of holding the others as infants resurfaced, differentiated not by the child but by the feeling of space: muted bands of streetlight against the Cambridge living room wall, a shadowy, pile-carpeted den in Newton. And what would it mean to begin here, to first learn the world at the shore? Sara had not witnessed anything, in Rome or elsewhere, and therefore seemed free. Say one could sift out what resided both in the others and between them, *that* June and its consequences, the half-buried thoughts: would Sara then encounter the clearest silences, unencumbered by absence, by the past? Say James believed this. Say he was partly right: she would first learn the world at the shore, begin oblivious. The past gave way to the future. Yet Rome, their Rome, also held its place, intangible, but dense with gravity. One could face elsewhere, resisting its tug, yet Rome and all that followed still silently whirled. Abstracted, like Molly herself—the space that had been Molly, or what, within each of the once-vacationing Murphys, had become of her.

Katy guarded the baby. Walked her, soothed her, slept in the nursery rocker or on the floor beside the crib, despite admonitions to stay in her own room. Natural, wasn't it? Weren't they all protective?

Yes and no. Katy would not hesitate to hand the baby over to Nora, but after a few months resisted giving the baby to James, or to Theo. One night, then another, the scenes repeated themselves: she'd walk the baby into another room, humming, ignoring James though he'd just arrived home, retreating when Theo greeted Sara. As if they were not to be trusted. *And who was holding Molly's hand?* James thought and tried to unthink.

When he confronted her, Katy said, "She's my sister."

"And Theo's sister," James said. "And my daughter."

Katy sulkily handed the baby to James and observed him for several minutes, as if he might drop her, then vanished up the stairs.

In the ensuing months, other hard moments accrued: Katy would ignore his instructions to turn off the television, or finish homework, or please help sweep the deck. More often, he'd be sharp. He did not want to be sharp; or, rather, he knew sharpness was no use. He tried to be more attentive, greeting Katy first when he arrived home, sitting with her over math. Waiting. She'd grow quiet, observing him, eventually becoming merely skittish.

"Katy's fine," Nora told him. "She's doing fine."

"Really?" James said.

"What do you suggest?" Nora said. "She hardly sees you."

"I'm just saying," James said. "She isn't fine."

And who was, Nora thought. Last week, she'd caught Theo with a beer in his bedroom, trying to drink, coughing, spitting beer onto the floor. Theo was mortified. Later, James only shrugged, as if sneaking beer at twelve were de rigueur.

Most days, Katy attended to her homework. And though she stuck close to Nora and Sara, that year she'd made a few friends, wary odd-duck girls who played board games and tape-recorded fake commercials, girls with strained laughs—girls who, like Katy, relaxed around Sara. They loved small animals, competed to pet the neighbors' puppy; they called to wandering cats and scooped them up. They were shy girls who eventually burst out with stories of family dogs and younger siblings. They visited the house after school, took turns holding the baby, at times confiding in Sara about slights or private disappointments, as if she were a plump little Buddha. In their presence, Nora recalled school years when her own life had seemed awash in girls, her sister Meg a daily companion. And if the thought of Newton or Lydia or Cambridge also arose, she'd refocus on the baby, or turn the radio to a pop station. Timid at first, the girls would sing along.

A DAY AT THE PARK

On a May Sunday, he took Theo to Fenway Park and discovered that Fenway Park remained itself. As it appeared in televised games, yes, but from those images who could make the imaginative leap to such scale and immersion? It seemed that after all, he and Theo could reenter Fenway as ordinary fans: that he could take a place in Fenway as he had for years. Here were their tickets; here were their seats. A sunny warm day, no sign of rain, a game against the Royals. Theo brought a transistor radio he held to his ear. He rattled off statistics with an intensity James recalled in himself.

When the game began, the day telescoped, pinned itself to the fortunes of the Red Sox, one pitch at a time. The first two Royals out, the third. The Sox began with a single; after a double play, Yastrzemski came to bat and singled. Yastrzemski, whom James had followed for more than a decade. Now, at Fenway, one could focus on Yaz at first base, and the Royals pitcher readying for the rookie batter, the dramatic moment when Yaz made his move to steal second and found himself caught out. It was, at least, early. The Royals scored a run at the top of the third; the Sox responded with a three-run homer from Bernie

Carbo, James and Theo shouting with the crowd. By then the world beyond the ballpark had dropped away: the world was the game, the crowd, the family beside them, the Little Leaguers in the next row, the man in front of them cheerfully insulting the umpire. One batter then the next settled into his stance; the pitcher wound up and threw, the ball flying into the dust or out toward the field, infielders shifting, outfielders in motion, catching and throwing almost faster than the eye could track, the umpire's emphatic gestures. And from the crowd the uncensored shouts, flashes of outrage, drawn-out resignation, flashes of joy. Here James and Theo were one more father, one more son, awaiting the next hit, the next swift realignment of the men on the field after the bat connected. A pure if temporary belonging. In the fourth a Royals home run, the Sox hitless. Theo and James drank cold sodas, watched for a sign. Then in the fifth another Carbo home run, another collective burst, Theo rising up, thrilled—as if, yes, thrill were again possible. Then the innings rolled forward, the rookie Lynn hitting a double in the sixth, the third out coming too soon. The Royals changed pitchers; the Sox held on, Rick Wise pitching the full nine.

Even when the game ended and the throng exited Fenway into the city, despite the crowded sidewalks and occasional shoving, James's elation did not end, not yet, but morphed into a sensation of contentment and possibility, as if he and Theo could go anywhere. Nothing distinguished them from the fathers and sons heading into restaurants or to evenings in unfamiliar towns: all seemed equal. Had he described it, James might have used the word *normalcy*, considered the day a return from exile.

When they arrived at the house, the late-day light was clear gold, the bay cobalt. Katy and a redheaded MacFarland girl raced bikes up and down the empty street; on the deck, Nora paged through an art magazine while Sara dozed on her lap. They had dinner; James drank a cold beer. Theo described the three-run homer; Nora laughed, reached over and mussed Theo's hair. A routine gesture of hers *before* but not *since*. It was and was not the same gesture; and the laugh clearly genuine, clearly hers but slightly altered, as if he had heard it from the next room. Was there, too, a missed beat? He paused, but then Sara threw her spoon on the floor.

"So much for the spoon," Nora said, and held out a pacifier.

"Next weekend," Katy said, "Lucy MacFarland's coming back."

The bicycling redhead? "Oh good," James told her. "How was your ride? Tires okay?"

"I won," Katy said. "But it didn't really count."

"You were fast," Theo said, apparently in a mood to like Katy.

And then James was clearing the table, and washing dishes, and working on financials for the New York office while Katy read from a textbook covered in craft paper, her name repeated in wavy emerald letters on the front piece. Theo hid in a novel. Nora bathed Sara and settled her in her crib.

Later, as James readied for bed, Nora smoothed cream on her hands, efficient and unself-conscious, and he could see then her deep fatigue, which of course had inflected her laugh. (Were there other inflections? He stopped at fatigue.) Recently, they'd begun to have sex again, gingerly, when not exhausted. He set out clothes for the morning: white shirt, gold tie, sepia shoes. She perched at the edge of the bed, watching him, her gaze shifting from the pressed suit to his face to the sepia shoes. Her thin blue robe adhered to the lines of her clavicle. "I'm pregnant," she said. She addressed the pressed suit. "I need this to be okay."

How astonished they'd been when she became pregnant with Theo; happy with Katy. And Molly, yes, they'd planned for three. With Sara, anxious, but too the hope of—what?—a redemption? A turning away from death. Say you make that turn; say you see glimmers of redemption. Now another child? For the first time, the news less welcome; for the first time, a wish to stop. And yet that turning away; and yet those glimmers, the wish impossible.

He and Nora were altered, this an altered life he could not steer. (Had he thought, for a moment, he could steer?) But okay. Nora was pregnant. Nora was waiting.

He affected serenity. "How are you feeling?" he said.

"Tired."

He nodded and crossed the floor to the bed. *Do this*, he thought, and mussed her hair. *Do this*, he thought, and kissed her.

SMALL GIRLS AND KATY

At first Katy would have to remind herself, almost daily: *Delia Delia Delia.* They'd grown accustomed to Sara, the baby who was not-Molly, although there had been moments when one or another of them would slip, using Molly's name. It didn't happen often. You'd hear the name aloud, then a flat confused silence before a change of subject. "You're all Murphys," Nora would say. "Sara with a touch of Connor." No one argued. But the other baby photos revealed clear variations: Katy with the darkest hair, Theo fair, eyes deep-set, Sara's baby face more oval. Molly and Delia round wide-eyed babies you could not tell apart.

"Take a look at your Murphy cousins," Nora said. "It's all the same picture."

It was harder now to remember everything of Molly, even to say *that* laugh, *that* voice was Molly's, this one Delia's, because Delia too was a little wild, her happiness, her sobbing already dramatic, already washing across Molly's first expressions.

Molly as a four-year-old remained more distinct. Katy's memory diverged from Theo's, holding to different details and perhaps different Mollys. Italy blurred: a church, a heavy door beyond which a high ceiling appeared roped with gold, paintings of apostles and saints swooning. But there was more than one church, and another swooning on the street. Nora naked, washing. The back of Molly's dress, her legs moving, almost in flight. And now Katy couldn't say for sure where they were standing. Or sitting? She's supposed to keep hold of Molly's hand. Sometimes Molly shakes her hand away—so typical of Molly. Sometimes Molly lets go and holds out her palm, so that Katy can give her a coin. But are they in Rome? The flat palm, a copper round. In Newton, Katy gave Molly pennies.

And for a moment, Molly might have sat outside the church, but she did not sit on the bed with Theo and their mother. No one wants to leave the bed. Glasses of water appear. Katy will have to move from the spot beside her mother when her father and Molly come back, of course. The coveted space, the space she is always giving up; but where are they? It's taking too long. If they return, she will relent, offer the space without complaint. There are splinters of hot light at the curtain's edges, and she has to turn her head toward the pillow. She clings to her mother, and then her father returns without Molly. Every time he returns, it is without Molly. Here the story never alters, and here the same pinprick recognition: after the truck, the blood, how could she expect Molly back?

With the little girls, Nora was worn out, but she had also returned—the playful Nora Katy had forgotten. Nora's false laugh, the tinny one, erupted only around people she disliked, the real laugh until now a remembered thing they'd gone without. Katy waited for it to fill other moments, but nothing she tried made Nora laugh, and in the failure Katy found a thick clumsiness, and the sad puzzle as to why it took the little girls to bring her mother back, her own efforts doomed from the start. But the little girls called—*Tee*, Sara called her—and Delia reached for Katy, squealed when Katy entered the room. With them Katy too felt lighter, and part of her mother's lightness. When the girls were sleeping and she occupied a room alone with her mother, she was no longer as light. She was simply Katy.

And still there were moments when her mother faded out: you had to watch for lapses. She might start to make sandwiches, and then leave the room, forgetting, or might drive halfway to the market before turning and driving to the library. Dropping into the space that was what? Katy kept watch, herded the little girls whenever they went out. She would have liked to tell her father that her mother still dreamed in the middle of the day, but he was hardly home at all.

Between her parents, a rising disturbance. Their Newton way of fighting had been looser, more dramatic and somehow less serious, airy, the big gestures also self-consciously cartoonish: eventually they'd made bug eyes at each other, or stuck their tongues out. But this fighting was different, guarded and tense, the low chattering of dinner plates on a heavy wobbling tray, a rapid clacking punctuated by a stomp or a word—*no* or *lonely* or *go*—and blown through with shushing. Katy and Theo listened together, the fight becoming an approaching train, moving closer and closer and reaching a crescendo only yards away, then—as if their eavesdropping were apparent—retreating, *ssh clack ssh clack ssh*.

Weekends and evenings when her father was home his arms were full of baby girls, or he was reading his files, or speaking heartily on the phone. He was difficult to catch. In winter, Katy forwent the luxury of sleep and padded down to the kitchen just after 6:00 AM and found him alone with his coffee, already in his suit. He stood at the counter eating a muffin, scanning the paper. On good mornings he called her *K-kat. K-kat, what's up today?* Some mornings he kissed her on the cheek. Some mornings he mussed her hair. *Cereal for you?* he offered. She shrugged and poured herself a glass of milk. *Blueberry muffin?* he said.

It was the prize for getting up early, these moments with her father, the added prize of a muffin. But the moments were brief: the little girls woke early, and soon they were in the kitchen with her mother. Soon one or another of them was on her lap—Delia either cranky or lively, Sara quiet and vague—and Katy was coaxing them to eat Cheerios, trying to minimize the spills. The girls babbled and tossed Cheerios on the floor, and their city-bound father slipped away while Katy was distracted, forgetting a kiss good-bye.

NORA'S COLLECTION

It began haphazardly and remained on the cheap, the color values erratic. In high school, Nora kept a few of Meg's reprinted *Annunciations*; in college, she taped postcards and museum sale posters to the cinder-block walls, reproductions she imitated in her own first paintings. When she first lived with James, she'd save exhibit postcards friends mailed from abroad, or pick them up at local shows, or cut pages from old books or magazines. The Dutch, the Italians, a handful of the French, stored in shoe boxes she'd cover in colored gift-wrap. Rembrandt, Vermeer, Van Ruisdael, Da Vinci, Bernini. La Tour, Matisse, Vuillard. The Magdalens she'd call "sad Marys." The backs of many remained blank, as if waiting for inscription, though some had vacationers' scribbled messages, dates and stamped locations. On the dresser of the bedroom she shared with James in Blue Rock, Nora kept two small frames in which she displayed favorites; on the wall beside the north window hung a corkboard on which she posted others, changing them according to mood.

Rarely, she'd hang a portrait—say, a Vermeer—in the kitchen, above the girls' semi-fauvist paintings and drawings of flying kids and orange swans, or tiny boats skimming over the blue outline of a hand. Her drawings from school she kept in a thin brown portfolio in her closet. In a happier moment, two of her paintings—the ones Theo kept—hung in the upper hallway at Blue Rock. A pink-toned Vuillard-influenced interior, and a portrait of Nora's mother reading.

ANOTHER SUMMER

She dreamed of driving in the rain in what seemed to be Paris, though she was driving a station wagon. It was an uncomplicated plot: she needed to get home before the school bus carrying Theo and Katy; she needed to pick up Molly from the babysitter. She was running late—why was she running late? She'd been visiting her other life, a friend, a museum, something that James and the children had no part in. And now she was driving, and though brick buildings and green parks flashed by, she seemed to be driving in place.

How transparent, her dreams, but recognizing their transparency did not prevent their repetition or the accompanying anxiety, or alter her waking life. Of course, in this dream Molly lived, and waited at the babysitter's (though where were Sara and Delia?), and for a moment after Nora awoke, Molly still waited, and then the dream gave way. Wind gusts whipped the side of the house, and when they subsided she could hear the little girls in their room, Delia chatting then calling for her.

She did not speak to James about these dreams, believing he'd be irritated by their repetition or by her dream portraits of him: he was never there to pick up the children, never there to collect

Molly from the babysitter's (though in truth, he devoted week-ends to the family). But the days and weeks accumulated when they'd forgo not only talk about dreams, but anything beyond the tasks of the day, both of them in rigid traces. Some days Nora had no chance to shower, others no chance to eat. Often, James returned at eight, exhausted. Small daily affections, ordinary en-dearments—at first with subtexts of a promised *later*—took a perfunctory spin as the fatigue accumulated, the space between them widening. On bad days, "sweetheart" meant *What now?* or *Again?* or *No*. Not the first marriage sustained by etiquette, but after a while, you begin to lose track. Some days, James appeared to her as dreamless and drone-like, if also—and unjustly—im-patient. Her weeks seemed a cast-iron box containing the house and children, which she hoisted and carried without respite, few moments to acknowledge she was lonely.

Yet this: the salt breeze, the taste of salt breeze. Always she took solace from the shore—even returning from the super-market, you'd move from the main onto secondary roads and then, finally, near the cliffs of Blue Rock, you'd catch the first glimpse of the sea, the view as you approached unfolding, sap-phire and vast, once you crested the hill.

She followed the road along the cliff, which then veered inland and down toward the harbor, brilliant now too in the afternoon, sailboats rocking on their moorings, and in the dis-tance other white triangular sails cutting fast across the blue. The road led around and down to another access road, to the beaches, to Shore Road.

✣

There was one last good summer. As the weather warmed, the tensions between Nora and James began to fall away. He arranged for two weeks off, and the first morning left bed at sunrise and ran, before anyone else had stirred. There was, in both of them, a listening, something perhaps instilled by the sea, Nora might have said, though James would say only that the summer calmed him. They had not expected to return to each other so quickly, and did not mention it, as if saying anything might sweep away what seemed itself another dream. Yet, in that moment, it was as if they were younger, a sensation at once new and comfortingly familiar, James his playful attentive self.

Two weeks of runs in the mornings; two weeks of lounging with Delia and Sara on the beach. Once, he and Katy lunched together down at the harbor front; once, he and Theo rented a canoe and paddled along the cove. In the late afternoons, he and Nora had drinks with the neighboring MacFarlands; evenings, if the wind was down, dinner out on the deck. He and Nora did not argue; it seemed they had nothing to argue about. It had something to do with the air, the body giving over to the place. Blue Rock lulled him; in summer it had always lulled him. Soon there was little beyond the immediacy of the moment. In the morning, he would find the daily *Globe*, quickly skim it, and set it aside, shedding interest in anything beyond the requirements of the day or the house or the schedule of tides.

And in Nora, the rigidities, the resistances melted away: she found, then, the return of desire. The cumulative effect of the light, shifting from orange at sunrise to clear lemon, of the sky's cornflower blue streaked by high white cirrus clouds. The sea became cobalt, red tones tinting the waves late in the day; when the sky was overcast, a deeper green tipped by whitecaps. Sunsets to the west still splashed pink into the eastern sky and across the water, the clouds reflecting the pink and the water reflecting the clouds. There was the cumulative effect of the tidal lapping, the black starry nights and the paler black nights, the curved reflections of the moon; the cumulative effect of breathing, of no longer holding her breath, not knowing until then that she had been. The effect of her late-night stirrings, when she would slip outside, barefoot and in her robe, to the deck or even to the beach, downwind from the open house, so that the breeze would sweep away all sounds. Then she could let herself tumble, let a spasm of breathless grief pass through her, after which she again found the air, and leaned back and watched the stars. Sometimes James found her there and led her back to bed, and he was, then, her James, his the body she would fall into.

And when he began again his commute to Boston, the hours of light stretched long enough to give him clear pink early mornings, and the late hours of syrupy light, the shift through orange to indigo; more drinks with Joan and Pete MacFarland, easy dinners on the deck, the kids content after their days at the beach, Theo reading, Katy beading bracelets and showing them to James, the little girls climbing onto his lap.

August thunderstorms, predawn lightning cracking wide the black sky over the black sea, jagged lines to the northeast, and the felt-sense of water spilling over in the dark. The weather Nora loved to sleep in, and often could not, because the little girls would wake. There was a lull in the storms, the rain diminishing to a mild drizzle, when James got up. She would later remember wanting him to stay in bed with her, to make love before the kids woke, and after to loll in bed listening to the rain, as they used to. "Come back," she said, and for a moment he did. For a moment he lay against her, skin damp and smelling of soap and of James, the clove/shaved-wood smell she thought of as his. She could feel his weight, and wanted to stay like this, with the rain falling, and the sea sounds mixing in, and the world beyond the room asleep.

A moment. Then he was dressing in a wheat linen suit and blue shirt and striped tie, transforming himself into the citified James, and he was down the stairs. In a few minutes the scent of coffee began to rise. In the distance, a faint rumble, another storm coming through. The little girls would call any minute, and the morning's ease or difficulty would depend on how the storm affected them, how well they'd give over to a change of plans. Because there was in these storms a permission to ignore the day as you'd expected it would be, to break open the hours, follow their eccentric configurations. The lightning streaked over the sea, jagged but oddly delicate, followed by tremendous thunder. After dawn, the sea was gray-green and ribbed with whitecaps, and yes, she could hear the little girls, a somewhat plaintive "Mama," from Sara. And when Nora went to find them, Delia was standing up in her crib, facing the window, watching the fat streams of running water, her face ecstatic.

ROME

The Ecstasy of Saint Teresa
Gian Lorenzo Bernini (c.1647-52)
CHIESA DI SANTA MARIA DELLA VITTORIA

Northwest of the Piazza della Repubblica, against a swirl of urban traffic, Chiesa di Santa Maria della Vittoria: an aura of disturbance. Inside, above the main altar, thick gold clouds cluster, chunky and graceless, and small faces peep out, gold rays enunciate the heavy composition. To the far right of the altar, beyond the pews, a clear sarcophagus holds a mannequin: a bleeding young woman.

To the altar's left, set off behind a protective rail, the main attraction: Bernini's famous *Ecstasy of Saint Teresa*. She's nearly alive, the swooning marble Teresa, her skin luminous, the drape of her robes delicate, the flowing lines a superb deceit, as is her face, her mouth an O of pleasure and pain. In a moment, she may rise out of the stone. Gold rays splay above her, an aperture in the wall bringing in more light. Nearby an impish angel readies another piercing arrow; marble opera boxes line the upper side walls, galleries from which a marble Cardinal

Cornaro and other notable marble men gaze down. Below, along the wood guard-railing hang laminated pages from the life of Saint Teresa, describing in three languages her terrible exquisite pain, her rapture.

A rising into light—say, divine light—or an obliteration? Orgasmic bliss, here with the torturing angel, the scrutinizing men, and the text proclaiming the splendor of her pain. Do not forget—how could you?—the larger scene dominated by those chunky gold clouds, and opposite the Bernini, just beyond the pews, the bloody mannequin girl.

FALL

Yet once summer gave way, so did the relative harmony. Often Nora and James rotated through separate rooms of the house, and in the same room remained silent, and when in conversation spoke curtly, not knowing why, and in bed remained disengaged and separate. After September, when the hours of light shortened and the season's cloud cover thickened, James became restless, and spoke again of other towns. As if, seduced by summer, he'd forgotten about the colder, darker seasons; as if, after five years, the long commute came as a surprise.

Barely light—or still dark—when he left the house in the morning, full dark when he returned. The sound of the sea washed over everything as if it were the sound of darkness. He did not like living in a town of nightscapes, although in early morning, a calm settled as he quickly traveled along the South Shore. Until the last several miles he moved unimpeded up the highway and found reprieve in the solitude of the car, the blue air of half-sleeping towns dotted with floating colored orbs of traffic signals, convenience store signs glowing. On the radio, news from Washington, or New York; news from abroad, read without fanfare by an anchor whose steady baritone pitch knit a surface of reason over the chaos; or a string quartet, a duet for piano and violin, a bit of Paganini. Sweet coffee from the donut shop. A purposefulness would take hold as Blue Rock dropped away, and the highways extended north, and Boston's southern industrial flank rose into view, on better days the light still peach-inflected, momentarily lending the steel containers, the rusting ship hulls, the smoke-blackened warehouses and dull russet boxcars a candied gloss. And then Boston's downtown appeared, awake, and he left the highway and crossed onto the busy surface streets with their close press of cars, the rush of pedestrians in good overcoats and fine shoes, the women wearing lipstick and colorful scarves. His office waited—quiet, uncluttered—reports and notes neatly stacked, computer on, his calendar open. More coffee. The usual half hour of reading before phone calls and meetings began. The day's obligations streamed forward, and though they would become layered and chaotic there was still a logic, an underlying structure they did not lose. In this space he could think. In this space there was no feeling of diminishment (headhunters often contacted him; bonuses often appeared), no sea sounds, no wash of darkness.

And as the day unfurled, there would be other moments: camaraderie with his secretary Maureen, camaraderie with Parker, the senior VP, a brief smooth plane of tasks, the pleasure at the deal completed, the pleasures of passing conversations with Janelle, a brainy, athletic girl in legal, and Margaret, the dark-eyed HR rep he'd sometimes take to lunch.

Only a few blocks to the athletic club: Mondays and Wednesdays at six he'd work out, avoiding rush hour. Occasionally he took late meetings, or a drink with Parker before heading home. He did not hurry. As he left the city, he'd again listen to the radio, passing walls of city lights, which faded as he approached the shore towns, his discomfort gathering in dense nightfall.

He pulled up to the house and ascended the outdoor stairs to the deck. There was always the wind and the wash of the sea, and now infrequent stars. Opening the door was like opening a jack-in-the-box, all the energy of the house springing out in his direction. His thoughts seemed to scramble then, in the presence of his family—sparked by the near surprise that he *had* a family—his clear work mind now obscured. The little girls, if they were awake, called to him, running, and Katy, so quick to take offense, offered her skittish *Hi*, Theo—grounded for curfew infractions—barely nodded, Nora kissed James hello. It all seemed to happen at once, the wave of greetings, followed by baths and bedtime stories, and he'd promised Katy something—civics? Math? A report on district elections?

When had he begun to find himself aghast, stunned by the instant erasure of solitude? There had been a tipping point, now submerged. He knew only that while he was in Boston, his family seemed remote, as if they lived not an hour's drive from work but a day's; or as if they lived in the Blue Rock of another decade; as if in his evening commute he traversed both time and space.

A now-chronic disturbance: when he spoke with Nora, he could not name it, substituting *the commute*. And perhaps, yes. Perhaps if he were traveling home to Wellesley after all (his cousin Patrick lived in Wellesley; cousin Patrick seemed content), or simply to Brookline, the moment of arrival would also transform. The family had lived in Blue Rock since Rome, since Molly; perhaps each day then was an extension of the return from Rome, no barrier to stop the aftermath from seeping forward. It seemed plausible. And yet, despite his complaints to Nora, he could no longer picture himself in Wellesley at all.

Was Rome sufficient explanation? Even now, after Sara and Delia? It had become difficult to remember the living Molly, reduced, at times, to a girl thrown across the hot street. That, and the confusion of Delia's resemblance to her, the way the raising of one girl blurred into raising another. But even when he searched, he struggled to find Molly behind the name, *Molly* now so thickly wrapped in event and repercussion it seemed her center had dissolved: in this way, too, the girl ceased to exist.

Whatever mood James was in when he arrived home rippled out, changing the air in the house room by room—lately, Nora thought, a daily upheaval. In anticipation of his arrival, the kids became anxious and sullen, the sounds of the house strained. When James began to spend occasional nights in the city, she expected more turmoil. The first time, yes: Delia teared up dramatically, Sara sulked, Katy retreated. But Theo's petulance abated; he offered to read to the girls. Nora coaxed Katy out of her room with popcorn and a TV movie. No one woke in the night, and the next morning, Nora slept until six thirty. She discovered she did not object.

Yet city nights did not alter his mood in Blue Rock. James took to arguing against the house, as if the place had failed him.

Its inadequacies multiplied. The windowed living room—a play zone for the little girls, admittedly scattered with toys—was a pit, he'd say. Nora had painted their bedroom white and delphinium blue, hung long drapes over the window quilts. Yet it was *unredeemable*, James said, because of the drafts (he'd put off window replacement). He was fed up with storm damage; in the laundry room, they'd found mice. And from Boston—how could she disagree?—Blue Rock was much too far.

A long drive, yes. The bedroom *was* drafty; each spring gnats floated in the morning coffee. Yet Nora had painted and furnished each room, hung the art on the walls. It was Nora who filled the fruit bowl on the table; every day, as the closets, shelves, and drawers emptied, it was Nora who pushed back, tidying, washing, returning hundreds of objects to their places. The house remained a haven.

Hadn't it also been a haven for James?

❧

"Go ahead." The woman waved at the French doors. "Open them—you'll love the garden patio. Not the season, of course, but look at all the brickwork." It was as she said: the doors, the broad patio, the garden brickwork, and still the snow-filled yard beyond, and the old-growth trees. (You have to imagine *grass*, said the woman—Miranda, was it?—you have to imagine *plantings*.) The living room was double the square footage of Blue Rock's; the kitchen also; the dining room accommodated a table for twelve, though Miranda called it "modest," stressing the house's versatility—perfect for entertaining *and* for kids.

A finished basement with a rec room, home office, and extra guest room. "Brand-new listing—it's a great find, Nora," Miranda said. "It's going to go fast."

Fresh tulips on the kitchen counter; roses on the mantel. It was not hard to imagine grass; it was not hard to imagine the children in the various bedrooms. She'd driven through Wellesley before, lovely, yes, in spring. Even now, the neighborhood seemed well accessorized with red-ribboned wreaths on doorways and garages. Perhaps Miranda's enthusiasm meant Nora had successfully played her role, in the soft gray suit she'd worn once to a luncheon with James, gold drop earrings, lipstick. Only twice had she drifted off during their conversation; once in the kitchen and once in the previous house, a four-bedroom Miranda called "very nice" though not, of course, as versatile.

She imagined grass, those cocktail parties with James. Certainly it was a beautiful house. She imagined the little girls running loops around the first floor. At that moment, they were likely running loops in Blue Rock with Joanie MacFarland, Joanie the lively, scrappy, still-pretty neighbor whose father had sold fish. Nora imagined plantings; she imagined a swing set. She thought it unlikely her neighbors would be children of fishmongers; unlikely that she'd meet local artists. *You never know*, James used to say. Though not for a while.

"Wonderful," she told Miranda. "Let me bring James." They would see other houses, "Just in case," Nora said, "he has other ideas."

Saturday then? Or Sunday? Or both? Miranda said. Nora would call.

She drove back to the South Shore through sleet, changed into her jeans before picking up Sara and Delia. In another hour Katy and Theo returned from school, as if on any other day. James arrived just after seven. They managed a family dinner, Delia on Nora's lap, Sara on Theo's. James had things to say tonight: he remembered to ask Katy about skating lessons; he remembered to ask Theo about the school play. Someone had offered him Bruins tickets; at this, Katy glanced up from her chicken but said nothing. James did not seem to notice. "A school night, Theo, but what do you think?"

A holiday reception at the Hyatt this Friday, he reminded Nora (whether to insist she join him or warn her of his late return, Nora could not tell). "It's that season." Which meant he'd be off to other parties.

The household silence after dinner would be brief, Nora knew. For now, Katy took the girls to read stories in the living room and Theo disappeared upstairs. Nora handed James Miranda's file.

"I looked at some houses," she said. "Closer in. We can see them this weekend."

"*This* weekend?" James dropped the file on the table, pushed it toward her. "Nora, I've got deadlines."

As if deadlines weren't perennial; as if he could not forgo the Hyatt, or, if need be, the Bruins. Nora nodded toward the wall calendar. "When else should we look?"

He paused. She could see him stretching for an answer. She waited: she could wait.

Though here was Katy again—not in the living room reading stories, but toting Delia into the kitchen.

"Look at what?" Katy said.

"Oh, Katy, another time," Nora said. "Is Sara alone?"

"Delia's thirsty. Look at what?"

Delia reached for Nora, and Nora took her. "Dee, you want some water?"

James had the newspaper now; he seemed to be skimming Region.

"Milk," Delia said.

Katy picked up Miranda's file, flipped it open to "Arboreal Dreamhouse" near the Weston line.

"We're moving?" she said.

"Delia, sweet pea, let's get water. You've already had milk." Nora set Delia down beside the counter and took a pink cup from the cabinet. "Looking," Nora said. "We're looking."

"No," Delia said. "Milk."

"Theo!" Katy yelled.

Nora filled the cup halfway with water, and began to reach for a second cup. "Katy, where's Sara?" she said.

Theo appeared in the kitchen doorway.

"I gave her *Harold*," Katy said. "I'm not moving."

"We're moving?" Theo said.

James sipped his coffee and read, as if alone at a café.

Without further protest, Delia accepted the water.

"Theo, find Sara," Nora said. "Your father has a long commute."

"You can wait until I graduate, right?" Theo said. His face—was it the light?—a bit pale. "I guess I could stay with the MacFarlands."

"If Theo gets to stay with the MacFarlands," Katy said, "I'm staying at Amanda's."

"Who is Amanda?" James said, dispensing with Region after all.

Katy glared at him.

"Amanda. Sweetheart—you remember," Nora said. "Katy's good friend. The field hockey girl."

"Oh. *That* Amanda," James said.

"I have friends here," Katy said.

"Of course you do," Nora said.

"We both have friends," Theo said.

"Yes, you do," Nora said.

"Then why would we move?" Theo said.

"It's just an idea," Nora said.

"Just an idea?" James said.

"Where *is* Sara? Darling," Nora said to James, "would you take Delia? Let's get the girls to bed."

"So we're staying?" Katy said.

In the living room, behind the blue sofa, Nora found Sara patting storybook drawings of fish.

Later, alone in their bedroom—another night estranged, untouching—James asked her, "Did you set *that* up?"

"Oh, please," Nora said. She sighed. "Think what you like."

On Saturday, they viewed six houses in Wellesley—none "the right match" for James.

Christmas: Blue Rock harbor strung with white lights, the houses in the neighborhood sporting red-ribboned wreaths, candles in the windows. The briefest peace.

BLIZZARD

Early January: the remains of Christmas seemed like an abandoned theater set that Nora then dismantled. The moment had already slid beyond the holidays' penumbra, and with January came winter's harsh deepening, as if to complete the erasure. Near-constant, buffeting wind, sometimes a whistling, a kind of arctic speech punctuated by snow and freezing rain, and more snow, which spread and froze in drifts and wavy patterns along the beach. And in the stormy mix, the neighborhood became static, summer houses boarded up, year-rounders taking refuge indoors. On a clear morning, the sun reflected off the snow and the bay turned cerulean; Nora took the girls down to the beach, and later gave them cocoa and read their books aloud, the day's equilibrium momentarily restored.

That Monday, when James kissed her good-bye, he seemed blankly innocent (but of what, exactly? She couldn't say). By daylight, a gray churning sea, wind, the slight rocking of the house, snow by midmorning. And the dismantling continued: warnings of storm surge high enough to flood the neighborhood access road. It happened every few years, yet still the evacuation order surprised her. She had just cleaned the house, and the rooms smelled of soap and lemon oil. It was counterintuitive to leave. Even as she packed overnight bags and loaded the girls into the car, the snow falling thickly, the paradox rankled her, as if someone—town hall, the meteorologists, the local cops checking the houses along the shore—had misunderstood. Here was the warm kitchen, the fresh pot of soup; in the bedrooms, layered quilts and flannel sheets; there the stormy, snow-filled roads. You had to leap, unseeing, beyond your own perceptions.

The shoulderless two-lane roads near the shore had long since iced over, the visibility dropped to squinting distance—taillights disappearing two houses ahead—the car itself rocking in the wind. Roads improved a half mile inland, and she managed to collect Katy at the middle school, then drove the three girls to the high school, where a gym teacher and several boys—Theo among them—set up cots on a basketball court.

A teacher from social studies brought a television on a tall rolling cart and plugged it in near the low rickety bleachers: a meteorologist on-screen moved his hands in circles over eastern Massachusetts, as if polishing the map. There were cookies for the girls, apple juice. Along Route 128 and I-95 dense traffic seemed to have frozen. Around Boston the snow was falling at two inches an hour. The storm surge could be fourteen feet.

Only now, from the high school gym, could she picture the house afloat like a bath toy. And yet the impulse to stay had felt like intuition, or perhaps wisdom. How did one know when to trust one's own mind?

From a hallway pay phone, Nora left a message at James's office.

In one of Nora's bags, Katy found Play-Doh and set the little girls to making blue and yellow animals. Eventually, the staff put up a telephone message board beside the snack table and posted weather updates: the snow would fall through the night. Eventually, a message appeared from James: *Will stay in the city. Very glad you're okay, love to the kids. Love, James.*

Rare to see *Love, James* in handwriting other than his own—as if from a florist. And what had become of the authentic *Love James*, the original one? For a moment, it seemed possible that the authentic *Love James* had written to her from Boston, having bested *late day sorry James*. But then, too, she'd been swayed by a clean kitchen floor.

In television footage of I-95 the cars had ceased to look like cars and appeared instead as white lumps along a white line, bumps embedded in the skin of road, as the road itself became less distinct, at points blurring into the surrounding land or made visible by additional tall white clumps that once were buildings and trees. In the hotel, James was grateful for the silence, the carpeted corridors, the sustained electricity, though of course a blackout was possible. He requested extra blankets from housekeeping, in case the heating went.

Other stranded men in suits filled the hotel lounge. An atomized assortment: at the bar some watched television coverage of the storm, others in club chairs read, only now and then glancing at the TV, the live camera's wall of snow, the red-faced reporters in parkas, buffeted by wind and snow, huddling while the cameras swayed. Then the view changed to the coiffed anchors and the windless studio interior. James befriended the bartender, tipping heavily, bought drinks for three attorneys. Beyond the hotel windows, the heavy whipped snow fell from a different atmosphere, a snow globe reversed.

Peace at the hotel. Peace and scotch. When he thought of his children and Nora, they seemed to him untouched by the storm, as if the high school he'd phoned were nowhere on the forecaster's map. Or as if they'd all gone to watch basketball. He pictured the kids on the bleachers, drinking cocoa, an image now suffused with tender light. Yet when he imagined the life he wanted, he pictured tonight's arrangement: a city hotel room, single occupancy. Or a suite from which he could come and go. Not, he understood, a passing wish. He stilled in the face of it, as he traced the logic of the desire.

The storm abated: days, still, digging out. Days at the hotel, the high school. They'd been lucky: the house had suffered minor damage, though the street had filled with debris. On the phone with Nora, James spoke quietly. She was readying to leave the high school then. In his hotel room, the heater whirred; beyond his window, the city seemed a canvas of dream shapes, white on white. He told her he'd be home as soon as he could; he'd find an open market somewhere, a video store. Maybe he'd pick up wine, buy chocolate for the kids.

And then he left the hotel and entered a kind of tunnel, traveling slowly down the passable roads, detouring now and then, recorded piano concertos sustaining him. Walls of snow on the roadsides, higher mounds in the parking lots, wind buffeting the car. At the Blue Rock house, he donned his work gear and he and Nora bailed and pumped salt water from the ground-level storage room and restarted the furnace; cleared broken boards and ripped plastic and part of a rowboat from the road and the short drive, pulled armloads of seaweed, stray shingles, and fish from the deck. For dinner they boiled spaghetti, heated cans of soup. After, he read to the little girls; Theo and Katy watched videos. He did not—would not—think of the hotel.

Say that hotel wish, with its clarity and fervor, would pass: a fleeting, snow-infused dream. For a few weeks after the storm, he breakfasted with the kids every morning before work and drove home directly in the evening. On the weekends he finished house projects, necessary repairs. He remained in a kind of holding space. Now and then, watching Nora with the girls, or alone with her in the evening, he glimpsed the spritely, beloved Nora, and felt a cautious pleasure, a delicate thing he did not want to crush. In fleeting optimistic instants, he thought that might be enough. Small rushes of affection carried him for a time, yet they coincided with the sharpening sense that another James, the James he believed he'd once been, had loved another Nora, and while that James had not chosen to stop, now there were other Jameses and other Noras crowding up the landscape. And if there was a way out of the story, any way out of the Rome in which those other couples had for years continued to wander, it wouldn't—how could it?—be together.

HIGH TIDE

Nora paid scant attention when her sister described a Nova Scotia trip: clouds and tides, vibrant summer days, the northern lights waves of green in the deep night hours. But later the tidal images returned. Stealthy, those tides: a thin membrane of water lapping, then thickening with long waves, apparently incremental yet deceptive, so that from moment to moment the change appeared small, the final accumulation monumental. You could be caught out on the flats, too far from shore. And at high tide, the bay now brimming, those flats unimaginable. It seemed the mind would not acknowledge any state but the present.

When James told her he'd taken an apartment in the city—signed a lease on a one-bedroom in Cambridge—he said, again, the commute was too much.

"The commute," Nora said, latching on to *Cambridge*, latching on to *one-bedroom*.

"You know that," he said, but he pressed his lips and furrowed his brow, familiar tells.

"And the house search?"

He gazed at the space beside her, a midkitchen column of air. This she had not let herself anticipate. Despite the bleak contentious months, despite estrangement. For a few weeks he'd been present again. Of late, his attention faded in and out, though with less rancor. A one-bedroom? Sara was just four, Delia almost three, Katy and Theo still at home. James did not allude to weekends or pretend he'd return. Shouldn't she have seen this coming? (Once, hadn't she imagined leaving?) She'd taken his discontent for midlife flailing, damaging but impermanent. And yet to imagine such a thing—to hold it in your mind—and keep each ordinary day intact seemed beyond her. As had so much else. She was, she thought, an idiot, but how would it help to dwell on her idiocy? There were whole realms of thought she'd learned to avoid and now there would be others.

"Nora," James said. "This is what I'm doing."

James in Cambridge, as if he were still the former James-in-Cambridge. Or as if he had filched her desire, reshaped it for himself. What if, in Cambridge, there were after all some other Nora, a Nora who had not borne a child at twenty-four; or one who had left her marriage instead of traveling to Rome? Did it matter? If another Nora could exist, she'd continue to exist elsewhere, apart from the parenting Nora: once, say, a Theo exists, one cannot unthink Theo. One cannot unthink Katy, or Sara or Delia. Cannot unthink Molly.

A one-bedroom, and the lease signed: a one-bedroom for now, though it had, he said, a large living room, it had, he said, room for a sleeper sofa. A bigger place, he said, would be too expensive.

"What about the kids?" she said.

"We'll make it work," he said. "We'll have slumber parties."

His public face, as if she were a client. "This is what I'm doing," he repeated. "This is what I need to do."

It would be easy now to skid, the moment having become slick, the kitchen counter, the wall of drawings, the basket of washed sheets failing to give traction. Here the James who wasn't James; or maybe she had misperceived from the start. She would not strike him. Had never. (Though if they'd talked in the bedroom? Might she have? Later she would speculate.) She surmised he had chosen this moment—the kids all home—to prevent her from shouting.

"Watch the kids," she said.

"Nora. I have to go," he said.

"Your kids. Work it out. Watch them," she said (aware that Katy, fourteen, had been minding Sara and Delia, that Theo, seventeen, reading upstairs, would help if they needed him).

Here was her pocketbook, here her keys. She called, "Katy, I'm off to the store. Dad's here," thumbing the familiar keys, eyeing the table legs. "Tell Theo" and then she was outside on the windy deck, the sky a patchy gray. Down the stairs, into her car, wearing her kitchen sandals, ignoring for a moment the weather, forgetting about shoes. In the backseat she found an extra pair of sneakers, socks. Here was a crumpled blue sweatshirt redolent of grass and dirt, Katy's or Theo's, here a ball cap.

She drove, aimless, first west and then south, around the sand and rock outcropping of her neighborhood, to the next beach down. Empty but for a few boys throwing a softball, dog walkers, a retriever, two Dalmatians veering close to the running boys, then away, distracted by the neon-yellow tennis balls their owners tossed. And then she cut back north and inland, one town up, to the far side of the harbor and a plaza with a drugstore, a pizza joint, and a pay phone, into which she dumped enough coins for three minutes of Meg.

"Today first," Meg told her. "Order pizza. Give me a half hour."

☙

The red-and-white pizza boxes leaked warmth. But for the kids, she could have stayed in the car, driven around Blue Rock. She returned to the house, his car still parked in its gravel spot; she did not let herself consider it.

Nora carried the boxes up the wooden stairs to the deck. Through the small window she glimpsed Katy's face, and the door swung open.

Beyond, in the living room, James sat on the sofa reading to Delia and Sara, a once-familiar image. One could almost wedge the moment into a past, simpler day. They'd chosen the book about zoo animals; a zebra, he read, named Zachary. The girls were curled against him, rapt; how quickly he could charm them back. Delia and Sara were happy. Interrupt or not?

She paused, retrieved plates and cups, cleared the library books and house bills from the table. "Katy, tell your brother we're having pizza."

Sara and Delia glanced up, having heard her voice, having heard "pizza." And then James closed the book, saying, "We'll finish later." In that moment she felt both a flash of regret and a pinching satisfaction. And too, a quick shimmying self-doubt, a minnow-sized impression that she'd imagined the earlier conversation; that the one-bedroom had loosened from her own imagination and attached to James. Perhaps he would sit down and share pizza and forget. Perhaps he would ban the idea of a Cambridge place, as she once had—a passing blip, harmless debris from a life not theirs.

There was the business of supervising Sara's and Delia's hand-washing, and setting the table and pouring cups of milk, soda for Katy and Theo, all of which occurred with a startling lucidity—the rising swoosh of milk in blue plastic cups with fat straws, the melted mozzarella, the arrangement of round white plates on place mats the color of moss all more intensely themselves. She set the table for five while James receded. Footsteps drummed up the carpeted interior stairs and down, and down and up the weathered wood stairs from the deck to the narrow gravel drive. Nora heated the kettle for tea, stationed herself by the stove, calling over her shoulder, "Anybody need more napkins?" When she turned, his coat was buttoned, his hands empty, as if he were also just heading out to the plaza. He told the kids he had to take care of some things in the city, as if the kids had neither heard their conversation nor seen him pack the car. Theo and Katy chewed their pizza, and he patted Theo on the shoulder, saying, "I'll check in later," without saying exactly how or when or what the checking-in entailed. He kissed the little girls, kissed Katy on the head. Katy did not move, but gazed out the side window, toward the beach and the slate-blue tidal ebb, away from the door, away from James and the narrow shoreline road.

ROAD DAY

As if the mall had dropped off the map—her mother had forgotten. Nora had promised to take Katy to buy running shoes, but after they'd finished the pizza, when Katy said the word *mall,* Nora's loose backhand wave banished the idea. In that moment, Nora's universe contained no malls; why counter with the actual world? It wasn't about Katy: Nora had promised to bake with Sara and Delia, and that plan, too, dropped away. Flaunting house rules, Theo tumbled with the girls in the living room. Through the archway from the kitchen, Katy watched them, sandy-haired sprites, Sara almost willowy, Delia still more dumpling shaped. Nora had not once intervened, instead drinking cup after cup of tea, cleaning the kitchen with fast brittle motions before growing still and unreachable. Sara's somersault edged the coffee table, which Theo was only now pushing out of the way. In the cleared space, he swung one girl, then the other, in circles so their feet lifted off the ground— what they called *flying*—and when they grew dizzy he performed handstands. It was a clowning reserved for the beach.

When Aunt Meg pushed the door open and called, "Hi everyone," the girls ran to her—pink-faced, hair wild—and Theo began to slump. Nora slumped differently, a momentary sag when Meg hugged her, then after whisperings a compensatory physical stiffening. In a moment she was up the stairs, gone from the room.

✤

Aunt Meg did and did not substitute. She and Nora looked alike, the same pale blue eyes, blond hair cut short and beginning to silver, though Meg was rounder, seemingly more solid, seemingly taller (though she and Nora were the same height). More anchored, more earnest: she shared neither Nora's inventive play nor her distraction.

"Okay, sweeties," Meg said. She kissed the little girls on their heads and set them to drawing at the kitchen table, the sixty-four box of crayons and white paper spread over newspaper. Theo pulled up a chair and drew comics with pink stick-figure Saras, purple Delias. Then Meg carried her suitcase up the stairs to Katy's bedroom and set it on the twin bed opposite Katy's. This happened sometimes, Meg staying in Katy's room, which felt both intrusive and reassuring. No one else ever shared a room with Aunt Meg; Theo never shared a room with anyone. And Katy was fourteen now: that should count for something. But that day—rapidly flooding with loneliness—her silent objection was fleeting and weak.

"Your mom needs some space to herself," Aunt Meg said, confirming what no one had yet said aloud: Nora would have the master bedroom to herself.

✤

Once the day became strange, there was no going back. There would be other reversals. For example, Theo did not retreat to his books, but offered to take Katy to the mall.

"Let's go," he said, and drove her there. He walked her to the sporting goods store, waited while she paced the aisles and jogged in place in four different pairs of running shoes. What did she think of the players on her field hockey team, he wanted to know; he seemed to remember their names.

On the drive home, he turned up the radio, and they sped past strip malls and into the harborside neighborhood and to the long road down to the beaches, and the narrow access road to Shore Road, the sky increasing in size at their approach.

"What do you think?" she said.

"He took more than one suitcase," Theo said.

What's wrong with us? The phrase had again begun to form, though she did not say it aloud: she seemed to be breathing the question, *what?*—she and Theo both—*what*; sensing a rapid vagrant cracking, the tumbling of dominos their father had just kicked.

Here was Aunt Meg's red Chevy, parked on the gravel drive. Otherwise, Shore Road seemed entirely itself—a relief, a small betrayal. She stomped on the gravel near the Chevy, close enough that stones flew hard against the door. "I'm going for a run," Katy said.

How else to manage? The day had begun a plain day and now she was clogged and swelling and on the verge of kicking cars, wanting, it seemed, to vandalize the neighborhood, every closed beach house, everything that had been shut and left, and flee. In betrayal, she'd flee her mother too.

Katy glanced up the wooden stairs to the deck, her gear stashed in the now-disturbed house. She was wearing jeans, a sweater. "I'll just go from here," she said. She sat on the bottom step of the thick plank staircase and pulled off her shoes, laced up the new Adidas. No gauze to wrap her left ankle, injured in a scrimmage. Awkward, but she could still run. Like most days she'd follow the residential streets, leading farther and farther away, out of Blue Rock, to the next town. On those longer runs, you could escape almost everything.

Theo's face. Somehow they'd crossed into the old country of two, a skinny rough-bordered place you go because there's no choice, because you're both about to vandalize the neighborhood. Maybe they had always been this way, though less often in the shared country than in their thick-bordered, neighboring states. Even before Molly—before the end of Molly—if one could remember. A harsh speckling in the air around Theo would come and go, sometimes mixing with the static around James. After Sara was born, he tended to ignore Katy, or mock the things she liked. But now he was gazing at her, no detachment, no brotherly mockery: today it was sympathy mixed with outrage, and for an instant he stood close, tucking her long, falling bangs behind her right ear, as if she were Delia or Sara. "Okay," he said. "I'll go when you get back."

She headed up Shore Road, along the shuttered beach houses and the open year-round ones, gaining speed as she veered toward the town road, the salt marshes, the inland road leading farther south, beyond the harbor toward the next town, past houses with lawns and small groves of pine and birch, along roads where she knew no one, running until the tight skin of the world finally opened.

HOUSE III

Miniature horses and miniature sheep fenced into powder-blue pastures or waiting in a plastic barn; a piglet-sized velvet pig, rabbit-sized stuffed rabbits; a two-story, two-bedroom house you could close up and carry like a cheerily demented briefcase; the living room's minefield of colored wooden blocks—these did not change. Nor did the room's color scheme—blue and yellow and white—cornflower sofa, blue tufted carpet, pale lemon reading chair—nor the kitchen's broad oak table, the shells along the windowsills, the finger paintings pinned to the walls. By the kitchen door: piled running shoes and school shoes and boots. In Katy's room, stacks of hair bands, a poster of Colorado wildflowers. A fruit scent of shampoo wafted from the upstairs bathroom, spilling past laundry baskets of kids' shirts and jeans and socks, baskets of pastel and dark blue pajamas. The pungent scent of coffee in the morning, sharpened by noon, the scent of stewed beef or roast chicken, onions, green beans, baked sugar, hot chocolate. All the same. A clock on a living room shelf—once belonging to James's father—disappeared. In the bedroom, now Nora's alone, James's absence became apparent, his socks, boxers, and T-shirts gone from the drawers, the closet empty of shirts and suits. In the storage room, Nora stacked boxes of the things he'd left.

The brushing sound of turned pages continued from Theo's room, except on weekends when Theo stayed out with friends. Absent were James's predawn shower and kitchen rattling, the regular 6:00 AM opening and closing of the outer door, the revving motor. While other weekday sounds were unaltered, Katy's footsteps turned heavy. Not stomping: not so forceful. A thudding, as if a kind of speech addressed to each room, or to the road beyond the exterior walls, perhaps to Boston. Or as if the sound might echo back through the house to an earlier moment, before James left; or back to Rome, and to the house before Rome. More often now, Nora would sigh, sometimes in response to the thudding, the two sounds alternating jaggedly.

In the weeks after James left, the membrane of each day seemed to Nora so thin it might tear any time. She felt a kind of vertigo. As if, on a sleepy morning, while you stood in the kitchen brewing coffee, the laws of physics might lose force, gravity failing. In what direction would you fall? And when she thought of the day James left, she thought of the way he addressed the column of air beside her—later she found herself stepping into that space—as if speaking not to Nora but to himself, or his former self, or to some other Nora, say the part that had leaked away. Perhaps he confused her with a column of air, not recognizing where Nora ended and empty air began.

Yet without the leaching drag of James's discontent, the days became simpler. The trick was to stay in the traces of household routine. One night after she put the little girls to bed, Nora allowed herself a martini, and a second one, and the cocktail party scrim returned. She'd begun to buy packs of cigarettes and ration them, two or three a day, though that night she took her cigarettes and her drink out on the deck, at the east end, sheltered from the wind. She sat on the wood planks, knees bent, back against the house wall, and drank and watched the lights down the beach, and the stars between clouds, and fell into the sound of the waves. She smoked a cigarette and then another, let herself drift, and was for a short time almost peaceful. Eventually the cold and the stiffness in her legs drove her back inside. She'd paid no attention to the time; it surprised but did not trouble her that an hour had passed. Only an hour, and on the deck of her own house. But on the living room sofa, Theo sat rocking Delia, Delia hiccupping, her face tear-streaked.

"What's up, Mom?" Theo said.

Nora crossed the room to take Delia, and when Theo stood, Delia clung to him. "It's okay," Theo said. "Dee's okay, aren't you, Dee? I'll put her back to bed."

Only an hour. Only her own deck; but the feeling on the deck, the relief, the sensation of her body relaxing into some other place, her mind loosened from trouble, then floating— how lovely that feeling had been. Not exactly *necessary*, not quite. The next day neither she nor Theo referred to that evening; but how easily it could recur, how easily those scrim moments might accrue. She wasn't, she thought, sorry enough.

For now, there would be no more drinks. Cigarettes—rationed—but only when the little girls were asleep, or occupied by Katy or Theo, only when Nora was in hearing distance. Then Nora would open the window above the kitchen sink and blow the smoke out; so, too, those seasons in the house were marked by the creak of the window opening, and the increased rush of wind, and the hard click of the window latch. More days smelled faintly of tobacco mixed with salt air; more evenings only of milk.

II

ROMAN CAFÉ

The tourist districts echo with repeating arches—freestanding arches, arched doorways and passageways, ancient viaducts. Echoing domes, stone walls, stone streets. Dreaming shop windows—blue gloves, chocolates, soft leather shoes, silk scarves, mirrors edged in gold, small etchings, handmade paper, books of art, books of philosophy—like glassed-in still lifes, or galleries in the mind. And the markets: imported teas and coffee, cases of cheese, fat oval breads and palm-sized pastries; table-top patchworks of tomatoes, Persian cucumbers, eggplants, melons, spinach, jars of olives, tubs of egg-sized mozzarella. Stone pines line the parks; citrus branches rise above the walls of gated houses; trompe l'oeil windows overlook narrow and broader streets leading to piazzas with fountains, outdoor cafés, local bars; and in the road, the Vespas, speeding Fiats, Smart cars, buses, daredevil taxis, and trucks pass within inches of each other and the curb.

Basilica di Santa Maria in Trastevere, Chiesa di Santa Maria sopra Minerva, Chiesa di San Luigi dei Francesi, Chiesa di Santa Maria dei Miracoli, Chiesa di Santa Maria del Popolo. In the story of the girl and the truck, the church is called only "the church," the street "the street beyond the church." One can walk here all day, chiesa to chiesa, recording details, meditating in empty pews as if in *this* church, the Murphys will appear. Outside, the morning's misty rain clears off, leaving a sky the blue of robins' eggs, later brimming gold and flaming pink, softening before fading out. But after hours, after the Chiesa di Santa Maria del Popolo, out on the piazza, fatigue: here, now, the impulse to lie down on the stone street, give over and gaze up at the narrow rim of city, the framed variegated sky.

It's still that brimming gold moment, outdoor café tables filling. Perhaps they're at a café then, the Murphys—white tablecloths, the shade of umbrellas. James, Nora, Theo, Katy, Molly: the Murphys as they were one day in Rome, and at adjoining tables the various incarnations of them since, taking chairs for a while before returning to the respective moments they've stepped out of, hollowed from their lives in and beyond Blue Rock. Several Noras sketching or quietly smoking along the edge of the piazza; a rotating handful of Theos, each reading a novel, sipping a latte; a repeating James in a navy-blue or soft gray suit paging through the *Herald-Tribune*. Katy spooning lemon ice, Katy soaking biscotti in milk. Approach and they look away; walk among them and they'll continue what they are doing, gazing only at their cups and spoons, cigarettes and pages. A single Molly, intent on her chocolate gelato.

NORA AFTER JAMES

It was the body she missed most, the body she had to let go of:
perhaps separation was always this way. The same body housed
a different James, a not-James, a man who ought to be named
something else. That scent—shaved wood, salt, cloves, a musky
sweat—no longer meant the James of her bed, the body she'd
turned to, although she recognized the minor curves and cal-
luses, the tilt of the head, the eyelids in sleep, the circular scar
near the base of the thumb, like a capped lens; the oblong calf
muscles, bronze mixed into the fine hair of his arms; darker
line along his torso, the dark bronze pubic hair, the heft and
delicate curves of his genitals, thickening belly, thickening hip.

She had let go of bodies before, or tried: she knew what
steps to take, how far one might travel to relearn the meaning
of a day. But her own body betrayed her, once again dumbly
forgetting: a sparking impulse to touch him, say, when she
glimpsed him at the train station, and then the delayed knowledge. A vestigial loyalty, nearly canine—the tumultuous jerk
at the end of the leash, distraught owner yanking her back.
Over time she'd learned to guard against other unaffordable
betrayals (she did not think *Rome*; she did not think of the

unlived Cambridge life, although still, remotely, of untrammeled space, the far coast of the sea, a green field one could run through if one were not-Nora). James was not another window onto the sea, she told herself, he too was trompe l'oeil.

Had she herself painted him? Maybe.

She'd scoured the bedroom and boxed his things. New mattress, new sheets, fresh paint on the walls. But here was his voice on the phone, the business-world voice she wanted to puncture, speaking now about a joint account (fast shrinking, her finances alarming), his upcoming weekend with the kids. It was better to send written notes, or to go through the lawyer—the divorce proceedings went through lawyers—but there was no avoiding discussion of drop-offs and pickups, the calls to retrieve Katy's jacket, Theo's track shoes, library books for Delia and Sara, now past due. In those first months, a chronic insomnia had taken root: she slept in small bursts, then woke, and in waking found the same salt air and same wind and also the usual thrumming, and she walked barefoot down to the laundry room and began a load of towels; or made lunches for the next day; or if the wind had abated, pulled on boots and a coat and briefly—only briefly—stargazed from the deck.

She'd begun another kind of winnowing, gradually becoming a yet-sparer Nora—thinner, quicker. A snapping energy. There was an end to languor. To calm herself she smoked her rationed cigarettes and read novels on evenings when the girls and Theo visited their father: these were the sole moments she quieted and traveled elsewhere. How easily she was undone by the stirrings of arousal. She'd touch herself but in the release there was also a wave of loneliness. What she could push away, she pushed away, learning to forget, to build more locking rooms in the mind, closing off the *we* of self and beloved.

There were small saving graces. A job, part-time, at Ben Sundlun's pediatric office, near the harbor; occasional drinks with the MacFarlands. Calm weeknights of family dinners and homework and stories before bed; Theo's soccer games, Katy's field hockey and track. A fortified city of days composed wholly of kids and house and dilute office pleasantries, buffered by civilities from cashiers, clerks, the kindred beleaguered parents of Blue Rock.

ROME

Annunciazione
Fra Filippo Lippi (15th century)
GALLERIA DORIA PAMPHILIJ

First, the colors seduce—variable reds and blues, dense golds. Here is Mary, seated in the chapel, her robe a rich blue, her gown crimson; she raises her left hand in greeting or surprise as a red-robed Gabriel kneels before her, his right arm crossing his chest. Both of their heads are circled in gold. The background arch leading into the chapel curves beyond Mary's line of vision. It's aligned with Gabriel—at first glance, you may not notice the breaks in the arch's curve. Perhaps you're distracted by the dove flying toward Mary, but look: three sky-blue point-tipped ellipses follow the dove, identical in shape to three gaps in the gray arch. As in a dream, piece by piece the sky displaces stone. The top of the arch is open, and from two suspended white hands, a half ring of fine gold rays ripples down through the dove and onward toward Mary's belly. Her features are delicate, but her eyes are glazed: a somber doll. Her belly is already swelling. It's a private moment, this new awareness—but a private moment made public, heavily staged.

Still, it's hard to resist the rich reds and blues, all the repetitions in gold: Gabriel's staff of lilies, lilies rising from a floor vase beside him, fleur-de-lis patterns, the gold floral patterns etched onto the furniture, gold stitching in the carpet and along Mary's hem, the gold wall hanging behind her. A striking painting, despite the immobile faces of Gabriel and Mary, wellcostumed actors still learning their parts.

Yet finally what draws the eye: Gabriel's grand red wings. They are nearly as large as the sweet-faced, androgynous Gabriel. Each large red wing is tinged with gold. Although he kneels—his gold-haloed head even with Mary's—the wings are still too big, out of proportion, suited for vast open spaces. Gorgeous, but they may not fit through the archway. The longer you attend to the splendid wings, the harder it is to focus on the doll-like Mary and—despite divine hands and dove and gold rays—the slight billowing of her dress. The red gold seems to melt into Gabriel's robe and his halo, the wings tangible in a way that immaculate conception is not.

This painting's miracle: Gabriel's wings. A flying boy. And who can resist the possibility of flight?

The angel has, it seems, something else to say to the bluerobed woman, the one we're calling Mary: what is it?

Let's get out of here.

And maybe, to everyone else: *Stop staring at her.*

THE MURPHYS II

In different ways they were reckless, the older Murphy children, their recklessness sometimes hidden, usually spilling away from their sisters. Garden-variety drinking, occasional cut classes, occasional broken curfews. At times they turned on each other, though more often the resentments were silent, now and then supplanted by alliance. Theo was both more sanguine than Katy and more separate. In the months before James left, Theo's grades dropped, but after, when it seemed James had cut him loose, Theo excelled again, enrolled in AP summer school. He lettered in two sports, charmed most parents. For the first half of his senior year, he had a girlfriend; the second half, another. Pretty, well-mannered, college-bound girls. Acquaintances did not perceive him as a recluse who might retreat in favor of a book, or a run. When he ran long distances, he'd often run alone, ignoring bad weather, ignoring fading light; he'd take no money; he'd leave no note at the house with his route or his return time. Once when a hailstorm came up he was five miles out. He waited at a bus stop until the worst passed, the road now icy, and hitchhiked home in the dark. Once in hard rain, he sprained an ankle and walked three miles back. Katy watched the girls while Nora took him for an X-ray. He'd wear the orange vest Nora bought him, but not always. On his bike, he sped over badly paved and potholed roads; too often, he would zigzag through traffic.

Sex without birth control, at first, in the urgency of the moment: he was not ignorant. And he was lucky. A girl he slept with got pregnant later by another boy—it was a matter of months. Then he took care. Some. He learned early to love sex, to love his body's immersion, an ecstatic kind of travel that from the start seemed not to attach itself to one specific girl. Or to boys. Within him there was an apparent divide: he claimed to want a steady girlfriend. He flirted, always. The softness was slow to leave his face, but the clean line of his jaw, the high cheekbones, and the arresting cerulean eyes allowed him to lie about his age, and hold sway with women. In college, without conscious intent, he would become a player. Casually friendly, engaging, persuasive. Easy to misread.

He was, in many ways, kind. He was, in many ways, responsible. On papers or exams, he'd never cheat, but elsewhere his ethics would slide. More than once he stole a book he couldn't afford, or skipped out on a café tab. Present in one world, he could easily block out another, believing, it seemed, if one ignored a condition, the condition might vanish.

Only many years later would he speak to friends about Molly.

And Katy? She, too, took physical risks, though not in the company of her sisters.

In field hockey, a bold, aggressive player. Trained hard, extra workouts twice a week. She, too, would run distances, sometimes in harsh weather, though Nora knew her routes, and often she'd run with a friend. She stole but did not like her mother's cigarettes. In high school, she'd drink beer or smoke weed but only when she didn't train or watch the girls, which was rare. Too often, she'd ignore homework. When eventually she'd begin to have sex, it would be with one boy, to whom she'd be devoted. They'd share what would seem a dreamy wildness together—reckless certainly about locations and birth control. She was both defended and careless with herself. She'd diet strictly, then binge on sweets. At times, she wished her sisters would disappear, a wish that horrified her, a monstrous wish, and she would punch her pillows and mattress, and pinch her upper arms or thighs where the bruises would stay hidden, or might be taken for sports injuries. Until later, until the boyfriend, who would not be able to stop her but would stay. Would see her monstrousness and kiss her head and stay.

HOUSE IV

Late August, the dark peach end of summer: Theo stepped lightly through the house and took the little girls to the beach and grilled burgers for dinner. More often now he escaped the house, to summer parties nearby, beery evenings, bonfires. Sometimes a girl. Soon to college in DC, which seemed far enough to begin again, simply as Theo, a Theo set loose from Murphy history, from Rome and grief and divorce, at least for a while. There he was, sunburned and jocular, swinging Sara and Delia in circles over the soft sand above the high-tide line, Sara now five, thin and limber, Delia at four more compact. There was Theo rolling the big rainbow beach ball; Theo on the deck sliding burgers onto waiting plates; there splashing water at Nora and Katy in the kitchen. As if he'd just arrived. As if leave-taking, and this particular leave-taking, were a simple intermission.

Say you crane your neck and call it intermission, but it was more of an ending, a common one, palpable only after time. There would be thick smatterings of visits, but he would travel farther and farther from this house, choosing, he thought, what to carry forward, seeking a separate life in universities, seeking cityscapes that might in fact blot out Rome. Say he had always been alert to stories of leave-takings: his father driving toward the city; a fleet of boats sailing from Spain. Here was his chance. At his father's place, he'd already dropped a duffel and suitcase, a cache of books. He would leave Blue Rock with a small overnight bag and take the T to meet James for the drive. In this way, James was fatherly. But better that James avoid Blue Rock.

If what Katy felt was sadness, she did not say; or perhaps she did not recognize it as sadness. In the morning, after breakfast, Nora drove Theo to the T, and Katy and the girls—all of them cranky, the girls hard to distract—assembled jigsaw puzzles of cartoon characters, the pieces as large as Katy's hands. Later, running, she imagined her father and Theo gliding southward out of Massachusetts in a blue cartoon car, along a bright yellow tubular turnpike, speeding farther away from Blue Rock, which appeared on the map near the Cape as the eye of a mutant fiddler crab. It seemed that Theo and James were always together (although they were not); and it seemed that they were always on the far side of the road (in Rome, yes, and also elsewhere). And yet there had been Theo at the grill; and Theo who since their father moved out had been more ally than foe. Still the Theo who could glide through anything.

A house of girls, now. From Theo's bedroom window, Katy watched swans gather on the pond, and evening porch lights and distant harbor lights appeared. Relieved—wasn't she?— by Theo's absence, a felt-sense she did not articulate. Perhaps could not. She could not say if she loved him. There remained the dismissive Theo, the Theo who ignored her, the one paired off with their father. And yes: the Theo perpetually across the road, waving; and she the one perpetually losing hold of Molly. The bitter nameless ongoing thing. Were she to find a name, she might call it a curse, one weaker in Theo's absence.

Within days, Theo's room seemed to her a guest room, and soon her schoolbooks appeared on Theo's desk, her calendar on the wall, though she referred to the room as *ours*. The house *ours*, meaning Nora's and Katy's and the girls'. Katy slipped into an *us* that referred to herself and Nora, and was bound to the girls' safekeeping—another consequence of losing hold. The girls, then, *ours*. Say that Sara and Delia were another chance: Did it matter that, before or after, Katy had never wished for a sister? She did not allow herself to think it. She loved them. Sisters appeared: you could not avoid displacement by small girls. You cared for them or failed.

And, too, Katy claimed Sara and Delia in a way she believed that their father had not. She took them to visit James in Cambridge, and because he'd lost track of who they were in time—buying toys and books too simple or too advanced—she translated, bridged the gap. Demonstrating, perhaps, that they were firstly hers. On the best days, Sara and Delia followed her, vied for her attention. On the best days, she made them laugh.

A year after Theo left for college, Nora painted the guest room a pastel blue: it became Sara's room. Then Katy would visit regardless, as if it were still *ours*. She finished her homework while Sara paged through library books, watched the swans while Sara strung beads. In that room, in Sara's company, she felt content.

For a time, to Katy, household proportions appeared correct.

KATY IN LOVE

Say that her father had become a telephone. Some days a telephone, some days a receding car, some days an idea. Occasionally a man. If Katy had been able to say directly that she missed him, would he have assumed the form of a father? But she could not acknowledge that she missed him. She wondered if, had he been able to deny paternity, he'd be any kind of presence. For her? To Sara and Delia, he could be sweet. A sweet telephone.

The times she shyly told him about a track win, or hardwon math grades, he spoke heartily for a few minutes. Then the interest wore off, and his phone voice became perfunctory again and once more she felt like an idiot. Tim—now there was Tim, a breathtaking runner, a breathtaking boy—Tim did not think she was an idiot. Neither, for that matter, did Nora. But once she felt like an idiot, something else might go awry. She might say things. She might refuse a visit but despair when her sisters met James without her. She might hang up and hide in her room, fall into a pinching trance.

For months she did not tell her father about Tim, though Tim often visited the house. Summer mornings while Nora worked, he'd join Katy and the girls on the beach. The girls took to him, as did Nora: he was good-natured, easygoing. Most afternoons, he headed into work at the Blue Rock Inn, and Katy bicycled to the Harbor Café. After their shifts, he racked her bike on his car and drove to the house, and they lounged on the beach and drank beer and fooled around. On days off, he took her sailing; rainy days they watched videos.

Tim and James seemed to exist in separate worlds, or perhaps the split resided in Katy—one Katy with Tim, another with her father? She talked to James about her teammate Amanda, Tim's younger sister. She talked about *biking with friends*. James knew of him from Sara and Delia, perhaps also from Nora, but Nora spoke to James reluctantly. He did not ask Katy about romance (though why, she thought, didn't he ask?).

Finally, on the phone, she said Tim's name. She used the word *boyfriend*. She told James, "He's tall. He's worked on boats."

"Does he have a boat?" James said.

"His dad has a Sunfish."

"Oh?"

"Theo knows him," she said, although invoking Theo was backpedaling. Theo and Tim had played high school soccer, but the point was not Theo; Theo was a faraway cloud.

And Tim was the door to that parallel world in which she was beautiful. Tim's love for her (love, really, no matter what her father might say) had nothing to do with Theo, or her pixie-ish little sisters, or the tragic dead one.

"He's calm," Katy said. "Funny."

"So he's older," James said.

"Amanda's brother."

"How old?"

"Graduating," Katy said.

Which was, he said, a nonresponsive answer.

"You wanted a new start," she said. "Tim's my new start."

"Okay. Tell me about Tim's plans," he said. "After graduation." And James talked, as he often did, about "going places." Was Tim going places? Did Tim care about going places?

Going places, Katy thought, meant leaving other places. That's what James did. Once the family had gone places together; once they'd gone to Rome. "Like Europe?" she said.

❦

There was a kind of détente. A making-of-efforts. Even her mother said, *Make an effort.* Yet too often it seemed that James was provoking her. Wasn't he? Or at least he didn't know how not to. In the fall, a few months after she'd told him about Tim, she began to notice small changes at her father's condo—specialty jam in the refrigerator, English teas, a grocery list in a flowery script—each one emitting a tiny nasty shock. Another kind of provocation, wasn't it? A violation of *something.*

As if the jam and tea bags occupied entire rooms, cutting the space left for Katy. Long after James left Blue Rock, it seemed to her that he was walking out again, following the trail of flowery script. Again there was no recourse. Leave him back? She had tried. Had he noticed?

She could admit: at times, her making-of-efforts inverted. Say the day she arrived early to her father's Boston office and found him outside the building, inches from a woman he introduced as Charlene—younger, and pretty in a skinny blond way, nervous in her tight black suit and fur-trimmed coat. "Hi there, Katy," Charlene said. And Katy—in that moment another, bolder Katy—found herself touching the fur trim and asking if it was real. "My little sisters love animals," she said. "Better rethink that, Charlene." James insisted, then, "That's enough."

Yet even when she pretended otherwise, Katy missed him. Wondered if, had she been Molly, or a different Katy, he would have stayed. Found herself imagining him appearing at the sidelines of her field hockey games, in the scruffy crowd of parents huddled over coffee cups yelling encouragement. Sometimes when he phoned, he called her "sweetheart." Today he said it.

He said, "Hi, sweetheart. How are you?"

"Fine. Good," she said, almost ready to say more. There was more to say (a B+ on a pop quiz, a bike ride along the shore).

"I was hoping to talk to your mother."

For a time on her bike, the breeze was so light you could coast past the second jetty, the sky so clear the water stayed more royal than navy for a time before the wind kicked up bringing the wide white clouds and darkening the sea, before the cold set in. She had not yet started to tell him, but he was already on to Nora. How quickly she could hope; how quickly hope sank. No scruffy crowd of parents, no depth to *sweetheart.* He couldn't stop to listen: he'd become the retreating car. Stay in the middle ground, Nora would say—but never exactly how.

"Oh."

"Is she there?"

There and not there, both, often. Now at the mall with the girls. Still *there* in a way James wasn't. "Busy," Katy said, failing, yes, to mention the mall. But why should he—especially now with his secrets and specialty jam—why should he know Nora's comings and goings, or Katy's comings and goings? Had he taken a minute more, she would have offered her news. Steer him back? Unlikely. When he said, "But she's there?" Katy answered, "No. Out," then blurted, "Taking care of your kids."

James cleared his throat. "I see. Perfect, Katy. That's just great."

She did not take it back, and he said, "Okay then," and "See you next week." Said *good-bye, Katy* without *love*.

FIFTH BIRTHDAY

Sara and Delia were distinctly themselves. Nora would say this, believing it—yet still they remained not-Molly. Sara because she slipped first into the space Molly left, Delia because she so resembled Molly. As if she'd been Molly's twin. The similarity continued through Delia's toddler years, less eerily exact: the mouth slightly fuller, the face rounder, the eyes gray-blue and long-lashed and a bit more widely set. And yes, Delia's exuberance was not unlike Molly's, but absent the aggression, absent the pinching and petty theft. Delia seemed without guile. For Nora there had been occasional breathless instants—the sped-up sensation of losing and regaining balance—when, from the beach blanket, she would glance up at Delia, close by, sculpting sand with a red plastic shovel and yellow bucket, and instead see Molly. As if years had evaporated, leaving Nora again and always with the beach blanket and her youngest girl, the fleeting nearness of a morning at the beach with Molly, the fleeting glimpse of herself untouched by the impending calamity. Then Nora would stand and walk over to Delia: "What are you building, sweetie?" and Delia would gaze up, clearly now Delia, pleased by Nora's attention, and pat Nora's arm, and announce, "This fort!" or "Our house!" And Nora would offer to lug sand or arrange a miniature stone path, until the tasks of construction and design settled her back into the present.

Delia always the more exuberant, Sara more pensive, the two a tight pair. In moments when Nora might be housekeeping or cooking, letting her whirring mind momentarily float while her body sliced apples or sorted laundry, the breeze might stir, or the quiet might accumulate into a question, and Nora would glance up, as if waking, to find Sara steadily watching her. Then Nora would summon herself, step forward into her body, find her voice: she'd offer Sara and Delia apple slices, or toss a sock to Sara and say her name, or join the girls at the table with their crayons.

Sara elicited a different kind of breathlessness in Nora. If both girls were playing on the beach, the present did not collapse into the time before Rome. With Sara there, Delia did not become Molly, but on rare days Nora's vertigo recurred. The fact of Sara and Delia playing in the sand seemed to be the most fragile of realities, one kept aloft by hypervigilance and counted breaths. Any undetected random force might intervene and sweep them away. Nora remained still, waiting for the atmospheric charge to dissipate. And again someone would speak: Nora herself, or one of the girls, and the moment would flip, the day settling into a benign fair-weather day. Here was a bucket of water to splash; here was a neighbor's dog; here the stack of shells with which to ornament a castle. A few minutes later Nora might laugh, or make the girls laugh, the world again known. Now and then they would ask about Molly—where was she now? Why not here? Nora found herself scrambling, lamely answering "In heaven" and "I don't know." Sara asked if Molly might come back. "No, love," Nora said, and flatly changed the subject.

The night of Delia's fifth birthday, it was not the sensation of vertigo she felt, but something just beyond; what seemed to be the stunning relief of vertigo allayed, a surer balance. Because Delia was five. This relief had not arrived on Sara's fifth birthday—hope, yes, but not balance—only Delia's, because Delia was the youngest, and yes, because of the resemblance to Molly, the perennially four Molly. And even *balance*, Nora understood, was provisional, but that night balance nonetheless. She thought of James, and in that moment not the James who had divorced her, the James of legal squabbles and late support payments, but the James who had returned without Molly to the hotel in Rome. It was the Rome James she wanted to find. On such a day—in its way transcendent—the desire alone felt potent enough to summon *that* James, and by telephone, from the house in Blue Rock.

While Delia and Sara slept and Katy finished her homework, Nora dialed from her bedroom, and he answered.

"It's me," she said.

"Nora. What is it?"

"Delia's birthday."

"Well, I know," James said. "She got the little bike, right? Katy put her on the phone with me this afternoon."

At "bike" she knew that she had called the wrong year, the wrong man. Self-flagellation and a cigarette would soon follow.

"Yes," Nora said. "She's five."

"Nora?"

"She's five, James. Everybody's five. That's all."

"Okay. Everybody's five."

James sighed, perhaps in plain exasperation. Or—too late—spliced with comprehension? Did he think or not-think of Molly? Maybe in fact he could keep the past in place, Nora thought; or maybe steady avoidance had cratered his mind.

"The girls will see you next weekend," Nora said. "I'm going now."

Here again the recurring paradox; irrefutable, dramatic evidence proved James—the present-day James—was not the James she remembered or imagined, yet she could still lose track. How could she forget? It seemed a form of stupidity. And now the conversation seemed a rebuke she'd provoked. She left the room to check on the little girls, who were both asleep; downstairs at the kitchen table, Katy drew angles on graph paper. At the sink, Nora lit a cigarette and smoked as she waited for the kettle to boil, and the salt wind and the sounds of the waves swept into the room when she opened the window. On the counter, half a chocolate cake sat beneath a domed glass cover. If she could refocus on the house, the chores, the girls, perhaps the sting and self-abasement would fade.

Katy was quietly watching her now; at least today, Katy had been easygoing, sweet with Delia and Sara. She'd made a fuss over Delia, frosted the cake, read Delia's new books aloud after dinner. There had been, in fact, no brooding or thudding or outbursts over minutiae. Nora stubbed out her cigarette and brought her tea to the table and offered Katy more cake. It was Katy—as she pushed aside her angles and proofs and reached for a plate and fork, Katy who said, "Mom. Delia's five. You know?" and cut herself a slice.

COLD

Even in the flush, promising years of the marriage, when bonuses topped James's estimable salary and investments mush-
roomed, Nora was cautious with money. They saved—for
college, for retirement—and they lived in comfort; they did
not stint, but Nora budgeted, shopped for the fairest deals,
conserved. After James left, she did what she could to protect
joint savings, the girls' savings, her own. The joint-account bal-
ances dropped the week James left. She had not thought—and
why not?—to save more in her own name. She kept the house.
James agreed to alimony for the time being; child support, of
course. Enough for school clothes and medical bills, the basic running of the household, enough to keep up with repairs.
Nothing extravagant.

Yet by Theo's second winter away, money dwindled unpredictably. Late support checks, occasional missed ones, the
alimony separate and sporadic. It was simply a matter of cash
flow, James told Nora. A few more obligations. James hadn't
planned for Theo's bills; Theo's grades had been uneven—high
in favorite classes, low in ones he disliked—and he'd lost a
scholarship. Static fizzed through the phone line. They'd saved

for Theo's college, hadn't they? "How high," Nora asked, "were those bills?"

"I've taken care of it," James said.

"Good," Nora said. "How about the girls?"

"I saw the girls last weekend," James said.

And what did that mean? They could eat mac and cheese, pea soup, dinner omelettes, but in the heart of winter she could barely pay utilities. The house leached heat; she'd made new window quilts, but sea wind permeated the walls. On school days, she dropped the heat to fifty-five, sixty-four when the girls were home.

"What would you like them to live on?" she said.

"Okay," James said. "Enough." And then he promised, "Tomorrow."

That winter, Nora wrote letters she copied to her lawyer, informal notes she did not. Meg bought her a tank of heating oil. It was the beginning of the house as another kind of house, a house of cold girls. In the evenings, Nora would bake. The girls stayed in the kitchen, and dressed in extra sweaters, and drank peppermint tea, hot chocolate, hot milk. Major repairs would wait, one season and then another; house maintenance would wait. The trick was to distract the girls until spring; the trick was to hold on.

MISSIVES FROM NORA

Handwritten on dime-store paper, shoved into the nearest envelope at hand (sometimes used, x-ed out addresses like abandoned flags, gray spots thinned by erasure): in those years, her notes piled up on his glass coffee table, and by the telephone, and in his briefcase. Tangible objects trumpeting financial woes. Maybe, James thought, this was the nineteenth-century side of Nora, maybe her retro form of aggression. Admittedly she'd always used whatever was at hand: when they'd courted, she'd written him notes on scraps, half sheets taken from brown paper bags. She'd drawn comic animals and caricatured his professors. But since the divorce, she'd avoided leaving the short erasable phone messages so common during their marriage. Sometimes she'd send a letter with the girls: here was today's, delivered by Katy, on the broad-lined tablet paper the girls used to practice their alphabets. So it was Nora-as-Nora, sending him the notes, her hurried script: *Remember school clothes? I need the checks. The last is three weeks overdue, the next due by Friday. The lawyer will call. P.S. The girls weary of spaghetti.*

If only it were merely Nora-as-words, the past and therefore inessential Nora rattling around. But school clothes were school clothes, and today at lunch, Delia surprised him with news of a bad roof. Katy shushed her as Delia described wet feet on a rainy night, a plastic bucket she circumnavigated en route to the toilet.

"Has your mother called a roofer?" he said.

Sara, silent, traced and retraced her plate rim with her index finger. Delia shrugged, meaning *I don't know*, possibly meaning *What's a roofer?*

"She's working on it," Katy said, a note of warning in her voice.

"Well, she should be," James said.

"If you tell her that?" Katy said. "You'd better send her a check." Katy had become sharp-tongued—when had that begun? (Was it the boyfriend?) And too, she'd developed a mature woman's body, solid-hipped, full-breasted, vexing. Sixteen. Hadn't she been shy? Nothing about her seemed shy.

"How long has the roof leaked?" he said.

Katy shrugged. "A while."

And the image rose of a four-gallon bucket filling with water, a steady clear line from ceiling to bucket, dully pinging in the dark of the bathroom he'd retiled years ago.

"Wait," he said. "Isn't there a light fixture in that ceiling?"

"Oh," Katy said. "We don't use it."

"Fine, fine," he said, his face now hot. After he cleared the lunch plates and served the girls cookies, he wrote a three-thousand-dollar check to Nora.

"Perfect," Katy said.

He'd just paid Theo's tuition, the girls' medical insurance; each month he contributed to their college funds. The latest check to Nora? He had not meant to defer, but then—what? Months ago he'd been impulsive with investments—a stock gambit had failed. He'd been stunned by his misjudgment; at least it was private, not professional. And now? He needed to transfer funds; he had not stopped at the bank. Next week he'd be paid. He loved his daughters—of course he loved them. Still, one gap, then another, would open between intentions and results.

When he pictured the house (and often in those years he did not: his daughters simply appeared in restaurants or at the doors of train stations or cars, or in his own condominium), he pictured it as it had been before he moved out. If prompted, he could recall the flooded storage room, the seasonal wind damage, the annual need to regrade the drive and add gravel. But in his mind, the drive was well graded, and the house had neither a leaking bathroom ceiling nor a splintering deck. No, for James thick towels still filled the closets, along with new sheets, new boots, new coats; in the leak-free bathroom, amber glycerin soaps and pastel-handled toothbrushes lined the tile counter (these from the era the Murphys moved in year-round, after Rome, before Delia or even Sara—when Nora spent hours at the department store with Katy and Theo to distract them). What could he say of this? It was not the only slippage.

He'd given up his marriage. You leave: you keep walking. You do not look back. Yet now *back* was not what it should be. *Back* fragments and leaps forward and adheres to your skin. And the mind slips; attempting to corral the whole and lock it in place both exhausts and makes you stupid. But if you can't claim a present separate from the past? Then what? A kind of crushing. James could not have said how such a crushing might take place, only that a deathly sense washed over him. It was difficult to parse one story from another: how does anyone? No clean order, instead the tangled strands of boyhood and marriage and Rome further tangled with strands from his father, his mother, a line of dead immigrants and desperate farmers. But no. He had left. Leaving ought to mean leaving. Arriving ought to mean arriving. So again a boy escaped from a childhood apartment; once more a man reinvented his life. He had left, he had arrived: yet no matter. Nora's notes appeared, redolent of a treacherous bygone era; the exigencies of the present still showed up slathered in history. What did he owe?

The girls. His girls, his daughters. The younger ones seemed tall, though only compared to their younger selves: they were average height, or perhaps small for six and seven. Here they were, drawing birds and forests; here they were, playing Fish. A still point of clarity. Love: he loved them. But days later he would again feel suspended between lives, the bills for both too often converging, and again he'd defer, cross into a tightly fenced present, miss another due date. Nora would again send paper scraps, her messages hypercivil and snarky, *Would you agree dental care for the girls is a sound idea?*

And again he would send a check, and again recommit himself to his present, evidenced by the condo he was renting, the house he was considering, the woman he was falling for. His daughters appeared in the present, lived in a house that belonged to their present. He needed to be mindful. But you *could* leave, you *could* start again, couldn't you? Start, this time, with a patent attorney named Josie Brundige, thirty-eight and lovely, intelligent, single, free of trauma. He had taken her to lunches and dinner and the symphony, and three times made love with her at her Back Bay apartment. He'd been looking at houses along the North Shore commuter line. Maybe he'd marry again. Redouble his efforts. He would, he told himself, introduce the girls to Josie.

"How about the supermarket?" Katy said. He had tucked away his checkbook; he'd suggested mini-golf.

"That's what you want to do today?" he said. "Grocery shop?"

"Well," Katy said, "mini-golf later? But we could get ice cream—Sara, Delia," she said, "don't you want ice cream? And pick up a few other things."

"Mint chip," Delia said.

"Okay," Sara said.

In the supermarket, Katy filled the cart with premium brands. Provolone cheese and sliced ham from the deli, alba-core tuna, tins of cocoa, chocolate-covered grahams.

"That's a lot of cocoa," he told her. "A lot of ham."

"My coach recommends ham," she told him. "I'll just take the extra back with me."

She was, it seemed, as scrappy and canny as Nora—perhaps as scrappy and canny as James himself.

"Of course," he said. "Get whatever you want."

REPRODUCTION

The Magdalen Reading
Rogier van der Weyden (c. before 1438)
NATIONAL GALLERY, LONDON

A young woman ignores the drama around her; it seems she has learned to leave the room without her body. White head scarf, white book open in her hands, her dress a swath of green matching the grass beyond the background windows. A silent still point. The rectangular windows echo columns of text. It's as if her scarved head and the white book are contiguous; as if the text transports her out of the room. She's seated on a low cushion, immersed, though around her various red-and-blue-robed saints—Saint John, Saint Joseph—make their way toward the now-missing panel of the Virgin and child. But this panel, her panel, centers on the green, green dress and the young woman's face—a clear white oval, eyelids half-moons floating over the book, lips dark pink and closed. On the floor beside her stands a curved white jar, white as the book, white as her head scarf, curved as her body beneath the green dress, settled here in the room of walking saints, whose own bodies block her exit, even as she travels beyond.

She seems unaware of the saints, the painter, anyone else. Say she has the privacy of thought: perhaps the view out the window—a green field, a lake—reveals her interior life.

A distinctive face, luminous: study her the way the artist did and you might grieve the loss of her, this contemplative girl, whoever she was, the passing centuries thin as light. And say you recognize something about her? How might you find her again, between here and the fifteenth century? Between here and a verdant elsewhere.

SARA AT NIGHT

The quietest Murphy, at least in those years. Like Theo, she preferred the company of books; like Nora, she took up drawing
early. Shy, at times skittish. During family arguments she'd hide
or daydream. Sweet, people called her. *A good girl.* She'd make
drawings—birds, boats, flying beach umbrellas—she'd give to
family members; she'd leave sea glass on the windowsills, pick
rosehips and goldenrod and sometimes Queen Anne's lace.

She frightened easily: anger frightened her, including her
own. She did not know how to insist. She did not know how to
object. Mistreatment stunned her. In response, she would freeze,
or rush away, or, if necessary, appease. Unnerved most often by
Katy. A quick learner, an intelligent girl, and yet perennially be-
wildered. It seemed Theo and Katy and her parents shared a
knowledge—or a separate realm?—to which Sara had no access
and Delia was oblivious; perhaps there was no more room. Say
she lived instead on a tree branch nearby, one that might snap
and drop into the sea. Perhaps they would not notice. Her mother could be distractible, forgetful—how easily might she forget
Sara? Already, for small moments, it had happened. A discordant
silence came and went. Evidence of a deficit somewhere: was it,

then, in Sara? So it seemed. Call it an inchoate sense of missing. In dreams her body became a stranger's, her arms and legs went lifeless. She was still young when her sleep disturbances began; part of most nights she was awake while the others slept. During her grade-school years, she would wander the house—there was pleasure in wandering the house at night—and sometimes she'd doze in the living room or on warm nights watch the sky from the deck. Because of those nights, she glimpsed Katy and Tim half-naked on the deck, pressing against each other rhythmically, and later passed out on the deck chairs.

She studied her parents, her sisters, studied Theo, who seemed to assert himself the way her father sometimes did. Theo could be sweet to her: often Theo would make her laugh. And when he visited from college—and he did sometimes, especially in the summer—in the first days they'd play beach games with Delia, they'd go to movies and make sundaes and together they'd read books. At first, she'd feel bolstered, in some way brave. But after a time he'd become irritable, withdraw into his own books and squint at interruption; he'd squabble with Nora about the car and end up taking his bike—to the harbor, he'd tell them—and return the next afternoon. And in better moods, he would sit on the deck and drink beer—with Tim, when he was there. Then Katy would become snappish. Theo would ignore her, ignore Delia and Sara though Sara herself had not changed. The games and beach walks that had pleased him before had not changed. But maybe it was her lack. Perhaps he'd run short of patience for her; perhaps he had good reason. Toward the ends of his visits, he'd cheer up, but his happiness—like her father's heartiness—seemed staged and fleeting.

✤

His third year in college, Theo began to bring a girlfriend to visit. Between visits the girlfriends changed. Nora would shrug; Sara would move into Delia's room, giving her own room to Theo and his friend. In the day, the girlfriend might sleep in the sun on the deck or walk in the tidal shallows, dreamy and remote, like a girl in a painting. At night, Theo and the girl would retreat into Sara's room. As usual, Sara wandered. From the upstairs hall, she could hear Theo and his girlfriends, her own bed creaking and the women moaning, and her brother moaning. Whispered laughs behind the door. She wanted to hear and then unhear them; later she'd try to remember and unremember.

At some point, Theo's girlfriends ventured to the bathroom. Sometimes Sara was in the hall with her glass of water, and the girl saw her and waved an embarrassed wave—the girl maybe wearing a T-shirt, her legs slender, her toenails painted. Her bare feet appeared elegant and frank. The girl would duck into the bathroom, and Sara would hear the sound of running water. Sara would return to Delia's room, where Delia heard nothing; Delia slept through everything. And in the morning, Sara was tired, always tired, but alert, watching Theo in the kitchen, now the more ordinary Theo, and his girlfriend, who was showered and neatly dressed and contentedly sipping coffee. Theo flirted with their mother and with Delia and the girlfriend, he flirted with Sara, and she smiled hesitantly. *Lighten up, doll,* her mother might say, and Sara would stand close and let Nora pet her head.

Though there was the morning at breakfast when Sara answered the phone and a cheerful voice, a woman, a Shelley, asked for Theo. Sara held out the phone to him, saying, "Shelley?" and their mother glanced up, and the visiting girlfriend whose name was not Shelley paled and swallowed coffee in small rapid sips. Theo took the call on the extension, and Delia inquired with great seriousness about the girlfriend's ear piercings (sometimes, even then, Delia could step up this way). No one mentioned Shelley again, or the French-braided girlfriend, who never returned.

If Theo was in a hurry to leave—he was often in a hurry—Sara might find the bedroom strangely disordered, her bedside books and her embroidered pillow and stuffed animals lumped in a corner. As if it were still, or again, his room. The sheets were damp in patches or crusted and streaked with white stains, a gamy-salt smell rising, a slight low-tide reek. She'd push open one of the windows, let sea air rush in, pull the sheets from the bed and drag them down to the laundry room and stuff them in the washing machine before Nora got to them. Tucking in the clean sheets was harder, but Katy would help, as if in commiseration or tacit agreement to shield Nora (though from exactly what? Sara could not say). The disorder seemed at times a kind of aggression. She was eight. She felt a queasy buzzing, the heat that could precede tears. If anyone had asked Theo then, he would have answered, surprised, *I had to pack, I had to go,* certain that was the only truth.

Katy reminded Theo to change the sheets, but he didn't always, and then the mess seemed all the more deliberate. Sara would strip the bed and a mixed-up kind of shame would resurface. At least Katy would roll her eyes and clown. *Let's clear the air in here*, Katy would say, and sometimes, *Let's clean this place up and go for sundaes.* Like their mother, Katy could fall into distraction, her gestures slowing while she gazed out a window, her lips pressed together, brow furrowing. It didn't last long. Sara herself daydreamed; they all watched the sea. In those moments, loneliness would settle into Sara, persisting until she called Katy back, and until Katy shook off distraction and smiled, until Katy told her, *Let's go.*

AT THE PATRICK MURPHYS'

Before Rome, one Murphy family must have appeared a close
variation on the other: the men in successful careers, the homes
in well-off suburbs, three children close in age, Murphy dimples, deep-set Murphy eyes, often tending to blue. Patrick's
wife, Carrie, was also Boston Irish and slender, though dark-
haired and slightly taller than Nora. There were mirrored bits
of history: Patrick and James together at Blue Rock, Patrick
and James caddying. And then Rome—the paths radically diverged—and the divorce. But when you looked closely, the histories contrasted more starkly: Without Rome, would another
branching have occurred? Had she asked herself, Nora would
have thought so. James might not have seen it: he had worked
to bridge the gap, envisioned closer convergence. After Rome,
the Patrick Murphys called often, visited less; postdivorce,
James would meet Patrick for dinner or golf, join his family
for holidays. A certain boyhood reprise. For a time, Nora kept
in contact with Carrie, exchanging Christmas cards and well-
wishing notes, sending birthday gifts for the kids.

Better genes? Some families, Katy thought, even families
with your name, were charmed, surrounded by a force field of

safety and ease. How was it you could share a name and not the magic? A nameless failing. Or a curse? To her the Murphy cousins seemed free of trouble, or almost free. She knew, for example, that Brian, the youngest and most gregarious, had a reading tutor. And this year Pamela—a serious figure skater, pretty, well liked—had fallen and injured her leg just before competition (sidewalk ice, no one's fault). She'd hobbled around, crushed. But everyone else rallied; the fracture healed; she was back on the ice. She still got to be Pamela, the way she'd known herself to be. Her brothers—Brian born the same year as Molly—remained her brothers; her parents stayed together.

As long as Katy could remember, the Patrick Murphys had lived in the same house in Wellesley. Now she rarely saw them, but when she did it seemed she'd opened a children's book she'd once read every day. They aged but remained the same: Aunt Carrie's same perfumy hugs, Uncle Patrick's jokes and kisses on her cheek, Pam's shy waves hello. Each time, the boys—playing street hockey or watching a TV game—seemed to stop without resentment, and call her name and invite her to join.

The house itself: windowed rooms opening out into more rooms. Nothing was a single color, or even a color you could name: the sofas and chairs covered in fabric densely woven with several threads, so you could only say, *More blue than gold,* or compare the fabric to something else—a season or a kind of holiday. Polished wood floors, Persian carpet, Mexican tile in the kitchen. Bowls of flowers on the tables, potted trees near the den windows, beyond which the lawn appeared an almost iridescent green.

Pam and her brothers seemed blithely unaware of what it all meant.

Her father had always wanted to be like Patrick, Katy could see that. Who could blame him? It seemed the Patrick Murphys paid no price. But wishes did not matter, Katy thought. Her father should know: you didn't get to choose which sort of Murphy to be.

Now they'd been invited to a barbecue at the Patrick Murphys', Katy and her sisters with her father. Her father said please. He said, "Please come with us, Katy. I hope you will." He'd asked her on the phone. She'd paused. (Nora had recently told her: think. How? Katy asked. "Press your lips together and count to six," Nora said.) So Katy told James, "Okay," and pressed her lips a second time to listen to the details.

The day was, briefly, like a return to another life, one she had misplaced. The adults and kids milling through the house and vast yard seemed friendly, unsurprised to see her, as if she were another of the Patrick Murphys, as if in this place she might belong. Two eighth-grade girls hired as babysitters played with Delia and Sara: at the Patrick Murphys', Katy could do whatever she wanted. With her cousins and their friends, she played badminton. For a time along the traffic-less road they threw a Frisbee, and when they tired of running, threw the Frisbee for the dog. For a time she joined her sisters in the pool.

And the woman. How casual, the way Katy met her. Reddish-blond hair, willowy. Elegant. In shorts and a plain T-shirt, but elegant. She was at the picnic table; she gave Katy some tongs for corn, and spoke to Katy as if Katy were one of the Patrick Murphys. She had noticed Katy at badminton with the boys; she'd seen her running for the Frisbee. "You must play something," she said. "Or run?" She herself was a runner, a runner friend of Carrie's. She introduced herself as Josie.

Blue-gray eyes, a way of listening, it seemed, with her body: a stillness when Katy spoke. Though, too, an easy laugh. Originally from New Hampshire, near the coast. A small town. Katy talked. Told her about Blue Rock, the beaches off-hours, off-season, the best places to run. "Maybe with Carrie we'll do a run sometime," Josie said.

Later, Katy returned to the pool, now with Uncle Patrick and Pamela and the girls, and after a time her father. She threw a small beach ball with the girls and James, then floated, a happy, lovely kind of floating: a cornflower-blue sky, near cloudless but for thin silky bands in the north.

After the party, after she and her father had shepherded Sara and Delia into the car, back into the city to toothbrushing and washing and bed, when the girls were finally asleep, her father asked, "Did you have a nice time?"

"Yes," she said. Still happy. Still somehow afloat.

Her father was smiling, and not falsely; he did have a beautiful smile. "I'm so glad," he said. "And meeting everyone? How was that?"

"Fine," she said. "Totally fine."

"And Josie?" he said. "What did you think of her?"

Perfect, Katy almost said, but his gaze held a giveaway intensity. Had he been talking with Josie at the party? Katy could not remember them together, but she'd been playing badminton and Frisbee; there was the pool; the Sox were on TV. Yet he knew her. And what Katy felt then was a kind of curdling, and heat, at what she could now see as a setup, unfurling backward, and the presumption—correct, wasn't it?—of how easily duped she could be, how dumbly eager to be liked. When kids acted stupid, Nora called them *dumb as lambs*; adults were *dumb as posts*. And Katy? Lamb or post? Imagining Josie's interest in her for her own sake, even imagining—hadn't she, just a little?—that Josie might see in her what others did not. *Perfect*, yes, but it was never Katy they wanted—it was the little girls, or Theo. Or if they'd heard the story, Molly (even dead, Molly claimed attention). Now James. Maybe Katy herself preferred to be duped: maybe she had it coming, knowing better but falling for the ploy.

"You like her," Katy said, one stupid fat tear rolling down her cheek.

"Didn't you like her?" James said.

A clogged feeling behind her face began to expand and she walked very quickly to the condo's guest bathroom and locked the door, then leaned into the wall beside the stack of matching brown-and-beige striped towels and pinched her upper arm until the sting pulsed on its own. Kicked the cabinets open and shut. Under the sink found a box of tampons—not Katy's brand. Josie's then? Katy unwrapped one experimentally, whipped it by its white cord against the towel rack, making a dull whap. Against the wood and the porcelain tub, the sound was more satisfying. When she grew bored, she curled up on the bath mat and pulled a dry towel around her and closed her eyes, pretending to be in the bathroom in Blue Rock.

She didn't expect her father to call her out of the bathroom, or to try to speak to her from outside the door: only Nora would have. But when she finally emerged, he was still sitting on the sofa with his water glass.

"I do hope you had a good time," James said, as if she hadn't just been whapping the walls of the bathroom.

Katy pressed her lips and counted. "I'm going to sleep now," she said. "You are meaner than you think."

NO CAFÉ

Say the Murphys have left the café; or say they never found it. Perhaps they are hiding on the Palatine Hill; perhaps hiding from each other. Or searching for the moment before the moment. It's a terrible relief to be alone. Separately they all fall under white trucks; separately they lie on city sidewalks reflecting on the sky; separately they retreat into hotel rooms. Bells ring heavily, then quiet.

The city repeats itself. The Murphys do not speak the language, and are in fact no longer "they": only the vaguest and most attenuated notion of *they* or *we* or *us* persists, a fading ray aimed back toward a fading concept, sometimes called Molly.

Say their steps displace small stones, tear bits of fallen leaves—gray chips, gold specks, russet flakes. It's January. After days of rain, light floods the city. Gardens and paths throughout Rome echo and echo with Murphys.

NEWS

James called to tell Nora directly. October, a windy Saturday afternoon. He called, and there was a moment—there often was a moment after long silences between them—before time caught up with her. A moment of hearing his voice and answering in an unguarded way. This could happen when she had been reading or sleeping or alone for a long while. The unexpected voice, the voice of her marriage, warm now, her lack of defense. He'd been dating someone, he said. He said they would be marrying.

She was in the still, cool kitchen, filling the kettle. Swans on the pond, the pond reflecting the moving pink and violet clouds, swans swimming through the colors' reflections. She listened. His announcement and patter were rehearsed, though a stranger listening might not think so. He could memorize speeches and deliver them as spontaneous eloquence, something Nora recognized; she wondered if the new woman detected the difference, or would ever detect it. One more bit of intimate knowledge Nora hadn't lost, one way in which the alien James was not a stranger. A further insult, it seemed, to witness his new life, but she saw no way out. This was why,

Nora imagined, parents kidnapped their children and moved to Brazil.

"We'll take it slow," he said. She did not know whether "we" meant James and the woman, or James and Nora, or all three of them. Next summer, he said. Perhaps midsummer.

"Okay," she said. "I see," she said, and more than once repeated. She'd let herself think in the near term only, had veered away from his private life—as long as it was separate from the girls, she'd told him, it was his business. And the kids had said nothing. But now she knew and would have to find space for this knowledge, a way to navigate it daily, with no apparent end. It seemed you could in fact start a second life, if you were James: you could walk away from the prior life, the one that had anchored you so utterly. And if she'd left, before? After Rome there seemed no other path. Before that? Would she have left the children with James? No. She'd have to reel back further, before Theo.

The girls had met her as a guest of Patrick's, James told her.

"Patrick. I see," she said. So, too, the likely end of her remaining Murphy ties. "Do they know?"

"Katy," he said.

"And Theo?"

He and Josie had taken Theo to dinner on Theo's last visit.

Which explained too why Theo had been so adamant about her private life. Didn't she want to date? If she met someone, why not? She'd said she had no time. "If it's what you want, Mom, there's always time," he'd said, but no, she'd told him. He could not understand. How tightly scheduled her days, with Delia and Sara and Katy, her job, the house; how catastrophic ordinary car trouble could be. The endless searches for bargains, the errands and repairs packed into the days the girls spent with James. To make him understand she'd have to say too much. "But if it's what you want," he repeated. At one of Katy's games, Theo watched from the sidelines with Nora and the goalie Ellie Burnham's father, Lloyd, who joked with Nora and Theo and shared a bag of pretzels. When they said good-bye, Lloyd Burnham kissed her cheek—"See you, hon," he said—and kissed Katy's cheek, and shook Theo's hand.

In the car Theo said, "What about him?" and Katy snorted, "He's married, Theo. Remember the sail club lady? Ellie's mom? Didn't you scrape up one of those boats?"

"Okay, so not him. Someone else," Theo said.

"Get me a new dishwasher," Nora told him.

And when Theo brought it up again later, she said no. A vehement no that seemed to take Theo by surprise. They were at the kitchen table drinking tea, and a flat silence hung over the room for a moment before Theo said, "Okay," and Nora said, "I need to look after the girls. Don't worry." But it seemed to Nora that Theo was confusing her with the Nora of the cocktail dresses, or the one who took him as a small child to cafés; or even the Nora who had rediscovered pleasure with James one last summer. Maybe Theo saw the Nora of that summer or maybe he imagined she could step back into that moment, the inevitable betrayals of the body notwithstanding.

And perhaps she should be grateful that Theo could not see the hairline fractures that might with one more collision, one more betrayal, become unbreachable fissures. Though Theo no longer lived in Blue Rock; Theo could be wishful; there was plenty Theo didn't see.

Nora could not explain herself. The steady small physical attritions were not what kept her alone, but they troubled her more as the plain facts of Josie Brundige's life unspooled, and Josie herself became a presence: a woman younger by a decade, lovely, her body a lovely body. There was a youthful lushness about Josie, and a surety to her movements Nora could not remember in herself.

And how was it that the body of another woman could within minutes make one's own body seem alien? On an ordinary Sunday, she picked up the girls at James's condo, and Josie was there, just leaving: the passing of ships, a handshake. Josie wore jeans and a sweater, but had the look of a Lord & Taylor ad. The girls called Nora, ran to Nora, she hugged them; Josie left, and the moment ended. James walked Nora and the girls to her car, careful, polite. As she was leaving, he handed her an envelope, a check for house money. As if he were buying peace, or reasserting severance. "Next week," she said.

She did not want to imagine James's desire: she imagined James's desire. And her own, the idea of being in Josie's presence, the way one might feel if one were not Nora. What her children might feel? And although Nora knew better, knew that no one escapes loss, Josie in the hallway with her equanimity and her red-gold waves and still-taut curves appeared free, and therefore more haunting. If James had not been in love with Josie, would Nora have seen Josie this way? Maybe not. Or in that moment, seen herself as almost without gender, at least not one she recognized? Strangely exiled, if on a familiar coast.

ROME

Pauline Bonaparte
Antonio Canova (early 19th century)
GALLERIA BORGHESE

In this moment, nothing is a problem for Pauline. A woman in her twenties, naked to the hip—high breasts, trim belly, now stretched sideways on a chaise longue, so that to the shoulder her body imitates the shape of the chaise, enunciating the angled curve of her waist. White fabric drapes her hips and thighs, her right leg extending forward, left slightly back, exposing slim calves, shapely ankles and feet, the second toe extending beyond the first. Still her back appears straight as she leans into the pillows, her elbow propped, fingers touching the side of her face. Neck curving upward, she gazes forward as if surveying the room, curls and longer tendrils of hair piled onto her head. A bracelet on her forearm, an apple in her left hand, which rests on her covered left thigh. Her skin is white, luminous, remarkable; she is Pauline and also a Greek goddess, an assessing Venus. Self-possessed, and in that self-possession, that luminous body, undeniably seductive.

Pauline Borghese, born Pauline Bonaparte, sister to Napoleon. Perhaps she's contemplating her desires; perhaps her lovers. Her chaise is set in the center of the room: now stationary, it once rotated, the marble Pauline surveying her visitors.

Reach past the museum rope and one might run a hand along her waist, belly, breasts. Or feel an impulse to lie beside her on the chaise. A wish to fall into her, or to embody her, as Venus, a woman who takes her pleasure; a woman who does not hide her body or desire, who in this vision does not bend to the desires of others, or fear the consequences of exposure. Maybe there's a dreamy moment when desire rises into the air of the gallery and mixes with the sense of possibility. Maybe a moment others witness.

A body in stone, a legacy in stone; somehow, also, Canova. It was Pauline's moment, a body and moment sustainable only in sculpture. And then the moment passed; the later Pauline inhabited another body, tubercular, dead at forty-four. Maybe the late Pauline, the shadow Pauline, is the haunting one. The one who is and is not herself.

And at what point might desire return to stone, or become stone? A question ribboning one's wakeful nights. If you asked Nora, she might not answer. She might tell you there are rooms inside your mind. Might point out the light beyond the trees, a line of orange, a milk-blue cloud.

DRESSES

An alternate constellation of Murphys, or near-Murphys: James in his khakis and polo shirt, Sara and Delia grade-school girls in sundresses, Katy in shorts and a summer blouse—and Josie, also in a sundress, mint-green fabric, finely ridged. Early June, a Saturday. They strolled the expanse of the Boston Neiman Marcus, past the cosmetics counters, past a glass case of Swiss watches, as if they might have frequented this place together. Say it was there—with all those mirrors, all those glinting vials and chic designs—that they most convincingly appeared as a well-heeled family. Though James did not consider it performance: he'd stepped, he believed, into the life he wanted. His wife—or soon to be. His children. His upcoming wedding (and soon, a move to his new house). He breathed differently now, didn't he? Still fresh, his gratitude, his happiness, though the balance could later tip—and would, as it sometimes had—from amazement at good fortune to an assumption of just rewards. The day, like the summer ahead, seemed to expand. His family strolled through the Neiman Marcus. They—this other, newly possible *they*—seemed to belong here (even Katy, her footsteps almost light). Had he taken the girls and Josie to the

Public Garden, perhaps the Garden would have been the site of such belonging. Not impossible. But they had come to Neiman Marcus to buy dresses, the collective moment and its associated dreaming inextricable from the fine objects with which one might furnish a life (what James called "living well").

For Katy, shopping as if a family was not deliberate pretense, or not *all* deliberate pretense: more the tug of a vortex. She'd been drawn in the moment Josie stepped into the car and settled in the passenger seat beside James, having first confirmed the three girls' comfort in back. On the drive to Copley Square, her father narrated as he always had, pointing out landmarks and rehashing local history as he drove, affirming himself as Dad, the girls as his kids. Initially a matter of Josie fitting into the puzzle, wasn't it? The substitute mother. Maybe this happened more often than Katy recognized, roles switching up? What if the absent Nora and Theo were to stroll Filene's—or a museum?—flanked by a substitute James, three substitute daughters? Substitutes were imitations. Obviously. But you tumbled into the role anyway.

In August, Sara and Delia would be bridesmaids. Josie had asked them: they had said yes. She had also asked Katy, and Katy declined (in what was for her a triumph of tact, she had offered no reason). For the girls, Josie had picked out graceful and unfussy dresses: a melting pastel blue, delicately patterned flounces at the bottom of the skirts. Sara tried hers on a bit timidly, Delia with more glee. James kissed them; he twirled them around, called them "gorgeous." They laughed, even Sara, even Katy. Though she did not laugh when the saleswoman—in a navy suit, silk lemony blouse, curled hair in a style Katy thought of as "wig"—referred to Sara and Delia as Josie's daughters, to Katy as "the young lady."

Other sales staff shared the same language; she was more loosely attached, her place less defined. A niece? Stepdaughter? (Yes and no.) Maybe an au pair? Yet Sara and Delia would be Josie's. Josie corrected no one. And if the woman had called Katy Josie's daughter? Would Josie—or Katy herself—have set her straight? Or would she have played the part? Though she was *already* playing the part, or trying to. They'd all been playing family. But the saleswoman called Katy out. The others could be a family without her.

Still the phrase: *young lady.* Still the Neiman Marcus attention. At least, Katy thought, the saleswoman noticed her. The tone—Katy had to admit—had not been snide. "What would you like?" the wig woman asked, as if offering free cake. Against her will, Katy began to relax, and to discover, yes, there was something she wanted. Some magnificent thing. How quickly, she thought, she could betray her mother.

Her father put a hand on her shoulder. As if comprehending, he said, "Sweetheart, let's find something gorgeous for you," and told the suited wig, "My daughter Katy wants a dress." So he claimed her, and in that moment attended to her first. (All day, of course, he'd claimed them, herding them and hovering and commenting.) His smallest gestures seemed grand and inclusive, shoring up the deceit of belonging together as well as belonging here. Irresistible assertions, Katy thought, had sped his rise in business.

"We'll pick one that matches the bridesmaids' dresses," Josie said. "You can always change your mind."

And so in the dress department, Josie consulted with the women attending to them. Dresses and more dresses arrived for Katy to try (privately—she was grateful for the dressing room door). Out she walked, and Josie and the saleswomen exclaimed over Katy in each dress, as if she suddenly merited their praise. Her own image surprised her; she did appear as another, more elegant girl. Was that also herself? Pleasure, a subtle glee in trying on the dresses—more betrayal? A thin shadow of doubt hovered, but receded as she marveled at the sheen of a V-necked indigo gown that made her look lovelier than she knew herself to be. Say she could, in this high-end shop, put on a dress and become someone else. She felt a small burst of happiness, pleasure modeling the dress for James, pleasure at his smile, his extravagant praise. Okay then. She would have the dress: she'd be the young lady.

After the deflating reversion to her usual self—her shorts and cotton blouse from last season—there was still the matter of shoes. In their pastel blue dresses, Sara and Delia had twirled for the mirrors, but they did not last long in stores. Did James remember this? Sara would tire and wander off alone. Delia might disobey, whine, or sulk, or huff off in search of the car. When she was exhausted, Delia's lips would tremble: she'd fight off tears but demand to call Nora. Katy told Josie, "She'll lose it if she's here too long," and the clerk glanced over at Josie, who nodded almost dismissively. As if it were a familiar risk, Delia in fact her daughter, Josie-as-mother now minding the clock to avert the kind of meltdown she'd witnessed too often. *I know*, Katy wanted to insist. *You don't know my sisters.* But there was heat in Katy's face now, and she stepped away, telling Sara, "Let's look for a water fountain."

And when Katy and Sara returned, Josie steered Katy away, suggesting she help Katy find shoes to match the new dress. When Katy hesitated, Josie squeezed her hand. "James will play with the girls. Let's find you some shoes." And Katy nodded dumbly, sensing—despite the display of elegant heels—that something had been taken.

Afterward, her father walked in the city with his arm around Katy. Then he walked with Josie: you could see that with Josie he was happy, but as Katy followed behind with the girls the remaining lightness seeped from the day, and in its place the familiar despondency took hold. Finally, what did *they* have to do with *her*? In three months she'd begin college: wouldn't they grow closer, she further away? Delia tugged, "Listen—are you listening?" A Rollerblader wove through Copley Square, a guy in a tank top and shorts, dodging cars and pedestrians, as if none of them made a difference. James said he'd booked a reservation for Italian, and drove them to the North End. When they returned to the condo, Josie took the T to what she called her "old place." But at James's place she was present in the small details, the fluted coffee cups, framed photographs—an apple tree in bloom, a white farmhouse—potted basil in the kitchen window, the orchid James tended. When had he ever cared for plants?

And when Katy later described the visit to Tim, Tim seemed to her obtuse, if undeniably *hers*. "He's still your dad," Tim said. But she could not find the right words to convey the dress and the shoes and the awkwardness, and the thick sorrow she'd felt the next morning at the condo, sorrow that in other moments had sparked fights with her father. James kept offering her waffles and eggs, which made it worse. She poured orange juice for Sara and Delia, but couldn't drink any herself, or eat ordinary toast. She'd brought her math textbook with her and retreated to the sofa while the girls ate. The math final, she told her father, was the hardest one. Very very tough. No, no eggs, no toast. She'd eat something later. No thanks to applesauce. Right now, she wasn't hungry. Sometimes, math could be like that.

HOUSE V

As if the rooms contained more space, the air seemed clearer, easier to breathe, after Katy left for college, though no one spoke of it aloud. But Katy's tom-tom thuds abated. Static abated. Bright chill days on the beach; cold nights, the coldest black spread thickly with stars. Nora would make hot chocolate and read at the table while Sara and Delia finished homework and drew, or layered blankets on the sofa and watched movies. The girls now traveled from room to room without hesitation, the house more fully theirs.

Though a house that appeared more ragged: Nora repaired the roof and managed a loan for a new furnace, but the siding was badly worn, one of the outer banisters split (for a time held together by white polyester rope from the marina). Inside along the carpeted stairs and upper hall, a flattened gray path darkened; accumulated coffee and ice-cream stains wore into the sofa fabric. The dingy walls she could repaint on weekends when the girls visited James. More window quilts, in blue and white; the framed black-and-white baby photos still on the kitchen wall above the side windows. Weekday evenings, while the girls slept, she'd use the big oak table to do Ben Sundlun's accounts.

The beach adjoining the house had lost almost a yard over the past decade, but the town repaired a half-mile stretch of seawall, including their section, and dredged the pond of storm debris; for several days the displaced swans congregated on the shallows of the bay, a white cluster shifting back and forth, sometimes brilliant, sometimes cream or tinged with pink or violet. You could watch them from the living room windows, or bundle up and head down to the beach, and pick up bits of sea glass or gray stones ribboned with white.

With Katy's move, Rome, too, seemed less present. For the first time, each of the Murphys who'd returned from Italy now lived separately from the others; say each carried a spinning interior Rome, a shifting interior Molly, that intensified in the presence of the others, receded in their absence; the sorrow rarely alluded to—as Rome, or Molly, and meaning precisely neither—also seemed to recede. Perhaps, too, each Murphy carried an interior blueprint of a house in Blue Rock—for Nora saturating waking life, indistinguishable from the current house—arising separately in each of their dreams, a denser, smaller eastern star.

When Sara wandered the house, she listened for the older silence, at times imagining a drifting patch of space, a persisting disquiet veiled by ordinary salt air, scents of coffee and soap, exchanges over breakfast, as the patch slid like light beyond the visible spectrum. It seemed—as it had always seemed—she could not apprehend the form. Anything could be a clue; anything could be the answer. Though not for Delia, who claimed to hear plain silence. She said what disturbed the air was low-tide kelp.

Sara studied Nora more deliberately; this Delia also did. Often now, while Nora worked outdoors or downstairs, Sara snuck into her room. On the dresser: a lace doily, a wooden jewelry box, a blue glass bowl of white stones. Beside the bed, shelves of novels and art books and shoe boxes. In the corner, a locked file cabinet, a small writing table, a cup of pens. A queen-sized bed that seemed like a small lake—pale green duvet, white pillows. In the closet, familiar wool blazers and pants and low-heeled shoes Nora wore to the office. Back of the closet: fancy party clothes, sleeveless satiny things, a black off-the-shoulder dress with rhinestone buttons, black patent-leather heels, backless silver sandals. A portfolio with Nora's drawings.

Delia would comb through the jewelry box and touch the rhinestone buttons and try on the silver sandals; on rare days, she'd try on a silk dress. Sara returned to the bowl of stones and the shelves beside the bed. The boxes held Nora's postcards and small reprints: Vuillards and Vermeers, Magdalens—a La Tour, a Caravaggio—Van Ruisdaels, Turners, a few Hoppers, a few photos by Cartier-Bresson. These Sara examined repeatedly and sometimes briefly filched. A Morisot, a Hopper. For several days, a Vuillard. For several days, a Raphael.

AWAY

Perhaps because Katy could easily visit the house and find her room as she'd left it, at first she did not miss Blue Rock. Nor did she consider the consequences of absence, the changes in daily life that would accumulate without her knowledge or implicit permission. She trusted Blue Rock to remain the Blue Rock she'd known. On the quaint campus outside Boston and through its leafy suburb, she ran in the mornings, and every day she spoke to Tim; on days off he visited campus, and on weekends she'd take a bus to Boston and stay in his shared Kenmore Square apartment. During his shifts she'd study, and after they'd drink beer and hazily make love. On Sundays they'd lounge in bed, his hands on her, stroking her, his fingers inside her, mouth at her breast; the day a-spin with jolting pleasures, the room for a time no longer the room, the city having peeled away, and he'd enter her then, and the room was Tim, dense muscle, exquisite rippling of light that was both a rising and a descent into him, as if she had moved beyond his skin, beyond his rib cage, into a place of liquid and muscle and bone. A salt tang, a pale gray drifting until the air cooled, until he stretched and curled around her for another hour, and she was not lonely.

In that first, elating year, when she visited Blue Rock the girls ran to her. Nora fussed over her. Those moments seemed precisely right and therefore went unremarked. But in summer, when she again lived in the house, the girls paired off and fell into private communication, or immersed themselves in books and solitary games, ignoring her. Why would they ignore her? Had they ignored her in the past? (She thought not. She did not consider her own preoccupations.) She'd coax them out with treats, which they'd accept, but soon enough they'd return to their twosome, or their solitary pursuits, or play with neighborhood kids. The girls' ability to engage with Katy for a moment, then disengage for hours disturbed her. Her resulting agitation had the cast of a low-grade fever, those small confused moments bloating, their sting persisting and leaching through the day. It did not occur to her to ask if something was wrong (though in the past she'd asked about their disquiet); it did not occur to her that these might be established habits. Her tone with them became sharp, surprising everyone. When she looked after the girls, if she enforced house rules, they'd talk back. It happened when Nora was out. No, Katy said, no more television; no, the sea was too choppy today for a swim. Perhaps they would stare at the whitecaps and shrug, and compromise by wading in the shallows. Perhaps they would balk, suspecting an arbitrary decision. One afternoon, Delia rushed ahead of Katy toward the beach road and the parked ice-cream truck—not in the road but near, and running. And when Katy yanked Delia back, it was with an excess she could not stop: her manner too stern, her hand braceleting Delia's bicep too tightly. Delia yelped.

"It's too close to dinner," Katy lied. Having lied, she found herself insisting. Delia swung her free arm back and forth like a pendulum, coins still clutched in her fist. Squinted at the sand. "You don't live here," she said.

"Oh yes I do," Katy said. Not for the first time, Katy's body seemed to be in charge; she grabbed Delia's swinging hand and forced the coins out, then marched the girls back to the house. At dinner, they pointedly ignored her: the next day they both insisted on staying in the house and reading and playing jacks. By then one panic had blurred into another. Nora returned the change to Delia and announced broad ice-cream hours (a short pre-dinner exclusion). Privately, she told Katy, "Oh, it's summer. Let her have what she likes." It took days and games on the beach with Katy and Tim for Delia to become, again, affectionate.

And of Nora herself? There was never enough. After the girls' bedtime, Nora would type medical insurance forms and calculate accounts and houseclean until she disappeared behind the closed door of her bedroom. Daily she and Katy spoke, Nora noting the weather and town events, sorting out the child care, asking when to expect Tim at the house—but Nora might have been speaking to anyone. Apparently Katy-as-Katy had the presence of a cereal box. When Katy mentioned taking time together—say, when Sara and Delia next visited James—Nora would say, "Sure," and smile and call her "doll." For a few days Katy would hope—lunch in Boston? a picnic and a walk?—the hope gradually fading. Nora made no plans, and eventually Katy's café job hours increased; her nights with Tim increased.

Each successive season, each semester, a flickering uneasiness about Blue Rock intensified, as if she were slipping toward its fringe; or as if the house itself were slipping away from her. By Katy's third year in college, the feeling rarely abated. On weekends when she stayed in Blue Rock, Katy sensed that while she occupied the space—even her bedroom remained unchanged—she was not *inside*. As if there were—after all these years—secret rooms to which she had no access, or as if a separate identical house existed within the house, this second one occupied by Nora, Sara, and Delia. She studied the girls— sometimes affectionate, sometimes contrary, Sara more silent, Delia blurting. It was then that Katy too began to roam and search the house: one afternoon, Sara found her napping on Sara's own bed. After another visit, the girls found their comic books and novels disarranged, bookmarks set at the wrong pages.

Katy too rummaged and sifted in Nora's room, checking Nora's closet, Nora's dresser, as if the clothes racks and drawers held a nameless elusive part of her mother. Once, when she was sorting through the plain white bras and plainer underwear, Nora walked in.

Her eyes focused on Katy, assessing. "Katy, what do you need?"

Katy froze, confused, deflated. She was wearing a thin cotton sundress. "A slip?" she said. "Something."

TRUCK REDUX

Until Sara was twelve, the Rome stories were hardly stories at all, only truncated phrases of Nora's: *accident* or *traffic accident* and, later, *a traffic accident, and then she was gone.* This last phrase Sara would sometimes recast as two separate incidents: a four-year-old Molly strolls the piazza (pink sundress, matching shoes) while on a nearby street (sometimes paved, sometimes cobblestone) two cars collide. At impact, a cracking boom rings out, and Molly absents the piazza. Pink smoke drifts. The drivers gesture extravagantly as they argue on the sidewalk. How easy then to imagine Molly reappearing elsewhere, lost but vibrant and intact. Long after she knew *accident* implied horror, Sara retreated to this picture.

To her, it had seemed Molly was always and never at the Blue Rock house. Not the ubiquitous lack Sara had grown accustomed to, but not entirely separate. Privately she'd speculated about who Molly might be now, were she still Molly, how like or unlike Theo or Katy, or Delia, her baby look-alike, or Sara herself. Whether, if Molly were still Molly, Sara would exist at all: she'd concluded she would not. So maybe, she thought, the missing thing was the gap between who Molly had been and who Sara had—or had not—become. The price of living, she wondered, because someone else did not? Could the space you occupied be fully your own? Born after the fact, yes, but it seemed she was still implicated. And although Delia was the youngest, Sara never wondered about Delia's existence. To Sara, Delia was rooted and permanent, definite in ways that she herself was not. Nor did Delia worry about her resemblance to Molly. They were sisters: they looked like it. But even at twelve, Sara was not fully visible. As if her body had less density or clarity than her siblings'. As if part of her were somehow in Italy; as if she'd been too faintly printed.

She and Delia had just been to the mall; now Katy was driving them home. Near the highway exit for Blue Rock, traffic halted, then crept forward. Flashing blue lights: a squad car, and beyond it an ambulance and another rescue truck, and two partly ruined cars, empty of people. Difficult to tell how ruined the people might have been.

"Who was driving?" Sara asked. As if Katy and Delia would also be thinking of Molly; as if all accidents led back to her.

Katy squinted.

"In Italy," Sara said.

"Oh. No one," Katy said. "Well, the truck driver."

And then the picture changed, the two-car collision and the flawless girl in pink now and finally swept away, replaced by a screeching truck and simultaneous thud, the body of a girl for one instant airborne, the next thrown to the ground. Sara first accessed the sounds, then the increasingly detailed images. The question of what happened to Molly's body became immediate and splintered into more precise and graphic questions and the unstoppable—compulsive—speculation about what Molly felt (did shock protect her?), and what she might have known.

Katy turned onto a secondary road and changed the subject to swim practice. Back at the house, a pitcher of lemonade sweated on the counter. On the living room sofa, Nora sorted coupons and read the news.

For months, Sara replayed the scene in Rome, which emerged more vividly as Katy let drop more details of the story: a church, the bright hot air when they emerged. Nora, Katy, and Molly together. Theo and James out on the street. A sports car—parked. Molly running. In those months, Sara and Delia frequently compared notes, occasionally found moments—in the kitchen or on the deck at a holiday gathering—to corner a vaguely responding Aunt Meg. With Nora or James, they brought up Molly only rarely, usually through the back door of Newton. From the living room cabinets, Sara dug out photos of Molly, some of which Delia took and hid in the pink lacquered box where she kept her swim badges and birthday cards. Years later—and from Theo—they learned of Katy holding Molly's hand. The waving? That came sooner, and from Katy, a muttered aside: *Why did they wave?*

On a subsequent weekend, Nora let Sara and Delia take a North Shore commuter train to meet James. It was winter; there had been snow, which stretched untouched over the fields beyond the tracks, blanketing the rooftops. Just as the train arrived at the stop, James pulled up to the loading zone across the tracks. Half a dozen other cars steamed in the parking lot, engines running, hazards blinking. As James emerged from his sedan, he waved to Sara and Delia, and Sara imagined another wave, in that other city, to that other daughter, the one who did not disappear in pink smoke.

"Hey, there's Dad," Delia said. She'd already waved back. She jumped.

REPRODUCTION

Interior: Woman before a Window
Edouard Vuillard (c. 1900)
FROM A PRIVATE COLLECTION

On the far side of the living room, she faces the long window, her dress a curving pale pink column leading to the paler curve of her neck, the dark upswept hair, the white cap. A wall of curtain sheers, wide white brushstrokes. Beyond the window, beyond the canvas, Paris, which appears as blocks of color—the blue windows of a nearby building, the white sky. Surrounding the woman and the window, opening out toward you, the airy salon: the sofa and chairs upholstered in white-and-gold striped fabric, a vase of white roses, ochre walls, all flooded with light. A tapestried carpet spills across the right front quadrant of the canvas; indigo, sepia, milk-blue blossoms and vines over a carmine plain. From the upper right, the frond of a potted palm reaches toward her, the glass-framed city, the light. Not unlike a viewer, happening upon this color field—from one's own glassless window, waiting for the woman to turn.

Say the woman—a certain Madame Fontaine—gazes out not in waiting but in reverie; or if she is waiting, waiting not for the arrival of guests, but of thoughts, a greater clarity. The room is blissfully quiet. Perhaps she waits for another life to unfurl.

Or imagine that after a century, the woman in the painting—held aloft, long after Madame Fontaine's death, the salon's dismantling—still waits for the room to reassemble full scale, here in the living world. What if? Did you also, as a child, enter an unknown brilliant room? And in your rush of happiness presume that, in years to come, you'd return? That of course you'd live here.

KATY'S PLACES

First: the house in Newton, which in memory seemed to slide backward and shrink, the way her father had even then. As if James himself were the departing car, the receding lines of a midsized sedan, dark blue, spinning tires, red taillights, the rear window through which, each morning, one might glimpse his silhouetted head or only the reflections of trees. The sound would diminish, abate; in the evenings she'd wait for the reversal, the engine whir emerging from the weave of kid sounds and dog barks, leaf raking or snow shoveling or lawn watering along the block. In Newton, early on, the bay window: she could sit still then and wait, holding but not reading the illustrated book from which she remembered a forbidding gray castle with a cylindrical tower, the princess only a blur of pink.

For Katy, the house in Newton first defined *house*. Her room painted yellow with white trim, a low wooden bed covered with stuffed animals; beside it, a dresser, a bookshelf, two bins in which she kept the toys of the moment, mostly miniature figures, human and animal, from various tableaux—farm scene, medical office, grocery—a postman in a blue uniform and a doctor in a white coat. For a brief time a Raggedy Ann that later became Molly's. On the opposite side of the room, Molly had her own wooden bed, her own stuffed animals and dolls, her own bookshelf and dresser. Nora had painted yellow daisies on Katy's dresser, pink ones on Molly's. The house itself seemed indistinguishable from Nora: the most satisfying room the room Nora currently occupied. Though Katy explored, she did not stray far. Even when Nora hired a mother's helper, Katy would trail Nora through the house.

Theo seemed to care only that Nora was home. He did not wait by the bay windows for James to return from work—as if, confident their father would find him, he did not need to wait. Or as if he did not need anything. Theo's room was from the start a separate realm into which Katy wandered only in his absence. Library books on volcanoes and stars, baseball cards, a dead butterfly, stones. Valuable because they were Theo's.

From the living room bay window she could see the Kellers' blue house and the Santa Lucias' white one, the O'Malleys' lawn next door. She had lived there *always*—the same *always* occupied by Toby Keller and Elena Santa Lucia—a singular extending present interrupted only by summers in Blue Rock, where her father appeared not as a retreating car but as a laughing man.

When the house in Newton emptied itself onto a truck, she ran back and forth across the unobstructed floors, tagging the walls, tagging them again, speeding past the sounds of her mother's protests, as if her mother were a speaking television. She ran the stairs, the running becoming its own buffered sphere, like the interior of a car on the highway, a fast-moving bubble you stayed in apart from the world. You could go on forever, not expecting to be plucked from the driving rhythm, your body pulled straight up, grabbed and lifted by your father, today a full-sized man whose arms had you straitjacketed against his chest: *Your mother said stop.* But how crucial the motion, and you slapped at his arms, *Katy, stop it,* and the straitjacket seeming to tighten and you kicked and he kept saying *enough now* until you went limp and teary, after which he set you down, and Molly stood in the doorway watching while your mother told you to go get in the car with Theo, right now. And in the backseat, Theo watched you kick at the upholstery, until your mother brought Molly to the car. Out the window, the houses and trees began to pass as in a movie, and then a movie about highways and cars, one of them somewhere your father's.

After Italy, no one visited Newton again: for a time the house remained in her mind a space she could picture but never find her way back to, and one where Molly stood in the doorway, where Molly might still wear the pink pajamas and eat her toast alone. Eventually, in Blue Rock, the images from the Newton house began their retreat, becoming opaque and unpleasantly shadowed, like pond water in October.

Later there was only Blue Rock, the *always* of Blue Rock the only apparent *always*—though always, too, the place her father was leaving behind (in her mind his car forever the same retreating sedan). It was the Shore Road house, pitched at the edge of the sea, Katy presumed to be indelible, her point of orientation not only from her college dorm and Tim's Boston apartment but also from the string of increasingly large, well-appointed condos her father lived in, which she thought of as motels. In their North Shore house, James and Josie kept a bed-room they called Katy's, a peach-and-white guest room with floral touches, *hers,* but only in relation to the other bedrooms or common spaces of the house: here she could close the door. Yet it was a room she entered only on scheduled visits, a house to which she did not own a key, in a town near the sea but not her town—and, strangely, not her sea. The beachside roads of Blue Rock, its cliff-side and harborside streets, the sand-filled town center became the measures by which she judged any elsewhere: Blue Rock or not–Blue Rock, Shore Road house or not.

KATY WITH TIM

When she and Tim agreed to live together, she first imagined Tim as he appeared across a polished table (the image from a bar downtown); and Tim in his bedroom (Tim's body). The rest—to the extent that she imagined the rest—was borrowed from her father's first condo in Cambridge (well if sparely furnished, fine natural light, the building brick, off Harvard Square) and bits from Blue Rock—her own bedroom, with its pastel walls and thick white bedspread and windows facing the sea. She'd finished college; graduation implied adulthood in a way that college had not. Tim arranged for a summer sublet, close to the T. They could move in together *now*, he said. A vital point: her paralegal job would begin right away (downtown, a high-end firm, thanks to Patrick Murphy). "A one-bedroom, a sublet, just for the summer," she told first Nora and then James over the phone.

Only the morning before the move did it occur to her that *one-bedroom* and *summer sublet* might have different connotations for Tim; or that the space she envisioned might be pure invention. Enough time to brace for the actual sublet, on the second floor of a saggy three-story building, its walls a patchwork of tattery brown-and-white wallpaper, one closet door punched in, mysterious stains on the ceiling and the mustard carpet. She managed to say nothing. She spent the first weekend scrubbing down the place, spread a sky-blue cloth on the kitchen table, flowered sheets on the bed. But it was a cardboard house, in a cardboard neighborhood, with only the sheerest divide between interior space and the overpacked block. In the heat, everyone's windows stayed open. Walls hardly mattered.

How was it that when she walked in Boston with Tim—on crowded streets, or the Common, at Fanueil Hall—she rarely considered the proximity of strangers? Most—even strangers right beside her—were unobtrusive. She'd attend to city pleasures, the familiar weight of Tim's arm over her shoulders, Tim's athletic grace. She'd forget about time; it later seemed those days of forgotten time were *real life*.

But *real life* she could not access from the apartment. She and Tim worked opposite schedules, and the early weekday commute became a reprieve: here was a moment—if one without Tim—of leaving the house and that gray street for the broader and busier streets and the T, the air still cool; and then the buzz around Government Center, and the sense of possibility and purpose, into the river of women and men in suits and skirts and purposeful strides. At the office, the secretaries and paralegals poured coffee and shared pastries and greeted her by name. Her workdays felt clean, the time itself inflected by the well-groomed space and her research tasks.

Yet at the end of the week, as the other staff collectively leaned toward the weekend, she faced a kind of exile. For the first month she spent her city weekends in the mysteriously stained apartment alone while Tim worked dinner shifts and stayed until close. The street—the street that had become, distressingly, her street—had no green space, no shade. The heat would rise in a haze above the gray pavement.

And over the course of the day, the haze transformed, it seemed, into noise: occasional shouts and throbbing music from apartments and from junk cars with bad mufflers and choking engines, party noise escalating at night. Tim remained untroubled: the apartment was temporary, and the worst noise subsided by the time he arrived home. Real life continued for him without disruption.

The Friday the neighborhood noise reached its apex, Tim worked a double shift. Next door a skinny girl named Lori and her drummer boyfriend Todd threw a party that began at ten and each hour seemed to reach a grand crescendo only to extend to a later, grander one. It seemed as if partygoers had projected themselves into Katy's sublet, smoking up the dingy kitchen and dank living room, stupidly flirting in her cramped bedroom, the flat air filled with the pounding of hard-soled shoes, amped-up guitar, an angry male cawing. Then a cloying jasmine incense—a failed attempt to mask the pot?—wafted in. Katy kept her lights off. The sound grew palpably weighty, both crashing and climbing skyward, until close to two, when a squad car arrived. A long-limbed cop stepped out, then a shorter one shaped like a turtle. The music went dead; the crowd dispersed almost instantly. One guy ran down the back alley while Todd was talking out front with the cops, head down, nodding.

And after the cops had left and the party apparently shrank to a few loyal stragglers smoking cigarettes and clinking beer bottles on the porch, Todd yelled—from the middle of the street—"Who called the cops? You suck." Pivoting slowly, 360 degrees. "You really suck."

Did she? The accusation seemed true, though she'd called no one. How was it that Todd had caused the disturbance, and she was a pariah? Yet the sensation remained, even after Tim returned from work and they'd made love, even after a short night's sleep.

On Saturday, when Tim left to pick up coffee, he ran into Lori and Todd outside, their voices floating up through the sublet's windows. Too bad, Tim said, he couldn't make the party. "You guys free for a while now?" Tim said.

When he reentered the sublet, Tim offered Katy the coffee, kissed her on the mouth, and took a six-pack of beer from the fridge. "Hey, sweet pea," he said, "you want to have a beer with Todd and Lori?"

Katy pressed her lips together. "No thanks," she said.

He shrugged. "Okay, then," he said, and left with the beer.

Fleetingly, it seemed the water stains, the sticky heat, and the vegetable rot from the outdoor trash might emanate from Katy herself. As if she were a squalid thing in the squalid box she now resembled. And *real life*?

She counted to twelve. Then she called Nora. "It's just so hot in the city," she said.

"Honey," Nora said, "how about a cool shower? Why don't you take a shower and drink lemonade."

Honey.

"Katy?" Nora said.

"If I take the bus down, do you think you could meet me?" Katy said.

✣

That day, the house in Blue Rock was quiet but for faint shouts carried from the near beach. The girls were babysitting down the street. Katy drank a lemonade and slept for an hour in the room that was still her room, the bed that was still her bed. Awoke again herself—which suggested, of course, that she had not been herself. Who then had she been? The question hovered, casting a weird buzzy shadow. She could not answer. She was thirsty, but there would be more lemonade. And now, yes, she was home. She was herself. She put on a bathing suit and sat on the deck. Late that night, Tim drove down to the shore, and the two of them stayed at the house through Sunday dinner.

For the rest of the summer, Katy spent the weekdays in Boston and tried to detach from small daily shocks: bare feet in urine drops Tim left near the toilet, a mouse drowned in the saucepan she'd soaked overnight. Each weekend she spent in Blue Rock.

✣

In late August, she and Tim moved to Cambridge, to a place she'd found on a side street not far from Porter Square, a large one-bedroom apartment in a solidly built house, beside other well-tended houses—houses with rosebushes, scattered maples, patches of grass, window boxes of geraniums. The apartment had good floors, good light, a white kitchen. Here she could be herself, couldn't she? Live her real life? She found a running route through the upscale parts of Cambridge and around the Harvard campus, and sometimes she'd follow along the river. Tim worked Tuesday through Saturday; on Wednesdays, she'd meet James and Josie for dinner. On Fridays, she'd stop by the law firm's happy hour.

Still, her loneliness and all of its shadings surprised her. Even in the short days of late October, she felt the Friday rush hour impulse to find a bus to Blue Rock, or ride the red line to Braintree and catch a local there. Just before Halloween, she returned after work to the apartment, the streets already dark, the air already chilled, and found the familiar disarray—Tim's running gear on the bathroom floor, unwashed dishes, beer but no groceries—and with it arrived a familiar despondency. No wildflowers or bowl of apples or shells on the kitchen table, no note for her, nothing like Blue Rock, where each room seemed to be as Nora left it, casually ordered, clean and unfussy.

She'd thought—what was it? That she and Tim were together, which meant not only the sex and goofy singing but also—was she wrong?—that together you were in *it*—a shared space, a shared state. Once in Blue Rock she and Nora had been *in it together*, hadn't they? With Sara and Delia. The *it* that was both house and more-than-house. Before the girls, there'd been another *it*, nameless but marked by the church steps in Rome, steps with Nora and Molly, then only Nora. Her father and brother seemed to recede into the distance, always, beyond a divide she could not cross. And if that divide began as a street or piazza (did it? she could no longer tell), it had long since metamorphosed. She'd never pictured Tim on the far side of that same divide—and still did not—but implicit, now-visible limits bounded whatever *together* she shared with Tim; apparently other divides existed. In truth, one might be separate and alone.

Yet when Katy imagined her mother, Sara, and Delia together, she imagined them as a single unit, theirs the house within the house. Another *us*—or *them*—none of them alone. The *house within the house* seemed an undifferentiated space free of loneliness: if one occupied that space, one would, she presumed, be equally free. Here then the dream, or the impasse: the question was how to return, step inside, go *back*.

And now through the apartment windows, the Cambridge trees appeared to be stage props. Here inside lay the crusted dishes, here the dirty laundry, despite her efforts. Again disorder had replicated; again the day confirmed that her simplest desires—the clean space, a conch shell on a bare wood table—were irrelevant; she herself irrelevant.

She was failing, wasn't she? Here, proof, in the face of which—what had spilled on the floor?—she found herself blinking. How pathetic her hopes, how plainly stupid. Not everyone is deserving, it turned out, some people, yes, but some are deluded, some cursed—how long can you pass? A clean space, a bowl of apples? No. She'd be denied these things—perhaps always. Even Tim, who loved her—or said he loved her, and in those moments seemed convinced—even Tim denied her these things. And how, yes, stupidly, that same day at the office, she'd laughed with her coworker Ava. A passing joke Ava made, a Halloween reception and a creepy senior partner—*he can go as he is*—Katy had laughed, both of them had laughed. As if she belonged in that office; as if beyond the office she possessed something, *it*, a home, a clean room, windows and trees, a table and a bowl of apples, a shell, perhaps a note signed *xoxo*, or yellow mums on the windowsill. No clothes on the floor, nothing dousing the little hope from Ava's laugh, or trumpeting that Katy's good things were dumb luck about to vanish.

On his break after the dinner rush, Tim called. And how to explain anything to him?

"I was running late for work," he said. "Katy?"

She was still teary, her voice clogged up and ugly.

"Oh, don't be sad, Katy," he said and promised to be more mindful (for a few days, he would be). He'd market tomorrow; tonight he'd bring her pumpkin pie. The next week, they'd decide to elope. "Be patient, sweet girl, just wait," he said. He sang to her on the phone, an improvised riff about waffles, the maple syrup he'd bring home for breakfast.

REPRODUCTION

Magdalena Poenitens (Penitent Magdalen)
Joannes and Lucas van Doetecum after Pieter Bruegel
the Elder (1555-56) Etching with engraving

This time, there's a kingdom and beyond, craggy mountains and outcroppings of rock, quiet valley below, a curving river briefly divided by an island, banked by groves of trees etched as round and flame-shaped puffs, snug houses tucked in among them. Look left in the distance: at the river's edge, here's the fortressed town, on the bluff above it, a castle. Another bluff, another castle. In the right foreground stands a tall tufted evergreen, like a dancer's ruffled dress. Singular, just not quite outsized, this tree—larger than the distant mountains and hills, the background castles, the rock outcroppings. The evergreen marks the edge of a hilltop forest: along the bluff runs a curved road. Two mules, one with a rider, make their way around the hillside.

From all of this, the woman has secluded herself. In the right corner of the foreground, nearing the edge of the print, she's tucked away in a rough shelter of spiked logs. Hidden from the road; nearly hidden from your view, and closer in scale to the tiny mules and their rider. She's in shadow, though here's her illuminating halo, and a small glowing cross. Here's the ubiquitous skull, the open book.

Her face is barely visible, her features suggestions. She reads—her book a world, or a doorway to a world?—ignoring the visual splendor, the mountains and river valley, the fortressed town and castles. In the distant sky hangs an orb with an elaborate cross.

Say you contemplate this world as she contemplates the world. Does the long view, the parallel act, bring you closer to her? Here is her arm—slender, white—her hand holding open the book. Here a foot, poking out beneath the hem of her dress as she sits on the ground. Tiny, in the corner. But the lines of the dress echo those of the hills and valley—and send you back to the expansive landscape, away from her single small corner. Again you study the print while she studies the printed text. In solitude, here outside the living world.

JAMES BY THE SEA

Spring. At least you could say that about the day: the North Shore crab-apple trees a frothy pink, lilacs in pale and deep violet blooming along the roadsides, the unfurling leaves a rare pale green. Thicker petals of ornamental magnolia, magenta and white, would bloom for one spectacular week, then scatter in the grass. On the weekends, James had turned ground for a small garden, vegetables and sunflowers. Only in recent years had he become a gardener, since the move to Beverly with Josie. Last summer when Sara and Delia visited, they seemed amused by his efforts, but they'd happily picked the cherry tomatoes, happily eaten the green beans. Sometimes while he gardened, they played soccer with Josie; sometimes they helped.

So he could anticipate, at least, a summer garden, more visits. Today he would have, on his way home, a wash of sunlight, time to walk along a North Shore beach—the thought like a distant plane approaching, still a speck, only a speck, as he drove north out of the city, not to Beverly but beyond it, toward Manchester-by-the-Sea. School buses now clogged the secondary roads, crossing guards in bright orange and black, like huge caterpillars, stopping him with a raised hand, small towns busy with daytime routines of marketing and bakeries and dog walking, kids on Rollerblades and skateboards, kids on bikes, and at the playground, on swing sets swinging. The crossing guards waved him on.

More roadside deciduous trees, tall old-growth oaks and maples and high banks of shrubs, more pastel bursts fronting the lawns of grand houses on the route to Singing Beach. There, toddlers played in the sand, ringed by young mothers and nannies: at the far end, a gaggle of teenagers leaned together and smoked. James's first thought had been Blue Rock, even now—the far beach as he'd known it with his father. But he liked Singing Beach, the intimate scale of it, the blooming, well-to-do town, in which, as a stranger passing through, one could forget the outside world. Residents commuted to Boston just as they did from Beverly, men not unlike himself, executives, attorneys—but today he was not himself. Today he was a man in a car, and at Singing Beach he was a man on a bench watching the navy-blue sea, the lace edges of the fallen waves, the small whipped peaks in the distance. From the town came the muted whistle of a local train approaching the crossroads station. The shoreline had reconfigured since the last time he was there, the shoreline he remembered—one curving sweep of sand, a broad uninterrupted pie slice—now appeared as sand lobes riven by receding seawater, as if sliced by fine branching rope.

An emptying. He had not called Josie. He would tell her tonight. Her sister Liz was visiting: he would arrive home at the regular time and tell her after dinner, after they'd said good night to Liz. In this marriage, in this way, he was different.

Do not squander routine contentment, he told himself; do not squander Josie's. She was for him an anchor.

Down the beach, the clump of teenagers broke apart, some of them running kites: an electric-orange shield, a rainbow-tailed dragon. The kites he'd once built were simple, white paper diamonds, the frames raw flat wood, the string cheap brown stuff that scratched and cut his hands. In Blue Rock one summer he flew colorful fabric kites with Theo and the girls (Katy. Also Molly? Later, Sara and Delia), kites with better line and flexible frames.

It was better to be a man thinking about kites than it was to be the man he was today in Boston, the man he had not planned to be, in Boston or anywhere, ever. Parker took him to lunch—not anomalous, lunch with Parker, but not routine. This was how it was done. A good restaurant—in fact, a very good restaurant, Parker liked him, and Parker liked restaurants, and at least there would be a good meal, if you could eat the good meal. "I want to tell you," Parker said, "I couldn't be happier with your performance," and James's quick flush of pleasure—even now—cut short by the news of reorganization. "We don't have much choice here," Parker said, though it wasn't clear whom he meant by *we*.

"I've been doing what I can." Parker leaned forward, lowered his voice. "It's a decent severance. And you know I'll back you up. You tell anyone to call me."

Parker appeared to be the same Parker he'd been when they entered the restaurant: when had the change occurred? Once there had been a different Parker: time, Parker announced, for a different James, not divisional VP but a kicked-out James, and a hot-faced, tumbling James, held together by his suit and by the heavy furniture and deep grooves of dining-club mores.

"Give yourself some time," Parker said. "It's a lot to take in."

"I wasn't aware," James said, "our division was involved."

"This wasn't my decision," Parker said. "They're going after senior people."

"What about you?"

Theatrical and stung, Parker's laugh. "Could be. I'd bet a year."

Something stilled in James, and he could see himself as from outside, an executive at lunch: he had done this before. The performing James, receding from the moment as he kept up the public face. And so he managed the dessert Parker insisted they order—a hand lifting a forkful of cake to the mouth, a mechanical chewing and swallowing—and the top-shelf cognac, more heat in his throat and face, as if it were a celebratory meal.

And as they returned to the building—Parker actually saying, "I think the world of you, James"—Parker keeping close, for an instant James wondered if the lunch had occurred at all, if in waking life he'd had the lunch he thought he'd had (nothing about the city confirmed the transformation, the tumbling, the sudden sham of his Italian suit, silk tie, the sham of his body, it seemed). Then Parker placed a hand on his upper arm as he opened the building door, and gently steered him not to the elevators but toward the approaching building guard, Ken. Ken, ex-Navy, a Red Sox devotee with whom James had swapped baseball and sailing anecdotes for a decade.

"Mr. Murphy," Ken said. "This way," and waved at the corridor to the delivery entrance. Parker shook James's hand and hurried—only then, clearly hurrying—to the elevators.

In the storage room off the delivery entrance, a set of boxes, stacked and labeled *Murphy*. "It's how they do this," Ken said. "Don't think it's personal. Sorry, James."

When he'd left for lunch, his secretary, Maureen, had been told to clean out his office—desk, closet, rows of cabinets— and box his personal things. With one of the senior officers observing, she'd copied personal files from his computer onto a disk (a letter to a realtor, ongoing letters to Nora's attorney, a hopeful note he'd sent to Josie when he'd first met her). In the box she'd left a handwritten note: she'd found whatever personal files she could and deleted after copying, the scrawled *P.S. They told me just before lunch. We'll miss you.*

The breeze at Singing Beach kept the kites aloft, though they dipped and swung back on an updraft as the kids tugged strings and ran along the flattened sand below the high-tide line. No help to wonder how long ago Parker began the paperwork. It was difficult, at first, to leave the bench, this smallest of way stations, and to leave the lulling crash of incoming waves, the ebbing, the next set. And then he did leave; here was his car. In the town center he lucked into parking and at the restaurant closest to the train stop, ordered coffee at the bar. A man passing through, drinking coffee. The after-work crowd was just beginning to trickle in, and it was comforting to hold the coffee mug while the bartender told him business had been better since Easter. You made the real money during the summer; but year-round the bar did okay. Much better than the last place he'd worked.

That morning, he'd still been a man for whom success had come to seem innate—as if the foregone conclusion of early struggles. Even after Molly, Rome, divorce, the notion had held fast. Because he was James. And yes, because he had worked tirelessly; because it had seemed that through sheer effort he'd escaped his mother's apartment; landed the Harvard scholarship; it had seemed that through sheer effort, he'd risen beyond. How easy to forget the raw luck, his uncle's phone calls, Nora charming the cocktail party crowds, Nora herself. To downplay the advantage of Boston Irish networks, Boston Irish clout. He'd resisted the notion that he might be a cog (everyone, Nora would say, is a cog); buried the suspicion that a sham—his—would eventually be discovered, the now and forever true James revealed as a grief-stunned adolescent whose mother lives on a couch. After years of money, position, praise—long since arrived, long established—why imagine they would stop? Love, yes. But not this.

The Beverly house appeared as he'd left it, Josie and her sister now at the kitchen table drinking white wine. Josie was still in her suit, no shoes, kissing him hello, saying, "Maybe James will make lemon chicken?" then kissing him again—"Lemon chicken, James?"

"Sure," he said. "Give me just a minute."

Later, the jumble of consequences. Later the odd realignment of his social world, and the piles of resumes and series of fruitless lunches, headhunters repeating that everyone is downsizing; later the lucky days gardening with Josie and bright days in borrowed sailboats; cross-country-ski days with Sara and Delia; and arguments with Josie and apologies to Josie;

later, when the severance waned (a good one, true enough), more weekly polite notes on dime-store notepaper arrived from Nora, and then on pricey letterhead from her attorney, requesting checks.

⚜

Tonight he found the little anchors, the soap and washcloth, the peppermint toothpaste, the chest of drawers in which he kept his T-shirts. Old khakis in the closet. The body took charge, though the house had an odd lucidity—in the kitchen the kettle almost announcing itself as kettle, the paper shell of the garlic feathery against his skin, tart slices of lemon brilliant on the counter. Steamed broccoli turned emerald. How odd that the world did not instead recede, that Josie and her sister did not instead recede. A normal family dinner, a good family dinner, with the usual social chat, and Josie musing about the weekend. He was listening. Mostly he was listening.

ROMAN CONVERSATIONS

The taxi driver Lorenzo, thirtysomething, sleeps with the windows open at night, hopes for a breeze from the sea. He says this as he dodges in and out of traffic, almost scraping a red Fiat, the wheel rim of a truck. Churches? Only to find peace does he visit, so he avoids the famous ones. If Murphys were here, he'd never know.

A waiter named Giuseppe says he understands Americans; he lived in New York with his boyfriend for years. Tourists don't comprehend cities; cities do not remember them. Who can count all the tourists? He blows air across his palm.

In the business district, a body on the sidewalk curls into itself: apparently a woman, apparently alive—full-length skirt, long-sleeved blouse, head scarf—a coin bowl beside her. Her hand darts out to take the coins; the hand retreats. People step around her; in an hour, she's gone.

"Oh," Giuseppe says, "she will be back. You worry she has no name? She has a name, and a bad story." He shrugs. "How many bad stories can I keep?"

"In New York," Giuseppe says, "I knew a Murphy once. Very handsome, a man called Sean."

CHURCH PANTRY

Nora waits in the South Shore church, her mind now in Canada, Cape Breton Island, where the coast is rockier, the sea wilder than anything she's known. In the 1920s, '30s, later, the place offers nothing for young men beyond the body-breaking mines or the treacherous northern seas: some families fish, others work the mines. A gorgeous, rough place, the light often transcendent, but who can live on light? Death litters the towns, each village isolated from the next, the nearest city days away. There is no money. The father: a lovely man, a sorrow-filled life. On Cape Breton, for the son, there is the father and the light. Stay or go? A kind of death to stay; another to leave. How blue the sea; how white the gulls wheeling over the wet black rocks.

"My wife, she reads. She reads all the time."

She blinks, marks the page with her thumb. The man behind her is fortyish, thin, a pale man in a light gray jacket, jeans, work boots. He's holding a paper coffee cup from a donut shop. Jittery: the cup trembles. Dark hair thinned as if to emphasize the furrowed brow.

Nora glances around. They're halfway through the line, ten people still ahead. A few small groups—women, mostly, one with a small boy—near the squared-off entry hunch together

and talk. Threads of conversation about a hair salon and a ruined party swim past her.

"Oh," Nora says. "Good. I think that's a good thing."

"Yeah," he says. Right leg jiggling. He leans in but doesn't
look her in the eye. She glances back at the description of the
wheeling gulls.

"This isn't my church," he says.

"No?" Nora says. The gulls fall away. "It isn't mine either."

"I go to church though," the man says. "I've been going."
He addresses her knees, her feet.

"People seem to," she says.

"Yeah," he says. "I do that. I do that but my wife, you know,
she won't talk to me."

They find her, these men, the lost ones. At the post office,
the DMV. And women—but more of the women seem benign.
"I'm sorry," Nora says.

"Thanks, yeah," he says. "I'm staying with my mother.
Now. She wants me to go," he says. He's on to his wife's story,
her hospitalization, a psych ward for weeks—and she's better,
she's better now, but now that she is better she won't see him,
won't talk to him, and so he prays, and he visits the priest, and
he tells his mother who doesn't want him there he's going to
church, and these bags of food are for his mother, he says, well,
his mother and him, but he's trying, you know? He's making
an effort, he says. It's as if the coffee cup is all that's keeping
him from flying apart. He's shivering, shifting from one foot to
another. Opening and closing his free hand.

Sometimes the smallest things can keep you from snapping:
a tabby sunning herself on the steps, a whiff of chocolate, a

neighborhood kid waving hello. Or a stranger in line willing to listen, someone who does not wish, as you might, that you were dead. Nora knows this. Still, she thinks, *Disappear. Please please disappear.*

Then he says he's got a boy, a boy and a girl, they live with his wife's sister now, he's going to see the boy in a week (so no, mustn't disappear, there's the boy, the girl). She's not a bad person, the sister, he knows that, she's taken the kids, but she doesn't like him, he knows she doesn't like him. Nora does not ask him why.

He's nice to the sister, he says, he's always tried to be nice, but these are bad days. Some bad bad days. "I pray," he says. "I talk to Father Thomas. I pray."

"He must be kind," she says.

"Father Thomas? Yeah. Yeah," he says. "But I need a place to stay. I'm staying with my mother now."

"You said," Nora says.

"Only she doesn't want me there," he says. "Bad days."

She does not ask why the mother wants him out; or why his wife won't see him; or what he did, or what he didn't do, or if his kids are okay; if he knows what can happen to kids in a minute; or how much it takes to keep them well; and if they are well, if he knows to thank, forever, the sister-in-law. After all, they're in a church. Now it seems that she is the calm thing that keeps his chaos from spilling out further. She does not want to be the calm thing, but here she is.

They're almost through the line, and when she picks up her bags and tells the man behind her "Good luck," he says, "Yeah," and then "Wait." But she does not want to wait: she rushes ahead, arms full, out to the parking lot. She's setting the bags in the backseat, and he's there, in the parking lot, behind her. His arms are full of groceries; there's nothing threatening about him, except his drowning. Maybe he is hoping for a ride. He's looking at her now, catching her eye. She is perfectly still. She wants to push him; to shove him hard, away, send him reeling back to his mother's house. For a second, his eyes widen, as if he's seen it, he's recognized how easily she could be cruel. Maybe he's not so oblivious. Or maybe he's now realized that she *is* a stranger, that he's latched on to her as if she were his wife or his mother or a sympathetic friend, but she's out of sympathy and he doesn't know her at all, the confusion shaming him.

"Good luck," she says again. It's flat and unlucky, the way she says it, and he steps back, shambling, gazing at the ground again. And then she's in the car, and she pulls out onto the road, and when she is a few miles out, stops to light a cigarette. It's as if she's caught his tremble. And on the drive back to Blue Rock, to the house beside the sea—who ever wants to leave the sea? Or Nova Scotia, that light? A father. How terrible to leave her own father—burying him had seemed just that, although he had gone—yes, terrible to leave her father, who loved her. In this life, how does anyone sustain kindness? And the island now so very far away.

HOUSE VI

Because of the money, Nora had said yes. At least, that's what Sara and Delia believed. Because Nora was scraping to cover the basics, and otherwise, why would she agree? It seemed shaming to ask; they didn't pose the question aloud. That summer, their father had begun consulting, but what did consulting mean? They were working, always, Sara and Delia, babysitting for several families; on Wednesdays, Sara helped at a garden center. In the early mornings, she swam at the high school pool. Almost no time in the house, almost no time on the beach. And with Nora at work, most days the house stood empty. Maybe the unoccupied rooms surprised Katy: maybe, Sara mused, she took them for an invitation. Because didn't she and Tim have a place of their own? And in Cambridge, with its theaters and bookstores and cafés.

When Katy arrived, Sara was babysitting near the harbor, Delia watching a MacFarland toddler at the beach. Had they been home, what would they have said? For weeks Katy had been repeating that Cambridge wasn't all she'd hoped. Cambridge was expensive. She'd been sad, some days, in Cambridge. And she'd looked sad—tearful, unsteady—but Sara could only say, "Sorry." She found herself repeating, "Sorry, Katy." Dread accumulated. It was like watching a B-movie plot intensify, a shadow closing in, Sara stuck in place. She was fourteen. She poured Katy another glass of lemonade.

She did love Katy, didn't she? Or couldn't imagine the world without her, which seemed to Sara, in part, what love meant. For years, Katy had watched out for her, cheered at her swim meets, found her babysitting jobs. But when Sara listed the things she loved about Katy—Rollerblading, Frisbee on the beach, movies and ball games with Katy and Tim—they all took place at leisure and outside the house. Inside the house, Katy seemed to breathe more air than everyone else. The quiet rooms rarely stayed quiet. When Katy was unhappy, her unhappiness seeped into every corner. Lately, a strange band of pressure had begun to settle in Sara's temples and expand across her forehead, then intensify, even to the point of queasiness. The headaches—many—coincided with Katy's visits. But there were other factors—poor sleep, surging hormones, death dreams, pilfered beer or vodka. "Air" and "unhappiness" were abstractions. The issues Sara pinned down seemed too petty to mention: on a Sunday, Katy would visit and finish all the peanut butter, leaving none for Monday lunch. She'd walk into Sara's and Delia's rooms without knocking. One could say, *Please knock, okay?* though who else needed the reminder? Nora did say, *Heard of knocking, doll?* But mostly Sara didn't respond, instead freezing, waiting for the moment to end.

Now and then Sara escaped, with or without Delia, to the Beverly house. After one headache-free trip, she turned down weekend jobs to spend time with James and Josie. She didn't want to abandon Nora—was visiting James abandoning Nora? But Nora worked on Saturdays, and Katy's weekend presence altered the house. These days James seemed quieter and more somber; he was attentive, easy to be with. She helped him cultivate a vegetable patch and beds of flowers ringing the house. When Delia came, they flew kites on the beach; Delia and Josie took late-day runs while Sara and James walked at a preserve. Together they all cooked dinner. They did not talk about money, but they did not go to restaurants, or to the tourist districts or to Boston. As if places they used to frequent had fallen off the map.

❦

The day Katy approached Nora, Katy did not disparage Cambridge: she only discussed her rent and the wish for a house of her own. Which was what she deserved, she told Nora. She and Tim. But they'd never save enough paying Cambridge rents, would they? And if they moved into the Blue Rock house? Temporarily. Just until they had a down payment. Even with the commute, it would be cheaper, and cheaper for Nora. They'd help cover Nora's bills: Nora could use help with the bills, couldn't she? And help with repairs? Tim could do repairs (in truth, he agreed but would endlessly defer). There were details to work out. Other than Nora's room, Sara's—once the guest room, once Theo's—on the street side was the most private. "More appropriate for a couple," Katy said.

"The girls need privacy too," Nora told her.

Of course. Of course. Of course.

Nora delivered the news by telling Sara, "Pick a color for Katy's old room. I'll paint it for you."

"Maybe Katy should paint it," Sara said. Then, "Oh."

Nora, sheepish, told her, "I'm sorry, sweetheart."

❧

It wasn't so bad, was it? Katy's old room looked out on the bay, stayed warmer than the corner rooms. Nora considered the furniture: perhaps she could find a good chair for Sara, a better quilt. But in late August, just before the move, Katy disclosed that she was pregnant. Three in one room would never work, not with Tim's schedule: they'd need a second room for the baby.

When Nora told the girls, Sara said nothing. Delia rolled her eyes. "Wasn't she on the pill?" Delia said. "Mom, tell her about the pill. Tell her the sperm-and-egg part."

Yet Katy herself had seemed nonchalant: she'd shrugged as she announced her pregnancy to Nora, as if it were a spring high tide or a thunderstorm, beyond anyone's control. In that moment, the calm of corporate dinners and emergency response had washed over Nora. With it, Katy came into sharp focus. Nora nodded and smiled her cocktail party smile. "Can you afford a baby?"

"Mom," Katy said. "That's the first thing you say?"

"I'm just asking," Nora said.

"You're not even a little happy."

"Honey," Nora said, "when did you find out?"

There was a thick elastic silence, as if in contradiction to the salt breeze and the calling shorebirds, the faint smoke from a grill a few houses down. The sea had turned a royal blue, gold light tinting the air. On a day like this, Nora had once gone swimming with the Murphy cousins and drunk gin and tonics on the deck. She missed gin and tonics on this deck; she missed the gold light now even as it fell. Maybe a glass of wine with the MacFarlands; or just a glass of wine alone, later.

She'd paint Katy's old room yellow, instead of violet. In six months, Sara and Delia would share the bedroom they'd shared as little girls. Katy would, Nora knew, lean on all of them to babysit.

"I'm thrilled for you, sweetheart," Nora said.

PREGNANT

An exhaustion in February they all felt. No apparent end to winter: it took a leap of faith and the awareness of the increasing light to keep going. Each morning Katy lumbered down the outside stairs—sand and snow blowing, the ice formidable—and clownishly maneuvered herself into the neighbor's Ford Escort, her ride to the T. Of late, months did not cohere as months; though this was the ninth month, by the calendar. It was difficult to sleep, and now the daily slog downtown from the South Shore was a feat whether she drove or caught an early train.

The discomfort and her own absurdity astounded her: in the office she squeezed past the file cabinets, a giant beach ball. Outdoors, the snowbanks, the ice, the near tumbles finally defeated her. Ten days before the due date, she stayed in Blue Rock. At breakfast, Delia eyed her from the kitchen doorway. Katy was in her rolled-up XXL sweatpants, rolled-up XXL Patriots sweatshirt, a pink headband Delia had given her.

"Has it started?" Delia said.

"No." Her swollen feet lay in the seat cushion of a second chair, like big, rag-wool sausages. Sad sausages. "Would you mind getting me a piece of toast?"

"Is it moving?" Delia said.

Sara appeared in the doorway and nudged Delia. "He," Sara said, and slipped past Delia to the kettle.

"He," Delia said.

"There's not a lot of room to move," Katy said.

"You're kidding," Delia said. "You're huge. How can there be no room?"

"There just isn't," Katy said. Her lips were pressed together as she blinked.

"Delia," Sara said.

"What?"

"Make some toast."

"Well, you look like you're going to rugby practice," Delia said.

She'd never been as slender or lithe as her sisters, both of them small and sandy-blond and fine-featured, like poster girls for high school gymnastics. There was something bitter for Katy about the sweatpants. In another life, she'd worn jeans. Leggings. Running shorts.

Tim did not let her pout. He sometimes rubbed her swollen feet and sang to them. But now Tim was sleeping; he was still chefing nights, this season at a high-end place in Cohasset. The owners liked him, and the money was better. It seemed he'd forever work nights.

Here was her toast. "You'll call when it starts," Delia said. "Right? Jam?"

"Mom will call," Katy said. "Someone will call."

Why was it she felt as if she'd been tricked into something? Though she couldn't say what, or who had tricked her. Here was her mother, pouring coffee; Katy could not say that Nora had tricked her, at least not in a way she could name. To the contrary: Nora had always been frank about sex, its consequences. In high school, after Katy's first dates with Tim, Nora took her to get a diaphragm *and* gave her condoms. Yet Nora still seemed part of a deception.

"Not too much longer, love," Nora said.

Her father wasn't off the hook, was he? It seemed the residue from old deceptions stuck to him. He'd never said, "Do *this*," his influence less direct. She thought of road closings: you detour and detour again, until you discover a surprise destination, or drive off the map. Yet now that she was pregnant, James called twice a week; now he'd ask, "How was your morning?

From his own new planet—California—Theo had sent a congratulatory postcard of the Golden Gate Bridge and a baby hat resembling an eggplant.

She deserved to have a baby—she and Tim—yes, that's what she'd said, that's what she'd told Tim. Her baby: she felt him press into her side, talked to him and hummed to him. Another world spun inside her while she buttered the toast. But something else had blurred, and in odd attenuated moments it was unclear why she was pregnant and Nora was not; why Nora moved as easily around the house as the girls did, and Katy did not. As if this part, too, Nora should have shared, the palpable wave carried over from before, from the girls as babies, and before that. They were in something together— she did not think *Rome*, but there was a sensation, a strand of thought that trailed back to Rome, to the moment of Nora and Katy and Molly instantly shifting to Nora and Katy, the

268 | Nancy Reisman

space that had been Molly a thick seal between them. Katy had protected Sara and Delia, hadn't she? Then and now. She and Nora had collaborated. Yet now all of this heaviness in Katy. This loneliness. She knew, apparently, nothing.

She wanted, she deserved.

"Sweet pea," Tim had said, "of course you do." September then: they'd come down from Cambridge with a truck.

"I get that's what you want," Nora had said.

"You should," Katy said.

A warm late summer day, the sea almost cobalt. Nora tilted her head and turned toward the window, as if speaking to the bay. "You'll be a beautiful mother."

"Beautiful," Tim said. "Fantastic."

REPRODUCTION

Magdalen Reading

Follower of Piero di Cosimo (1500-20)

COURTAULD GALLERY, LONDON

Her face is a kind of moon, a thin copper halo above, hair blond, partly braided, threaded with pearls. She's seated, facing the viewer, her attention riveted to the book she holds. Here is the clean edge of a table, here peripheral views of the surrounding garden, the scene—the garden, her dress—painted with brilliant color: violet, aqua, gold, emerald green. The chair frame's red seeps into the dark rose cloak draped over her arm.

In the book: bold and less bold script, columns of text echoed by the chair's rectangular back and the rectangular panels of garden flanking her. Look twice at the garden, the single huge purple iris on the left panel, a smaller, apparently distant tree marking the edge of a bluff on the right; the composition suggests windows where none exist. A small white jar sits on the table, its curves echoing the woman's face and white neck. Her large eyes—with moonlike lids—remain trained on the book, but her mouth is tightly set: if she is aware of the viewer, this is the only clue.

Here you'll find overt love of geometry—even her jawline's squared—and a decorative tilt absent from di Cosimo's graceful original. The color is what draws you in—the rich green, the dark rose—before you observe her face. It's a close-up, unlike the Van der Weyden Magdalen, who appears as if on a stage set, unaware of the open fourth wall. Proportions have shifted: this garden Magdalen is much larger than the iris, the iris larger than the tree. She's a giant against the bluff, the distant sky. Nothing obscures her from view. Yet the close-up reveals emotional distance—her fixed concentration, that set mouth? Might she prefer to be alone? She is what we have of the moment: an unknown woman painted by an unknown painter. All the violet, the green, the gold. A color dream. But step back.

INTERIOR WITH CHEERIOS

Luckily he was a sweet boy, Connor. He had Tim's disposition, and the Murphy dimples; he was happy to be held, cooed at the girls. And they were sweet with him, relaxed, often doting: they'd been babysitting for years. But for all the playing and soothing, feeding and diapering, all the households to which they'd come and gone, neither Sara nor Delia had realized how much space a baby could claim. Now here was Connor, toys strewn across the living room, his extra changing space displacing the alcove drawing table; baskets of baby laundry in the kitchen, on the stairs, onesies fresh from the dryer dumped onto the sofa. The upstairs bathroom was overrun with ducks and blue boats (cute ducks, cute boats), baby wash, baby towels. Had Sara and Delia taken up as much space? (Yes and no.) Connor's cries carried through the house, even when they weren't babysitting: how could this be a surprise? They'd neglected to consider the hours during which they'd study or talk on the phone, the usual television times, the nights before meets or exams, when performance depended on rest; or that Connor's moods would be tied to Katy's. Together Connor and Katy were content; together they were miserable.

Nor had Sara and Delia anticipated all Katy's ways of taking command—habits picked up, Sara guessed, from attorneys. Too often, her sentences began, *Sara/Delia, I need you to* _____. At first, Connor's fragile newborn state seemed to justify peremptory demands. But they did not stop, and Katy's tunnel vision did not broaden. She might hand the baby to Sara the moment Sara walked in from her swim meet. Just before the girls' last visit to Beverly, Katy had called, "Delia, I need you to feed Connor," even as Delia buttoned her coat to leave.

"We're going to see Dad and Josie," Delia said. "Get Tim."

"Tim's sleeping," Katy said. She trudged upstairs to retrieve Connor herself, and from the stairs called, "When will you be back?" as if Tim was in fact awake.

Thoughtless but not angry, not Katy's worst: her yelling could be stippled with rage, which Sara could not bear. Out of proportion, or in response to issues Sara failed to see. In those moments, Nora might speak sternly to Katy, then ignore her, or Delia might snap back; as usual, Sara would freeze until the tirade ended, or involuntarily flee. She found Katy's melancholy less frightening, if as involving. You couldn't get away from Katy's discomfort: she needed, it seemed, to share every bit, as if her body were a country she couldn't stand to live in alone.

When they were not watching Connor, the girls retreated to their now-shared room, often with homework. This was no guarantee: Katy might walk in and sit on Sara's bed and begin with *I need*; or she might stretch out, exhausted, as if hiding out with them. Schoolwork was the best defense. Sara and Delia would leave textbooks open on their pillows, just in case.

This is my study time, Sara would say, *it's chemistry* or *it's history* or *it's math*, and Katy would leave her.

Away in the shared bedroom, though hardly away. The girls listened to headphones connected to Walkmen. They were in a pink phase, Delia in particular: pink lip glosses, pink nail polish, pink stickers on the headphones. A pink-and-white bedspread (Sara's plain white). They wore jeans; their hamper filled with pink and gray running clothes. Swim goggles hung on the doorknobs, blue varsity jackets, pink swim caps, pink sweatshirts. The pink and the goggles lent them the look of candied Martians. They took to keeping Cheerios and other snacks in their room, so they could hide longer when Katy's moods filled the house, or when they needed to dodge unscheduled child care.

About Katy's encroachments, they said nothing to Nora, who could see it all well enough for herself and had been up several nights with Connor. She smoked off-brand cigarettes on the deck, bought discount Cheerios again. No-Cheerios, Delia called them. Now and then Tim brought leftovers home from the restaurant, which counterbalanced the weirder foods their mother picked up: off-brand peas, dried kidney beans, canned mackerel, generic mac and cheese. She'd gone to a pantry somewhere. Once in a while they'd run out of milk, and a thinnish papery-tasting stuff appeared in a jug in the refrigerator. It turned the tea gray. At least, when Katy found it, she'd shop for two-percent.

Consulting, James repeated. For support he sent token amounts, or brief notes to Nora instead. No one talked about the college funds: Sara and Delia had snooped around in

Beverly, they'd seen some of the bills. At least at James and Josie's, they could relax; at least they always ate well. The girls did not ask for money or food, but late at night, while the others slept, Sara would raid the Beverly kitchen, just as Katy once did, slipping granola and maple syrup and sometimes cans of beer into her book bag. Did James notice? Josie said nothing. Here was one more kind of silence; most weekends, Sara found new jars of crunchy peanut butter, fresh boxes of granola, more Cheerios, and Delia's favorite jam shelved in front.

PARTY NIGHT

It happened on a Saturday, a long late night. A party at which a friend of Delia's became terribly drunk. Got into trouble—too drunk around drunk boys. One of the boys tried to take her somewhere, another room, though she was stumbling, and not speaking clearly. In the house on the bluff, Delia was looking for the friend, and found her in a bedroom, and stomped and yelled, "Get away from her, fuckhead." Yelled, "I called the police." A naked boy covered himself, and Delia pulled her friend from the room. From the kitchen of the party house, Delia called Sara, who was just home from babysitting, their mother asleep. Katy had stretched out on the sofa: the TV poured blue light on the carpet.

"Something's wrong," Sara said, "with Delia's friend."

"What." Katy said it flatly, as if to deter interruption.

Sara said nothing more. She took Nora's car and drove up the bluff, the sky starry, the roads dark; then the girls were in the car too, and she drove back down the bluff. Trying not to turn quickly, because the friend, Caroline, was sick. They stopped for Caroline to be sick; after, she was crying. Time seemed to slow as they ferried Caroline to the house. She would sleep in

Delia's bed, they decided, Delia would give up her bed (later Delia would share Sara's). First, though, a shower. They tried not to wake the baby or Nora, but Nora appeared nonetheless. Without reproach she took charge of Caroline, Delia with her.

Sara carried the soiled clothes downstairs to launder, the living room TV still pouring light. On the sofa, Katy appeared pale. Everyone was pale, Sara thought: she might be Caroline in the car, or Delia in the bedroom doorway, or Sara driving. *What can happen*, Sara thought. But Delia, magnificent Delia yelled, *You fuckhead*, and Sara drove. Bad but not the worst: Fuckhead had just gotten started. Now their mother was rinsing the sick from Caroline's hair.

"Mom thinks she'll be okay," Sara said, and set the laundry basket down.

Katy closed her eyes.

"Katy?" Sara said, but Katy rolled away into the sofa, feigning sleep, waiting, it seemed, for the moment to end.

STORM

Early winter. The low barometric pressure and dropping temperatures drugged them all: no one wanted to get out of bed. That morning Katy was rushing, half-organized at six thirty, but Connor had been up at three, as if alert to the rising wind, the stronger gusts soon buffeting the house. She'd pulled a T-shirt over her stockings and skirt and managed to start breakfast while he was still asleep: now she was cracking eggs, toasting bread in the oven, spilling coffee grounds as she measured. At the counter, Nora made sandwiches, packed brown bags for the girls. She and Katy were both quiet, alert to the uncalm air. Nora stepped over toward the sink and opened the window to strong damp gusts. She stood with her cigarette and black tea, blowing smoke out, the wind pushing it back.

There had been pre-storm warnings, local broadcasters photographing the sky and then cutting to cheerily colored maps of offshore systems, and men with pickup trucks buying gasoline and road salt. High storm surge predicted for coastal towns, which would mean water in the street, seepage in the basement, and another neighborhood evacuation. The access road still dipped low and rose and dipped again, and heavy storm surges could swamp it, cutting off their street. Last year they'd had damage to the north-facing siding and shutters, the roof. Already, Nora had fastened the storm shutters, taped the interior windows, filled the freezer with ice for the power outage ahead. Though there was the off chance they'd spend a night in a motel or the high school gym.

No Tim: Tim had closed late and stayed with his friend Sal in Hanover. And when the phone rang and Nora answered—calmly it seemed, despite the cigarette—it wasn't Tim, but the neighbor Joanie MacFarland saying the evacuation order came early, town trucks already on the way.

"Girls?" Nora called from the bottom of the stairs. "SaraDelia, pack it up." And then Connor's cry—the unhappy shock of first waking, the awareness of Katy elsewhere. "I'll get him," Nora said.

Katy poured the eggs into the skillet, listening. If she could just have eggs, coffee and toast and eggs, she might be able to think.

Upstairs, the girls thumped, murmured, and Connor's crying ceased. "Okay, angel," Nora said, and then, in a louder voice, "Don't forget your eyedrops. Delia, grab Connor's hat." A string of reminders. Katy pulled the toast from the oven. "Get that heater. Sara, lights. Would you take him?"

In a moment Sara appeared at the bottom of the stairs with Connor, Katy's round, pink-cheeked boy. He was happy; he was reaching for Katy.

"Hi Connor," Katy said. "Hi baby boy." She held him for a moment, and he pulled at her T-shirt, reached for her hair. "Good morning," she kissed him and motioned toward his bottle. Sara took him back to feed him, and Katy poured the coffee.

Buttered toast, eggs on the plate, milk into the coffee. "I'll be right back, Connor," she said, and carried the breakfast upstairs. Connor's packed diaper bag leaned against the wall outside her room, the bedroom itself chaotic. In an over-stuffed drawer, she searched for a clean bra, clean stockings; in the closet, she found her empty overnight bag. But her handbag?

"Delia, almost?" Nora said.

Delia's murmur emanated from the bathroom. "Which lip gloss?"

"Love," Nora said, "just take both."

And from downstairs, Sara called, "I think the town guys are here." Katy could hear Connor fussing. "Hey," Sara said, "hey hey, wait, that's dirty, you'll get it back. Okay?" And louder, "Mom?"

The bell, loud knocking on the kitchen door.

Hooking the bra, buttoning the blouse. Jacket. Shoes. She'd have to wear boots. Delia and Nora headed down the stairs, the diaper bag now gone. From the bathroom, Katy grabbed a makeup case and toothbrush, then followed.

Here was the town guy, Joey Connolly, two graduating classes before her, in his shining yellow slicker and boots: the sleet was blowing in now. Just past low tide, he said, and already they had ponding at the end of the road, a thick film of water creeping up the street-side outside the house. At the door, he took Connor from Sara—held him securely enough—and Sara and Delia hurried with their bags down the stairs to the wet street and Nora's car. "I'll keep him with me at work," Nora called, and followed them out, Joey carrying the baby.

Where were Katy's keys? Handbag? And once she found them (living room) and pulled on her boots, she slid the eggs between two pieces of toast and into a paper sack, gathered her overnight things and coat, and hauled it all down to her car. Joey Connolly waited until she'd turned the motor and started down the street, toward the two orange-flag-waving guys directing cars to the access road.

Atrocious roads, atrocious sleet, a blurry two-mile backup at the highway ramp. After several minutes, Katy turned around and made her way through the sleet to the doctor's office at the harbor. Inside, it was quiet. At the reception area, Nora held Connor on her lap while he chewed a pink teething ring and drooled on her jacket. She'd tucked the phone receiver against her shoulder; she scanned the computer screen, typed. In the waiting room, one toddler and mother sat on the floor, stacking blocks; most of the morning's appointments had cancelled. Katy took Connor to an adjoining play mat, Connor oblivious, happy to smash a blue plastic block against the mat, and when he tired of that, happy for Katy to read to him. After stories of friendly pigs, a sledding holiday, and a magic bicycle, Nora announced she'd booked two rooms at an inland motel.

By late morning, the office had closed, as had the local schools and most of town hall. Nora collected the girls, Katy following as they inched along the slick and jammed-up secondary roads.

✣

Strangely boring, the storm: for the first several hours, Sara watched TV movies and weather reports with her sisters and Nora, took turns entertaining Connor. Had she been alone, or just with Delia, she might have napped. But Katy made no move to take Connor to their room, and the TV chattered on. They ate pizza; Nora phoned neighbors at other motels, left a message at James's office. Finally, Sara and Delia brought their home-work to Katy's unoccupied room. Then, for a time, Sara slept. When she awoke, it was full dark and thickly snowing, only the nearby donut shop's lights cutting through the murk beyond the window. She had begun to picture Shore Road as a fast-moving creek, the house's storage room filling with water, high enough to swamp the furnace, leaving the yellow beach chairs and sand buckets floating above sunken metal shovels and bench tools. Dead fish and seaweed might wash up on the outside deck, along with drifts of sand and ice. She pictured the second floor: spongy wet carpet, a flooded bathroom. There had been television re-ports from the region—footage of gray waves and white foam and, through a veil of snow, somebody's seawall, somebody's roof, more crashing gray waves against sand, but nothing from their neighborhood. When she returned to the other room, her mother was on the phone listening.

✣

It was not news they understood. There had been surge dam-age all along the road, the worst at the far end, where shutters had torn off and rushing seawater burst through windows; and then the access road, which had flooded badly, potholed, lost a two-yard bite of pavement. Their immediate neighborhood had held up better, though there would be expensive repairs. But from the bluff looking out, someone had seen smoke, a glimpse of orange. Hard to confirm until a lull, but then, yes, fire and already far along. Which made no sense, the water seemingly all around. It must have looked like a burning boat. "Even in the weather?" Nora said. Yes, in the weather. "And the surf?" Despite the surf. Well, the surf's what might have put it out in the end. What there was to put out.

For several hours, Nora lied. "There's damage," she told the girls, "but nothing we can fix tonight." She helped Katy settle Connor in their room, and told the girls to sleep, and crossed the parking lot to the donut shop.

What was true or not true? They were in a motel room; they were taking the word of Joey Connolly, or someone just like Joey Connolly. They were taking the word of a guy who waved orange flags. Easy enough in winter storms to misidentify a house. It might have been a neighbor's house (no one wished that on the neighbors; mistakes are made). Say it was in fact a boat, a large boat, blown too close in—even to the seawall, where boats don't belong. You might mistake that for a house. The Murphys' motel room appeared as it had when they'd arrived; news or not, the house must still be as they'd left it.

Electrical, of some kind, no telling the source for sure—no matter how many times Nora asked, then and in the weeks to follow. There had been roof leaks; they'd had two upstairs rooms rewired, the contractor cut-rate. A leak in the siding Nora had tried to seal herself. Hadn't the girls run a heater? Turned off, yes? And unplugged? "I turned everything off," Katy said. Once she said it, she could picture herself turning off the burner and the oven, the coffeemaker, and the space heater in her bedroom. And when she later repeated it to Tim, still the picture—but in it, was she wearing the T-shirt and skirt? Stockings for work or plain socks? An image from another day?

At 4:00 AM, when Sara woke up, Delia was sleeping, Nora still out. Beyond the window, visible under the streetlights, thick flurries.

MOTEL

In that life—the life they'd momentarily entered—the donut vendor played a key role. He was wiry, his face creased and weathered, as if he had been a fisherman before he'd become a donut shop manager. Taciturn but not unfriendly: he'd put extra chocolate creams in the bag when he found out they'd evacuated their house. And after the news, when Sara returned and sat by herself at a table, he poured her free coffee and stationed himself several feet away, neither close nor far. She thanked him; she ordered donuts to go. He asked if she needed a box, and she welled up. Ridiculous. A box. Was it the kind tone? Or just the fact of offering—napkins, creamers, sugar, anything. A stranger could offer things you didn't need and still help you.

The motel bathroom: perfumed white cakes of soap, miniature bottles of amber shampoo, bleached washcloths, hand towels, undersized bath towels the girls called "half baths." Two double beds, two faux-wood night tables, an armchair, a desk. A compact refrigerator, yellowed coffeemaker, instant coffee, tea bags, sugar, a grainy powdered creamer, red plastic stirrers Connor wanted to grab. A large color television perched on the bureau. Gold polyester curtains covered the windows, which faced a parking lot: motel lights dully reflected on cleared car hoods and icy puddles.

Katy's state should have been plain when she'd first maneuvered to stay in the same room with Nora, insisted on being near her. When Sara walked in with the donuts, the static seemed visible. From the bathroom, the splash of water, Delia's voice trotting along to "Old MacDonald," Connor's monosyllabic babbling. Nora's arms flapped in frustration; Katy, red-faced, tearing up again. It appeared to be a play. "Wake up," Nora said, and her arms flapped again. Katy slid onto the far bed, tucking her legs under her and turning to face the wall.

"Kathleen," Nora said.

Katy didn't answer. Couldn't, it seemed.

"Beautiful," Nora said, in a hard unbeautiful way, and stepped outside into the wet cold to smoke a cigarette.

"Here's your bear," Delia said from the bathroom. "What do bears say?" More loudly she called, "What *do* bears say?"

"I think they growl," Sara said. She carried the donut box into the bathroom, closed the door, and sat on the toilet seat cover. "But not that bear."

For a moment one could pretend the world outside the motel bathroom was the same one it had been yesterday. Just another baby bath. Just another box of donuts. "I got crullers," Sara said. But then Delia seemed to deflate, though her face seemed puffy; there was an odd congruence between Connor's round face, pink from the bath, and the puffy pinkness of Delia's, their eyes the same shape but different colors.

Sara took Delia's place at the tub then and pulled Connor's towel from the rack, the baby smacking the water with the plastic bear. And she and Delia talked loudly to Connor and quietly about Katy, whose meltdown could easily migrate to him.

Sara was pulling Connor's thick leggings up over his diaper, Connor tugging at her hair, when Nora returned and knocked on the bathroom door. "Okay, angel girls, I'll take him." Once she'd bundled Connor up, Nora carried him with her back to the donut shop.

Sara left the donut box at the foot of the far bed, otherwise ignoring Katy. On the widest section of carpet, she and Delia shuffled a deck of cards, played rummy, and speculated about the day's schoolwork, books left at the house, and what their father might know.

Still just a bad rumor, until you saw for yourself—although it would be months before Sara revisited the neighborhood. It seemed that she and Delia played rummy for an hour, though it couldn't have been more than twenty minutes before Nora returned, Connor asleep against her shoulder. At first, her face appeared sunken.

Katy was still curled up on the bed. And who didn't want to curl up on the bed? Or hide at the corner table of the donut shop, or lose yourself in sleep. Despite Nora's pallor, her voice remained the same. "Oh, honestly," Nora said, or Sara remembers her saying. Murmuring. Or perhaps, as sometimes happened, it was Sara's own editorial, posited in her mother's voice.

POST-FIRE

How quickly after they left the parking lot, the motel and donut shop dropped away—as if upon retracing the route you would not find the plaza again. From the car speakers, chamber music asserted an idyllic and precise order, which seemed at once absurd and necessary. Low clouds pushed east, the roadsides piled with snow and ice, snow-crusted buildings and signs, but the highway had been cleared down to dry pavement. In the suspended hours of the drive, it was easier to think of nothing, to take in the flying images of snow-streaked cars and white and graying snowbanks, and the curve of the plowed highway. On the secondary North Shore roads, they found postcard views of white-blanketed roofs, the snow-lined branches of deciduous trees, consolatory evergreens, still-pristine fields. James's house was unchanged—if this house unchanged, then? And again the sticky logic tugged, the image of Blue Rock held in the mind intact, weakly contested by the anomaly of Nora driving the girls to Beverly. Here was the Beverly house, here was James outside, opening the doors of the car, hugging them in the driveway. Hugging Nora.

Today there was no Josie (Josie was at work) and the chamber music stopped and in that moment the quiet seemed a vast ice-blue plane, absent anything, even the often mute parental discord. No Katy: Katy was with her in-laws. James unloaded the heavier bags from the car while Nora copied phone numbers for the girls on a notepad she'd taken from the motel, circling Aunt Meg's. Nora would call the girls' school and set up a plan for their classwork. The class names themselves—chemistry, history—seemed like small birds flitting into the neighbor's spruce, but the girls promised to keep up. It had again begun to snow. Plenty on the South Shore to take care of, Nora said. (How could there not be?) She would call them later. There was no other plan. And yet, now in Beverly, James lifting Delia's suitcase, it stunned Sara that Nora would leave the girls there. That Nora would leave at all. As if her leaving carried meanings both threatening and opaque: as if *insurance agent* meant *international flight*. Perhaps Katy had sensed *international flight* at the motel. Why shouldn't Sara climb back into the car with Nora and Delia, restart the chamber music, return to the passing views? The impulse must have been apparent in her face: Nora walked the girls up to the house with James and quickly left. Inside, James poured hot chocolate; Delia shuffled a deck of cards.

That evening, Josie returned from work, also unchanged—in her slate-gray suit and elegant boots, her vaguely gingery scent, a fat briefcase in hand. She kissed them and handed them bags from Filene's, sweaters to try on. She'd picked up videos and Chinese food, and they sat in the den eating dumplings and watching comedies, as they had with her before. A calm evening, yet the air seemed pixilated: they did not know Nora's whereabouts. She had not called, and no one answered at Meg's. But Sara's panic would flatten out and begin to ebb near James and Josie, here beside the familiar oak flooring and vine-and-leaf-patterned carpet, reading chairs and sofas piled with throw pillows. Here in their known house: the airy kitchen, the bedrooms—the girls' rooms—painted white, paperback novels and beach stones on the shelves where the girls had left them, bottles of scented hand lotion and stacks of clean towels on the dressers, beds covered in down comforters with violet duvets.

Briefly, all of Blue Rock was out of sight, as it had been on other nights they'd stayed. The Beverly house steadied them; James himself steadied them, remaining close. Delia slept. Sara also slept, but she woke in the dark unable to locate herself. There was a brief sensation of falling, before the scent of washed sheets and pine pulled her back to the Beverly room. There'd been a dream: the dream had vanished. Hours before dawn, Sara carried her old comic books downstairs to one of the den's oversized reading chairs and practiced drawing characters on scrap paper. The sounds beyond the house were muffled by light snow, the wind just perceptible. A night like others after which she'd found deer tracks in the yard.

It was after 3:00 AM when James appeared in his robe. "That's a good chair," he said. Would she mind if he read on the couch? He carried in blankets, one for each of them, and an issue of *Time*, though he soon dozed. He appeared self-contained even in sleep—unlike Delia, who flung her arms and disordered the sheets, her face suggesting the quality of her dreams. Rare to see James sleep, so there was not much to compare. Might your sleeping self change over time? Maybe for someone like James, it stayed constant. Say you could enter sleep the way you could enter a beautiful room and close the door. Did anyone do that? The place she eventually drifted to was not a beautiful room but a calmer blankness, and when she later woke, her father was there on the couch, still self-contained, still himself.

A turn? Was that the moment? The day her mother dropped her off in Beverly, the night her father found her drawing by flashlight? Or perhaps the moment in which a turn became clearly visible. Other moments had accrued before this—those summer weekends? He'd been more attentive since the down-sizing. Still: James on the couch. Her father. In that moment (though for how long?) a father she might trust.

Perhaps the father Sara had glimpsed as a toddler and for-gotten? He'd never spoken sharply to Sara, at least that she could remember; he'd never been unkind. Had been, at times, affectionate and playful. But more often faraway, reduced to an idea. And what about money? *That* unkindness. The miss-ing support unavoidable now—but before? She had thought it foolish—at best misguided—to rely on him for anything that mattered.

⚜

In the morning James offered to make breakfast. Delia came downstairs in her pajamas and robe, Josie in her suit. Coffee brewed, glasses of orange juice appeared. And when Josie left for work, James called the high school to get the girls' assignments, insisted Sara and Delia make a schedule (including a walk, including snacks), and cleared the table for them to work.

And so they shaped those days, during which they received only short calls from Nora. In the late afternoons, Sara napped for an hour; nightly the den scene repeated. Delia grew quiet, and there was in both girls a strained attentiveness, as if they were listening for a distant bell. The Blue Rock house was lost but did not seem lost. Certain things Sara did not say, even to Delia, but a corner of the mind allowed: if in your mind, the house existed, might it also exist somewhere else? If you reached the correct universe, the correct highway exit. Say there was another space in which the house might still exist. Say that, like your house, your mother had dropped out of sight: if you were to find one, would you find the other? An alternate house, with an alternate Nora?

"Sweetheart," James said. "You really must sleep." He handed Sara a glass of milk with honey. "Maybe no more chocolate at night?" This time he patted her head, and walked her up the stairs.

Nora had never forgotten to pick up Delia or Sara; she was rarely late. Still—if she did not return? Meg's phone connected them only to Meg and Louis—both alarmingly gentle—who would take messages and then speak with James. Nora called sporadically. A few more days, she said. I might have a place. She told them to go to the mall for new clothes. With your father, she said. Remember hats. Remember gloves. She would phone again tomorrow. And for a time—a few hours—the strain diminished, and they would concentrate on their school-work, or cook for James and Josie, or shop for hats and gloves.

But only hours. They would want to speak to Nora again, and instead again reached Meg. They did not in those first days speak to Katy, who remained with Tim's parents in Blue Rock. Katy was fine, James assured them. Connor and Tim were fine.

After a few days, Delia began to miss her favorite jeans, a black-and-pink cardigan, long earrings made of dice, her suede boots; Sara a white lamb's wool sweater, her turquoise-and-coral pinky ring, her pale green robe. Other longings accumulated. For a few days, James drove the girls the two hours to school in Blue Rock, stayed on the South Shore, and drove them back to Beverly. Hardly a workable plan. No one mentioned transferring schools; for a time the thought hovered, unarticulated. But after a week, Nora announced she'd found a three-bedroom condo in central Blue Rock, near the harbor and the high school.

And when Sara and Delia returned with Nora to Blue Rock— the roads lined with half-melted snowbanks and slush and chunks of gray ice, the sky a matching diffident gray—town seemed exactly the same town they'd left, yet also (and deliberately) estranged. As if the town, downsizing by a fraction, had picked which house to burn, which residents were unnecessary. This impression persisted despite daily offers of help from neighbors and friends, the high school faculty, the swim team, the owner of the Harbor Café. They did not drive down to

Shore Road—though from the harbor at night you could see out to where the road approached the pond, and the cluster of house lights, and their pocket of dark space.

The condo was at first an undifferentiated emptiness, each room a beige-carpeted box. Beyond the windows, strips of snow-covered lawn bordered a row of saplings, the buildings nearer the harbor, the parking lot. Some days it seemed as if they'd been traveling, their luggage misplaced, their dislocation temporary as they waited for their possessions and the house itself to catch up with them. And in fact for months relied on card tables and folding chairs—which did nothing to break the illusion. In the morning Sara woke, still oriented to the obsolete world, then readjusted. She did not miss Katy or Tim or Connor, but the notion recurred, if fleetingly, of a waiting house in a parallel world from which they all had become detached.

She did not have language for this. None of them did. Delia referred to their lost possessions as "old," which made them sound outgrown, deliberately discarded. While Nora navigated the insurance (she'd kept up her payments, a small miracle), she perseverated about "value," of which there seemed to be many kinds. Other language dropped out: for weeks, no one mentioned the daily tides.

On the phone, Katy—now house-hunting—spoke confidently of square footage and school systems. It seemed that, if one Katy had fallen apart in the motel room, another—assertively pragmatic—had popped up after she left. No one spoke about the motel—at least not directly—but between Nora and Katy, that silence marked a new, decisive border.

A paradox: for Nora and the girls, daily life became easier. The condo's location simplified their routines—the walk to school, a longer walk or fast bike to the harbor, five minutes to the office. Perhaps, Nora mused, she should have sold years before (though now her windows looked out on a patch of brown grass and snow, a row of other condos); perhaps she should have rebuilt. She'd been lucky to get a high price for the lot; erosion would continue to wear at the near beaches and seawall and access roads, storms would tear at the houses. But that year without the sea—and after—she felt irrevocably diminished. As if the horizon had steadied her, somehow shielded her from the raw, workaday substrate of each morning.

Still, at first Nora insisted no one visit Shore Road even to see the MacFarlands, whom they would meet in town. Sara and Delia pretended not to care. But when the ice was gone from the roads, Sara biked to the beach. She could still see the lines of the foundation; she could almost imagine the house rising up, almost imagine Nora climbing the air where the stairs had been, or imagine herself floating where her bed must have stood. Now there was a clear view from the far side of the street and the more distant pond to the sea. From the air it must have appeared as a gap in the string of houses, a lost tooth. That day Sara gathered stones and shells from the beach: if she'd had a camera with her, she might have photographed the site, but by the time she returned again, it had already begun to change, new owners preparing construction.

With the insurance payment and the sale of the lot, money worries diminished. That spring, James became, again, an executive, now managing a startup off 128. A bizarre inversion:

the lost house, the found money. At the condo, a chafing normalcy insisted itself.

III

ROME

Apollo and Daphne
Gian Lorenzo Bernini (c.1622-25)
GALLERIA BORGHESE

A consuming desire; a desperate flight from that desire. Here's the moment when the chasing Apollo, eternally young, reaches the fleeing Daphne, their bodies muscular, graceful, both nearly breathing and nearly out of breath; and too the moment when in desperation she cries out. Not to Apollo: he can't hear beyond the rapid whir of his desire, the drive to possess her, but certainly possession will shatter her. She is not fast enough; his hand rakes her hip. They almost fly, her hair streaming behind her, her mouth roundly open in terror. It's her powerful father she beseeches, and in calling him escapes, her body transforming as we watch: her fingers now turning to branches of leaves, her toes taking root, one slender leg now covered by a sheath of bark.

White bodies suspended in marble, stone transformed to muscle and sinew, skin and leaves. It's her face one returns to, and then the astonishment of her body, the smooth belly and high breasts, and from her raised arms, the hands unfurling leaves, and along her slim leg, the spreading bark.

Forever she calls out to her father; forever he saves her—though she will no longer be herself—the story a soundless repeating loop.

And if he cannot save her?

Another story, another loop, a girl for whom desire and flight have merged.

And what if in Daphne's expression you recognize a haunting both nameless and familiar? If in Apollo's? No one can run fast enough. Down near the Piazza del Popolo, there are cafés, shops, ordinary conversations. A glass of wine? Count the days, years you've dreamed of stone and leaves.

THE MURPHYS III

Mistaken for twins on occasion, as young children. Later, even during high school years, referred to as "the twins" by neighbors who knew they were not. Neither Sara nor Delia would make the correction. At a distance one might notice only the sandy-blond hair, the slender builds and short statures, the fair skin; closer up the blue-gray eyes, one oval face with a slightly aquiline nose, one round face, a more buttonish nose, the same precisely curved lips. They were thirteen months apart, and some years that mattered; but no one would confuse Delia's face for Sara's, or Sara's for Delia's. To Joanie MacFarland, "Nora's girls" referred to all the Murphy daughters, "twins" to Sara and Delia only. Shorthand, yes, but also slippage from that early resemblance between Molly and the young Delia? At times it seemed "twins" conjured Molly too, referring to an approximate category centered around Delia—Molly Delia's dead twin, Sara her fraternal one, the number of pregnancies irrelevant.

To Sara, at times they had seemed a trio, though Molly appeared as a peripheral blur Sara struggled to define. Delia's curiosity—intermittent, less vexed—had focused on Molly's taste in games or food or color (did Molly also love jam?) and rarely involved Rome. Nor was Delia troubled by resemblance and mistaken assumptions. During childhood, if relatives slipped and called her Molly, she answered "Delia" in the lighthearted tone of a party hostess. As a teenager, and later, she too mixed up the baby photos. "Maybe my cheeks were fatter?" she'd say. "Hard to tell." Yet how fully Delia occupied her own body: for her, the questions ended here.

Paired, yes, but not mistaken. Acquaintances referred to Sara as "the quiet" one, Delia "the lively." In school, Sara earned straight As, Delia—bright but unpredictable—a few more Bs, the occasional C if the teacher was, as she explained to Nora, "a turd." It was Sara who remembered to bring their lunches to school; Sara who closed the house windows during storms; Sara who knew when they'd visit James. Delia planned beach picnics and baked cookies and lobbied for trips to the mall.

They were unserious competitors, though they joined teams and sometimes won (Sara mainly wanted to swim; Delia to socialize). Only to each other did they speak of disappointments in their siblings and their father; together they worried about Nora. Well liked, both of them; still, Sara could be morose, Delia clownish to a fault. Boyfriends. To Sara, Delia's resembled retriever puppies. To Delia, Sara's were dopily earnest or brooding and mute. As high school girls, both first had sex, Sara with a boy who lived near the harbor and showed her his boat designs and stole beer from his parents. He rushed, not needing, he said, a warm-up. "Oh, God," Delia told her. "I hope he gave you a beer." Though Delia's own first time was unlaughing, a constrained educational exercise with a boy from varsity soccer.

Not twins. After high school the moniker dropped away; once they left Blue Rock for college, they were plainly sisters, though only later could they sort the implications. Sara moved to Western Massachusetts; Delia stayed near Boston. They talked on the phone, they pursued degrees; in certain ways they mystified each other. Delia joined social committees: she event-planned, she networked. Sara hung out in cafés and slept with disaffected men. And mulled: really, did the mulling help? Would sports? Maybe she could try a local league, or pickup games; Delia played Frisbee and met a sweet guy named Mike.

High GPAs, both of them, and graduate programs. Delia trained in physical therapy; Delia wanted kids. In these choices, she was clear. Less clear about Nora, who'd sometimes be unavailable for weeks; less clear about the distance from Theo, to whom she mailed outlandish postcards and holiday gifts. He sent comic responses and expensive presents. It was something, a relationship of sorts, if from a distant sphere. Only once, when Theo had been out of touch longer than usual, Delia said, "Maybe I have too much Molly." "He's like that with everyone," Sara told her. Delia did not worry about her relationship to James: amicable monthly visits and weekly phone calls seemed enough. She did not worry about Katy, whom she saw often, and whose life her own soon began to resemble.

A marriage. Two girls. A house in the outer suburbs.

To Sara, Delia's life seemed lucid and precisely chosen and unimaginable. In college the subjects Sara studied—sociology, art history—posed abstract questions that led meanderingly to rare concrete jobs. She waitressed; she temped; she joined a community garden. Only later, after a master's and a return to

Boston, did the work improve. In the intervening years, Delia spoke to her with an apparent patience that continued even after Sara resettled and found what Delia called a "grown-up job" in nonprofit media. Delia at thirty sent rainbow-colored party invitations and thank-you notes; this Delia arranged family dinners—pizza, but dinners nonetheless—and invited Sara to block parties and birthday gatherings.

Sara could not explain Delia; neither could she explain herself. By her early thirties, her work anchored her as much as any work might. She too could write thank-you notes; she too remembered birthdays. It occurred to her that for Delia a spouse might be another kind of twin. Unclear how many such pairings a life might sustain, or how long they might last. A bond separate and distinct from the kinship Sara felt in friendships and relationships, though she'd been in love—or a state she understood to be love—several times. Men. Thrilling, at first. It was always easy, in the beginning, to lose herself in sex, but the more intimate the relationship became—and the more familial—the more she retreated. As if she were at first escaping into pleasure, but later (and more dangerously) began to vanish from herself. It had happened even in the most hopeful of relationships, despite apparent trust, elated future planning—that brief feeling of arrival as if the place of arrival might not also be a point of departure. And then? A growing disorientation, her body again becoming a separate thing. Questions arose, reasonable questions—other cities, children, how to shape a married life—and there appeared, again, a vanishing point beyond which she could not imagine or travel, and in its contemplation felt herself receding. It did not seem to be a matter of wanting or not wanting; she had never said, "I don't want that." She didn't know. It was as if she couldn't speak the language. As if she were hearing Russian: she knew only English and French.

At thirty-two, she left a man she'd been with for three years. Hadn't she loved him? He had not pushed for children; he too did not know. He'd studied architectural history. What he'd wanted, it appeared, was a worldly recognition she understood to be fame, though that desire was hard to parse from his dazzling curiosity and solid work ethic. He would not have used the word *fame*. He would have said *professional advancement*, perhaps correctly. The desire, the ambition, had nothing to do with her, but it appeared to take on a life of its own, like a permanent house guest from whose company she'd withdrawn. Maybe she could not judge; maybe her own desires were timid and sparse.

"Your own what?" Delia said. "Maybe you just don't like him anymore."

This sounded true. "I thought I did," Sara said. "I thought a lot of things."

"You did," Delia said. "I know."

SARA'S PLACES

The first time Sara visited Theo in California—before she started college, long before she really traveled—it seemed she was
flying to the edge of the world, a point from which she could fall,
or, if not fall, become lost in anonymity. As if, so far from New
England and Nora and Delia, she became unfamiliar to herself.
For a panicked moment, she imagined herself stranded there, exiled, unable to adapt or return. Then the panic abated; she struggled to explain it to Theo. They were at a café in Berkeley. He
nodded and kissed her on the cheek. "We all miss the house," he
said. He suggested sushi for dinner.

Had the house still existed when Sara finished college, like
Katy, she might have schemed to return (conjuring an early
September house, occupied by Nora and Delia). The longing
for the vanished house and those moments persisted. From
the years of the condo through her college years—and beyond—temporary perches became the norm, as they had for
Katy. James and Josie's Beverly house was an occasional refuge,
though the occasions grew infrequent. She traveled but held
fast to New England: here was the familiar coast, familiar small
towns and farms; here was Boston; here was Cambridge.

After she split with the historian, she found her own Cambridge apartment, a small one-bedroom off Huron Avenue near Fresh Pond. Relieved to live alone, though the place felt provisional. Perhaps it would always, despite her efforts—new paint, silk pillows, shelved books, framed photographs, tapestried rugs on the hardwood floors. Perhaps rentals always felt provisional: or would the sensation persist regardless of place? She could not see beyond the temporary, even when imagining a house. In the redbrick house where Katy and Tim had settled—solid, inland—she guessed one might believe in permanence, or Katy might; unlikely, it seemed, that Katy would entertain the question.

Yet possession seemed to make a difference: what if Sara owned a house? If she also bought a two-story, redbrick? If one owned a redbrick house was *self*-possession then a different matter? She could say without thinking, "my boots," or "my radio," but today, beyond her apartment window, orange leaves fell from high branches onto the hood of a small blue car that was, surprisingly, her own—a car she'd driven for a year. How had she arrived at this moment, in her one-bedroom apartment so far from the sea and from the houses and apartments in which the rest of her family lived? As if they'd all been flung from Blue Rock and yet remained in some ghostly orbit—orbiting, say, a dead star? Or if not in orbit, then what? Free-floating? If floating, one could merely say: here is a woman by a window gazing at a car on the street. There are other women and other windows; men and windows; various streets, various cars. Random flashing signals from random shifting points. Perhaps those other women, those men, were guided by stars unknown to her. Perhaps also floating. At this moment, should someone have phoned Sara—at the window, watching leaves, amazed by her own car—and asked, *How are you?* how would she have answered? Might she have cited the Blue Rock fire, her subsequent lags in cognition—months after, rummaging for a particular green scarf before remembering its place in the vanished house? The day of the orange leaves seemed the opposite: on the street, a car—apparently hers! How had it arrived? In response, Delia or Nora might have offered, "Do you need a new scarf?" and invited her to dinner. *How are you?* To Katy—she had few real conversations with Katy, even rarer ones with Theo—Sara might have answered "Fine," and marveled at the color of the leaves.

James? He called most days, not only since Sara's breakup but also before—since she first sensed the relationship's slide, though neither she nor James remarked on it. Apparently, he'd heard the telling note, or the muted one, she'd otherwise managed to conceal. Little alarmed him: lately nothing surprised him. If she'd mentioned the green scarf and the blue car to James, he might have recognized not their contrast but their common marking of displacement. *How are you?* Had she told him, "I'm not sure how I got here," he'd be the one to say, "I know."

For Sara, just as there would never be a return to Blue Rock, it seemed there would never be a complete departure. Or maybe whatever still tethered her to the earth would remain gossamer. Not the lost house but a ghostly aura expanding outward from the space the house once occupied. What is a place? Its inverse? Over time? She had no idea.

WALKING

"She's off birding or something," Katy might say—or Delia, more wistful, "She's in a studio class." Both routinely noted the ways Nora disappeared into the life they all claimed they wanted her to have. For months Sara had listened—attentively, she'd thought—as she had to other weekly news of child-care dilemmas and car repairs and workplace dramas. For her, Nora's busyness—the drawing classes and gallery openings and nature walks, the allusions to friends they'd never met—posed no problem (nor did Nora's holiday evasions). Nora visited with grandchildren every week: surely, for Katy and Delia, that had to count.

And Sara too had been busy; Sara too often missed holiday events. Every other week, she met Nora for dinner; every few days they e-mailed. Then Sara became single again, which seemed like a return from exhausting foreign travel: who might be there to greet her? Nora sent encouraging notes, bought her perfume, a merino sweater. "You call me anytime, sweet pea," Nora said, though Nora habitually silenced her phone, answered nonurgent voice mails with texts. Nora had plans and other plans. Like Sara, she was single—at least so far as Sara knew; but here Sara found herself stymied. They would not, it seemed, be single together—as Sara had somehow presumed. From what dream had she drawn that idea? As if upon return from her partnered life she'd find Nora as, say, the Nora of her college years, frosting cake for her arrival (only once had there been such a cake). When Nora declined invitations—*Oh doll, I'd love to meet for (dinner/a movie) but I'm going to a (potluck/ museum tour/birding group)*—Sara was taken up short. The once-sufficient e-mails and voice mail messages now seemed flimsy representations. Too often—message or not—Sara couldn't really find her.

With her sisters, she frequently commiserated.

There was a comfort in shared commiseration, one thing, at least, she had in common with both sisters. Exchanges about James were more fraught: Katy brooded, Delia sighed, but Sara was not unhappy. She spoke with James several times a week, brief friendly calls she did not mention to her sisters. Nor did she disclose that after her move, she and James began to take Saturday walks while Josie visited her sister Liz. James did not mention the walks either; nor did he take walks alone with Katy or Delia. The walks seemed a delicate if ordinary thing; she did not want them ruined.

First they walked on the North Shore beaches, in September, when the weather was still mild and the clarity of the light had increased, even as the days began to shorten, the cold mornings giving way to warm days that chilled fast at dusk. The brightest afternoons the coastal sea turned cerulean or royal blue, deepening with violet or green when the clouds arrived; the beaches were mostly empty but for walkers in their jeans and sweatshirts.

At times Sara imagined Nora preceding or trailing them, a kind of shadow; at times simultaneously walking beaches miles south. Once Nora and James had walked alone together. Did anything of those walks echo in Sara's walks with James? As the leaves turned, she and James chose inland parks, followed wooded paths, visited Walden Pond and nearby conservation land. Invariably relaxed, those days. James knew local history, the sites of shipwrecks, the names of birds. On rainy days they picked historic towns and window-shopped, chose good restaurants, or strolled with umbrellas near the Beverly house and drank tea. By late fall they developed conversational shorthand, the habit of exchanging small gifts: mint from the yard, a waterproof compass, a chocolate bar, an archaic map. A strange happiness came upon her in anticipation of seeing him and when she heard his voice, and when she caught sight of him.

For months, they did not talk about love. Not about her failed relationships or his divorce from Nora, or even his happiness with Josie. In careful language, they spoke of her siblings' lives, simultaneously transparent and opaque to her. At times, James reminisced about his uncle Paul, who knew the South Shore beaches and the salt marshes, the birds and constellations and the shipwrecks offshore. Occasionally he mentioned his own early life, navigating his teenage years by walking the city of Boston when he did not want to go home, and taking beach walks in Blue Rock, until the walking instilled a kind of surety in him and his despair dropped away. As if the repeated steps asserted that there was solid earth and he would not fall off; that by walking your body learned the place, and your mind had the chance to catch up.

On the first mild Saturday in April, when they walked on Crane Beach, Sara and James noted seasonal shifts in the coastline: they talked about maps; they talked about latitude. They were just north of the forty-second parallel. The beach curved, it seemed, beyond the horizon. A few other walkers passed. Fat gulls approached and flew off; whitecaps appeared and melted into approaching waves. In Rome, James told her, once the EMTs had stopped trying to revive Molly, he'd felt a slight weight on his shoulder, as if her death were pressing down. Only when the ambulance arrived at the hospital did he realize it was the hand of the EMT, steadying him.

She did not tell Delia of this conversation, though for years she and Delia had shared information about Molly. With regard to James, Sara remained evasive. When she found herself in the larger family company, the easy rapport between her and James drew quick glances from Delia, lingering ones from Katy. As if it were a kind of affair, transparent to Josie but partly veiled from everyone else. Sara could see that Katy's version of James differed from Delia's and of course from Nora's, but she didn't always recognize those other versions. Who were her sisters thinking of? This James, the present walking James, was not a man she remembered from childhood. Maybe this James had something of the James Nora married, the hopeful one. Or now that he'd aged, more of his uncle Paul. Or maybe he was like the wandering James, the one who found solace at the shore, the one who knew, too young, what it meant to miss a father.

AFTER II

Often, Nora dreamed of her own mother as she appeared in the apartment in Somerville—without lipstick or jewelry, hair loosely clipped back, singing—what was she singing? She opened and restitched seams, let out a waistline, shortened a hem. In the living room a woman on a step stool held still, while Nora's mother pinned her dress. Another day, a coffee shop, Nora's mother in a corner booth leaning over a table to hear news—lipstick now, but also concern. The images were fast clips, not the elaborate stories Nora sometimes dreamed. Her mother crossed a city park. There was rain. Or there was no rain, but she'd disappeared into a crowd. She was in a movie theater, waiting for the lights to dim. Places she had appeared in life; places she had not. As she'd been in her forties, vivid, in her knee-length dresses with delicate prints, her brown eyes limpid; chatting or singing; and as she'd been in her fifties, in pink-framed glasses, still chatting but pale. There were spools of thread to sort; spools rolled from the table onto the kitchen floor. She was in her pearl-buttoned green cardigan; she needed hot tea; she needed a blanket.

In waking hours, Nora found herself addressing her mother, *What do you think?* a quick, habitual glance upward. Posing the question as if her mother were alive, or now Meg, or some alternate version of Nora herself; glancing as if the sky listened.

Late middle age. Perhaps her mother too had felt herself becoming more singular, marriage or no marriage—she must have, but at what point did she recognize her inherent separateness, its existential certainty? During her illness or before? Nora's own life now seemed distinct from her children—and more completely hers—in ways both stark and unforeseen. She felt, if anything, condensed, possessed of a clean practicality untempered by marriage or youth. After the girls had left for college, she'd cultivated both solitude and social worlds apart from the family. When she could, she studied art. She walked, always, as she had in Blue Rock, but now in other preserves, on other beaches, sometimes with friends who carried pocket sketchbooks, reference guides, binoculars. She carried her own. The naturalists knew her first as a Nora of favorite haunts and walking habits, with a gift for botanical illustration; a Nora independent of any other Murphy, or Connor, or neighborhood history. As she preferred.

Her girls wanted more of her. She visited, she helped them, but in their voices she still detected the mixed note of longing and dismay. Perhaps they wanted childhood, or a different childhood; or that she shape her life around theirs, even now. She could not say. Theo's expectations—from California or elsewhere—were usually minimal, though he claimed full attention during visits. Every week, she spent time with the family: Tuesday dinners and weekend visits with Katy's kids, or Delia's, and Katy and Delia themselves, the sons-in-law; dinners with Sara. The grandkids seemed to view her lovingly, ignoring the sharp boundaries she recognized in herself. She doted on them, then retreated. She had more time now, and less. She tired more easily; with effort, she saved the better hours for herself. She trusted her children to be the adults they were. Sometimes she'd take a weekend away in Maine, or Vermont, or the Cape. She might remember to tell Delia or Sara how to reach her; she might forget, and they'd leave messages until she remembered to check voice mail, eventually returning their calls.

So often Nora wished to speak with her living mother. However implausibly, the world had spun for decades without her, without Nora's father, without Molly. And for a time, their deaths defined the vast realm she recognized as *death*, news of other losses drifting at a remove, strangely hollow and peripheral. Yet now, again, illness riddled the nearer landscapes. Friends. The world as one knows it is only the world of a moment, isn't it? Then there is another moment, another world. Though you could be lulled—and repeatedly—into thinking otherwise, or imagining that a moment sustained in happiness was in fact the singular authentic world—the world compared to which all others seem false. Maybe the life in which you strolled through Cambridge with an infant boy; or a June predawn hour when you made love with your husband; or an afternoon tea with your middle-aged mother; a bakery trip with your young whistling father. Or, later, an evening with your friends on their deck, by the sea. Say each bond is composed of moments compressed into words. So the hours on the deck and the wine disappear, but these new words exist—and the years of words accumulate, and the language steadies you, and then your friend dies, and you are the lone speaker of that language. Over time, you remain the lone speaker of how many languages? It happened to everyone. How to prepare? Or for one's own disappearance?

What had Nora's mother done? *What do you think?* When Nora's mother began to confront these moments, Nora had been in high school, then college, busy falling in love with James, busy with a baby. Toward the end her mother was weary, the liveliness sapped, Nora determined to cheer her up. Offering visits with a tiny Theo, delivering flowers, telling jokes. Vital small pleasures, but had Nora listened enough? It seemed she had not. *What do you think*—about any of it? Nora hardly asked. She'd tried desperately to entertain. And how could she go back now—this late—to listen? Who ever caught up with the past? How necessary. Yet *back* was only in the mind: *now* was what she had.

HOUSE VII

For all of the Murphys, the house's shifting manifestations would blur, stray details and perceptions surfacing without context, others forgotten. The last photos, some of which captured the house, had disappeared with the house itself, though older ones survived in James's file box and in albums owned by the Murphy cousins—black-and-whites, square white-bordered snapshots in colors faded or skewed yellow. A few objects had survived with James or Theo: the clock that had belonged to James's father, cereal bowls and mugs Nora had given to Theo; two of Nora's small paintings and a handful of her sketches, which Theo had taken west.

Proportions would slip. For Sara and Delia, *home* had first and always meant the shoreline, the odd birdhouse silhouette, the wind, the radically altering sky, and at times their memories of the house seemed tied to language, to apprehending the world itself. *Banister* would first bring to mind the sealed wood along the stairs rising to the deck, and the polished, nicked one inside—the foundation of every other reference to banisters.

And too, Sara would remember the house at night, the way the dark transformed the spaces. Rooms melted into the air beyond windows, furniture into walls. In the deepest dark she rarely stumbled, her bare feet against the brushed carpet, the cool linoleum and smooth wood floors, the pinpricks of sand. Later, in other houses, she might close her eyes and walk barefoot across similar floors, and for an instant the night house might flicker.

In Katy's memory the rooms seemed larger than their true dimensions, an expansiveness she could not explain; her later views of the house seemed plucked from summers when she first dated Tim. She tended to forget the tensions with her sisters, or the atmosphere toward the end of her parents' marriage. Nor would she contemplate what becomes of an atmosphere held within a house—the precisely charged air—when the house is gone; if the atmosphere might remain at the houseless site; or move, intact, to an unrelated place; or dispel. Still, before the new owners built on the site, she too had returned, walked the perimeter, studied the seawall, the remaining foundation. There had been for her a flat emptiness. She too had searched without success for familiar objects, something tamped beneath clotted silt or wedged in the nearby rocks. Most of the debris had been swept out to sea or down the road toward the pond; the town and local contractors had combed the property. A tablespoon, a bracelet might have been swept into the murky pond, but it was easier to find a duplicate at a flea market. Yet what she wanted wasn't the spoon; rather the house reconstructed around the spoon. A house reconstructed to match surviving keys. Still, after a year, when Katy and Tim moved into the redbrick, she fixed her attention on its interiors, which gradually supplanted Blue Rock's.

When the Murphys were together, conversation about the house retained a surface lightness, as if it had always been a summer holiday retreat; or as if the winter storms had been comic adventures recounted over cocoa, the wind a character from a children's book. Rarely did they mention the failing structure or deferred repairs, except to joke about Nora's improvisations—the white fisherman's rope along the outer stairs by which Sara and Delia identified their house to arriving visitors; a yellow bucket briefly hung from the leaking bedroom ceiling, like an art installation or a sloshing bell. Theo tended to talk about his running routes, which did not involve the house at all, or his shelves of books, most of which left with him, or moments with Sara and Delia when they were infants. Like Sara, he recalled in detail the art that Nora hung, and the photographs, the postcards taped to the refrigerator. If he dreamed of the house, he didn't say; just as he rarely spoke of Newton or of any early memory of Cambridge, or of Italy. Perhaps California had supplanted them all; perhaps they were sealed into a geologically separate past.

For Nora the house remained nearly present; the feeling of the house returning to her often, like a scent, or the dreams of her dead parents and of Molly, images blown into the current moment like confetti. For her too, the house would shape-shift but never beyond recognition. Normal, now, to carry so vivid a sense of the place, she might travel there, if not for a weak prohibiting memory of its demise. More often the worlds she carried in her mind lacked physical analogs, or survived as artifacts. If she met old acquaintances or strangers who shared drifting bits of the past, she felt surprising kinship. With Meg or Somerville families who'd known her parents, she expected such moments. So too when she encountered a girlhood friend of Katy's, or a host from a long-ago party, or a neighbor from Newton who'd known Molly: the past sparked brightly for an instant. She could not explain this fleeting return or the subsequent longing any more than the undeniable attritions. She missed the house and yet something persisted; she was relieved for the solitude of later apartments, preferred to walk beaches elsewhere. She imagined Blue Rock, or what Blue Rock implied, as a kind of true north as she traveled in other directions.

For James there was the memory-house of his uncle, and the house he and Nora renovated, though they often merged: in the cousins' sleeping room, light fell through the white sheers Nora hung years later. Some details slid and some remained static: the blue sofa was always backed by windows to a cerulean sea, a clear midday sky, the unchanging weather of vacation photos. He imagined meals with Sara and Delia not at the oak table he and Nora bought, but at Aunt Brenda's, topped in white-and-black enamel. Neighbors from Newton sometimes showed up as neighbors from Blue Rock before finding their proper place.

When he was working, stray images arose during his commute, as they had earlier in his life; later, when his heart trouble began and he stayed home to rest, he missed the house, summoned views from the deck and from the windows. At times his reading concentration waned; he grew impatient with his sluggishness, stunned by the ways his body had betrayed him. As if his body were for the first time separate from his conscious mind and his will, and now defying him. But you waited while the body languished or healed, accepted small pleasures—a pear, returning daffodils, radio jazz. Old images surfaced, collected shortcomings exposed, as if one room in the mind after another had flung its doors open. Perhaps a summer moment with Molly at Blue Rock, her blankets and stuffed toys a pale pink smear beneath a bright window, or a window beyond which the sky had turned indigo and Molly herself stood drinking water from a cup. Though he could also conjure Sara dragging a pink blanket, a tiny Delia standing at a window.

Always the house in its earliest forms remained clearest to him, along with the varying skies: pink dawn reflected on the bay, dense clustered stars or the thick cloud cover and bracing wind. Difficult, but not impossible to push away the most troubled notes: the saddest Blue Rock might still revert to a distant point in a larger landscape, the size of a freckle, a leaf bud, a wren's surveying eye.

REPRODUCTION

Interior with Pink Wallpaper I, plate five
Edouard Vuillard (1899)
ART INSTITUTE OF CHICAGO

She's tucked toward the back, the blue-clad woman in a small arched doorway, a slice of blue room receding behind her—but here is the room you want, fifteen-foot ceilings and pink-and-red wallpaper—think of falling cherries, falling rosebuds—a shell-pink ceiling, tiered chandelier. One side table, a small lamp. Traces of blue echo through the room, but the point is the open space—how it holds the light—the sea of pink, the vivid red drops. A room in which you can breathe. Say you choose this room to replace the missing rooms: why not? A room you might enter in place of a bedroom now gone and untraceable. Look: such lovely high ceilings. If you might step into this chosen elsewhere? Say you could keep these colors, this bright air, the perpetually falling roses.

Perhaps there's space on the table for sea glass. Something from a former house, resurfacing on the nearby beach, a smoothed bottleneck or broken tumbler, washed out in the storm. Any bit of glass might once have been yours. A shard from a blue bowl, the shade of the woman's dress, once kept on a chest of drawers. Fragments like it wash up wherever currents run. Still, how is it that objects you thought lasting are ephemera? Fragile as origami.

Rooms disappear. But might they appear again? What if, like the salon of Vuillard's *Waiting*, this *Interior*—the woman standing in a doorway, the pink walls blooming with roses— nonetheless awaits you? At least in the mind.

STOPPING MAN

You might choose some of the rooms you occupy, but how many? They appear; you walk through them; they disappear, soon or eventually. The strangest ones you rarely choose—say, a motel room near a donut shop. Or the hospital waiting room where Sara found herself with Josie after her father's heart attack. From the beige-and-white corridor, she left phone messages for Katy and Delia, Theo, Nora. Light fell in pale blocks onto the linoleum; Josie paced; they found two reading chairs, passed a crossword back and forth. From green cans, they drank ginger ale.

Sara had been on a bus, en route to the pool. Beside her, a girl read a book with a sexy vampire on the cover. A preschool-age boy kicked the seat ahead of him; his mother asked, "Are you a goat?" Josie called; Sara found the T. She arrived at the waiting room with her swim gear. Already he was in surgery.

She did not ask Josie, *Are you sure?* though it seemed germane; on Saturday, Sara and James had visited farm stands together. She'd bought apples: in her gym bag now, she carried one of them. He'd looked good; or she'd thought he looked good. She'd asked him—as she often asked him—*How are you?*

His energy? His routine tests? Their walks had shortened; of late she'd been meeting him for lunch and a harborside stroll, or at his house with Josie. But there seemed no route from A to B: Saturday, a visit to farm stands. Tuesday a heart attack, bypass surgery.

Tuesday. Josie offered few details: what was Tuesday? Less energy that morning? An impulse to stay home? Discomfort in his arm? And on the road? His chest? His breathing? He pulled over. He was alone in the car; he fussed with his phone, reached a hand out the window toward the passing traffic. A man stopped.

Crucial, that stopping man.

Tuesday: Her father waved. The man stopped. An ambulance arrived.

Now she and Josie waited. Katy appeared. Delia appeared. With or without them, Sara found herself caught in the elision between now and *always*. Monday evening she'd spoken to James by phone—no one could deny Monday evening. Surely a speaking breathing father was lasting proof of a speaking breathing father.

Later, in the ICU, James's legs were made vulnerable by, it seemed, the hospital gown. They'd lost muscle tone, appeared in that ICU to be partly bleached, miniature landscapes of scars and spots, burst capillaries and heavy blue veins. Diminished overnight? Sara had paid attention; she'd thought she'd paid attention. For years, he'd worn the same sort of khaki trousers. But she'd seen his legs, hadn't she? When had she last seen his legs?

The ICU. The hospital's parallel insomniac universe: his room, nurses' station, cafeteria, waiting room, a slow addled relay with her family. Say you've fallen into that world: there will be blankets. Hot and cool liquids, bells, screens—occasional TVs. Other families, also blinking and in limbo. What happened to Saturday? If you took the right elevator, could you find it again? *Let's get out of here*—but what might it mean to leave? No one can tell you. No one knows. Perhaps after a stranger has coded, you think, *Let's please stay indefinitely. May we move to a general-care floor; may I drink this bad coffee forever.*

ROMAN STREETS

One narrow street appears to be another: Rome will never be the Murphys' city. Or, rather, only their city of disorientation, the realm in which they are lost. The specialty market's grappa display is nowhere near the English bookshop; gelateria signs—a chain—appear as if by mistake. Here is a bridge; the river curves; a fresh start, another maze. Might the map conform to someone else's city? Perhaps it is a map of Madrid. Too soon fatigue sets in. Say the Murphys wander alone, apart from each other, unknowingly retracing each other's routes. At noon one rests at Campo di Fiore; another leans against the Pantheon. One crosses the Ponte Mazzini, another Ponte Sisto. Approach and they melt into the tourist crowds, emerging at intersections where the vendors hawking scarves ignore them. The hotel rooms are empty; they have not found the hotel. Perhaps they have stopped looking. Perhaps the object of the search has changed; perhaps it has changed again. In the evening lights float along the Tiber—lights and the reflections of lights—like unnameable dreams. Are they here? From the bridges and riverbanks, one Murphy then another peering out?

BLUE SUIT

In the middle of the wake, the Murphys adjourned for lunch. Appearing—as they had at other moments—an ordinary middle-class family, if extended now, asymmetrical, still handsome and poised. Well dressed, as if for a performance? They took up two tables at the restaurant—white cloth napkins, chrysanthemums—a self-possessed Nora settled with the kids at one end. Even Josie appeared normal. Or especially? Sara ordered like a normal woman. Should she—should any of them—have appeared sadder? Yet this was one thing they felt sure of: how to order lunch. For an hour the world became, again, knowable. Soup or no soup? Bread or no bread? (Yes for Theo, now distance running; no for Katy, on a diet; others equivocal.) A small bubble of time within the larger bubble into which they'd tumbled. They drank tea and coffee and milk and juice: they ate.

Then they returned to the funeral parlor. James was still there, waiting, it seemed—his physical presence, the fact that he hadn't *left*, an unexpected relief. He'd been laid out in a midnight-blue suit and silk tie, his eyes closed—as they might be, Sara thought, on a commuter train. The mild surprise that he did not sit or speak repeated itself; nonetheless here was a family gathering—the cluster of chairs occupied by Murphys—and here was James.

Like the other Murphys, she had begun to adapt to her father's appearance—the stubbornly closed eyes, the distinguished suit, the mistake of the casket. He had, at least, appeared. The trouble—as Sara came to call it—materialized when the wake ended and she could no longer see him. As if all events until then—the ICU with its bleating machines, the calls, the arrangements—had been edgy, eccentric theater. Then for her his body—James himself—became purely conceptual. The terms flipped; an air lock broke; the world emptied. And then a kind of numbing? James had been so very still, then gone, and Sara numb—should it surprise?—in Sara's zombie-mourner state, a little confusion about who was dead? (And why would burial seem a mutual abandonment?)

What could she say to the others? *Are you a little dead? This arrangement seems criminal.* Worth trying Delia, if she could find more palatable language. Delia, she knew, would make an effort, if only to keep Sara company. But it seemed that for each of them, a different James had died. After the burial, Josie and Theo visited with Murphy cousins; Delia collected her kids; Tim and Katy ferried out-of-town relatives to yet another dinner; Nora withdrew. Like Katy and Theo, Nora seemed both present and elsewhere—had the balance just tipped to elsewhere? More likely they'd remained the same. *Are you a little dead?* Sara herself was obtuse. For an extended moment, her father had been present. Then the moment ended. Now his absence seemed to collide with a shifting unnamed vacancy she'd thought she'd outgrown.

Calm days, at first, following the funeral—say it was the calm of shock. Or of distraction: Theo in town, staying with Nora, smaller gatherings with Murphy cousins. Every day Sara spoke to Delia and Katy; almost as often she talked with Josie, twice met her for dinner. Then daily life resumed; it always resumes, whether one is ready or not.

The chronic insomnia recurred. Whenever she could, Sara slept. On Saturdays, she began walking again, revisiting places she'd gone with James. As if she were waiting. As if he would call; as if he would appear in Concord, or in Marblehead. During the week, Cambridge seemed to imitate the Cambridge she lived in; normal routines seemed like imitation life.

And there were dreams, with and without James, often of the house. A dream, say, of opening a door to discover she's found the Blue Rock kitchen, Nora pouring tea, Delia lacing running shoes, Katy sifting mail. She walks upstairs alone and finds the hall is full of animals. A huge tabby sprawls in the bathtub. An enormous dog, heavily muscled, fur a bristly white, naps halfway down the hall to Nora's room. Sara's room is as she left it, but now the dog's awake, growling and barking beyond the door frame. She shuts the door, but it's badly cut, off by several inches, and the dog shoves his snout and one heavy paw underneath. At some point she is sweating and shouting. No one intervenes. At some point she wakes up.

Or the dream in which her voice mail has filled with messages: they must be from her father. But he can hardly speak. She hears only thick syllables—is that him? He sounds awful—then obscure pop songs spliced together. It's a code, isn't it? He's played the songs because he can't speak. But the puzzle's too difficult, she's not clever enough—she keeps trying, going back to the sad thick syllables, the quoted pop songs, discerning less and less.

And over those strange weeks, yet more insomnia: it seemed as if a kind of chasm had opened, and with it the confusion of absences she could not unmix. She tried to reach Nora, who texted back *Sending love. Let's talk soon.* So often Sara couldn't find her—it was terrible not to find her. Where had she gone? (Could she be lost?) And James was gone—dead—but what did that mean? Last seen in a midnight-blue suit; last seen unspeaking. The box in the ground explained nothing. Body, suit, box: more sleight of hand, more theater. James was a person: a person had to be somewhere.

ROME

La dama con liocorno
Raffaello Sanzio da Urbino (1506)
GALLERIA BORGHESE

Try to look away: how long before you're drawn back? The dama's young, maybe sixteen, eyes the aquamarine of an island sea yet the gaze grave, unflinching. Raphael painted her seated on a veranda: beyond her, an aqua sky, aqua brushstrokes suggesting trees along the low horizon. Set against all that blue, the amber and burgundy of her variegated skirt, her light amber bodice, the burgundy sleeves almost wide enough to be wings. Red tones echo in her hair, her ruby-and-pearl necklace. In the galleries, is there anyone else like her? So you take a moment to register that her tawny lapdog is not a dog at all, but a miniature unicorn—the small face equine, delicate horn tightly curled, the size of a fountain pen. Its dark liquid eyes focus in the distance, well beyond the gallery space.

Stand before her long enough and something in the mind begins to shimmer. The dama appears as alive as the soft-bellied guard pacing the museum. Here's another elision, one more liminal point: a hair's breadth of distance divides you from her. How vivid this girl, how mesmerizing her blue gaze, defying judgment. Perhaps she defends the unicorn. Perhaps she defends the unicorn's reality.

She is not at all dead. She is herself; she is covertly Raphael. And for the briefest instant it seems to you that she is *here*, nearly able to step from the canvas; not only visible but also conscious. As if in fact you see each other. In that moment, she might be as real as you are; or you as fierce and lucid as she.

ROME III

It occurred to Sara once, and then again—in that storm of other thoughts—that if she were her father, and dead, she would go to Rome.

And so she left from Logan, first to the crush of Heathrow, then to Rome on an early morning flight. She stepped from the plane onto walking ramps and into corridors empty of anyone but fellow passengers, and it seemed as if they were backstage, or as if bleariness veiled them from the city. But passengers from other flights began to appear near passport control, and then the space thickened irreversibly, the silence and murmurs now Italian silences and murmurs, and near her German and Dutch and Hindi. She was a kind of sleepwalker, moving through fragmenting and re-forming crowds, alert to the pressing details— baggage, euros, exit, taxi—while the voices and light, soon the morning light in Rome—seemed to wash over her. The taxi sped inches from the adjacent speeding cars, passing through what became for her the *first* Rome, highway giving way to utilitarian boulevards and ordinary modern streets, working neighborhoods and billboards for auto repair and cosmetics, graffitied concrete walls of apartment buildings, laundry lines on stacked balconies,

a Rome insisting on the present. Almost resisting the imposi-
tions of history—or, at least, the history Sara might impose. And
once the taxi reached the Centro Storico, that resistance gave
way to what seemed a ubiquitous past composed of countless
discrete pasts, tilting toward the light or stacked in shadow, exca-
vated or hidden, the present still elbowing in, the present spinning in the crowds and markets, the Vespas and Fiats vying for
lane space, the rush-hour buses, the street vendors selling scarves
at tourist sites, selling roses. And in the café beside the hotel, a
quieting and narrowing of focus: the immediacy of a cappuccino
and a biscotti, the barista's conversation, mellifluous and to Sara
incomprehensible. She slept for a day in a small hotel near Piazza
Navona, then began walking.

Say she was following a thread, or what she imagined to be a
thread, that might lead to James, or to Molly. To Nora, to Theo
and Katy as they once had been. Say she tried to apprehend the
contours of before and after, and what else they'd left behind.
Say that, in seeing what they'd seen, she might name what had
eluded her.

And yes, it seems possible to suspend the present, but only
for a moment; just as one might ignore the past—for a moment—without consequence. Off-season yet the streets buzzing
with ordinary urban life, the rush-hour crowds and students and
city workers, and the peppering of classical guitarists on bridges
and in piazzas, and the clusters of vacationing families in the
Piazza del Popolo; couples on holiday along the Tiber, American
students in Trastevere bars. Cafés and more cafés, flower vendors
hawking the long-stem roses so aggressively that couples pay
them to go away. The Pantheon fills with tourists crowding in

to photograph Raphael's sarcophagus; on the floor of San Luigi dei Francesi, an engraved stone marking a French child's burial. Outside this church, then the next, begging women, one with small children, another with a teenage girl. Dome after gilded, muraled dome, as if the heavens in fact are here, and outside the church the mirroring brilliant daylight, perhaps in confirmation. At the gelato shop off Campo de'Fiori a well-heeled family of five, a boy and two small girls: in a church in Trastevere, an Irish-looking blonde and two girls strolling.

Even now, in those rare retellings of the Murphys' trip to Rome, no one ever names the church, the street, the hotel. Perhaps would not. It's possible Katy and Theo do not remember; maybe after time Nora and James forgot; or maybe they imagined that by naming the place they would reify the tragedy. And so, yes, any church might be the church, any busy street the street. To ask—*this one?*—is to imagine Molly running. James and Theo wave, Nora palms an orange, Molly lets go of Katy's hand. Here? The immediate disastrous consequence. And isn't Sara, much later, another consequence? Of course for Rome, their story—and hers—is the size of a dust mote. There are so many lives, so much talk, so much other humming above the dense silence.

Picture them, the young Murphys. Nothing has happened yet. They've been sleeping off jet lag; say they linger at the hotel. If they do not explore Rome, and Molly averts her disastrous run, the years ahead promise some ease. It's unlikely, Sara thinks, that she herself will appear: they seem complete without her (though not, it seems, without Delia. She can't say why). They are at breakfast, drinking coffee and hot chocolate. It's not yet too late.

What to say to Molly? She is still only four. Sara would like to tell her, *Wait. Hold on to Katy's hand. Live.* But if she lives, will Sara? If Sara is predicated on Molly's run, how can Sara stop her? Given a chance, how could she not? Molly must not run. Sara must not vanish. If Sara could? She'd say, *Let's get out of here.*

Again and again on these days walking Rome, searching out the family for whom she did not exist, she has felt a pull toward the stone of the streets and benches, the bits of dirty grass, an impulse to lie flat and gaze at a sky alternately gray and Della Robbia blue, or a patchwork of both, or rimmed with orange. No one mentioned rain; she has not imagined rain, but it might have been raining that day too. She has only the church, the girl running, the truck, the quick erasure, the subsequent repeating loops. The impulse to see and resee.

The Murphys in Rome? They left decades ago. Say they are like memories of a house that exists only in the mind. Is it ever exactly the same house? And if it could exist untroubled? Or if the corollary exile might end?

Nora once kept a tiny print of Raphael's *Dama con liocorno* in a shoe box, the image cut from a magazine. Perhaps she saw the painting here: a skeptical girl with limpid sea-colored eyes and the perfectly rendered unicorn in her lap. A girl five hundred years older than Molly, and in the viewing moment, almost as real. In that moment, more seems possible, doesn't it?

Why not imagine that after all, with what remains, you can continue? Imagine that although James is dead, and Molly is dead, you are not. Say that, beneath this sky, in this or any city, you do not fall. You do not fall. You walk.

ACKNOWLEDGEMENTS

My profound thanks for the remarkable support, generosity, and insight of Gail Hochman; to Meg Storey for her lucid, intelligent editorial eye and dedication to this novel; and to Carin Clevidence, for her tireless manuscript readings, spot-on critiques, and sustaining friendship. Big thanks to Heather Sellers, to Rick Hilles, and to Rachel Teukolsky and Peter Guralnick for their thoughtful manuscript readings, conversations, support, and faith in the work. I'm happily indebted to Liss Platt, Claudia Manley, Mercedes Cebrián, Dave King, and Jenny Humphreys for their insights into art-making, writing, and the city of Rome; to Sarah Van Arsdale, Elaine Sexton, Robin Messing, Raymond Johnson, Natalie Baszile, Susan Choi, Melissa Zieve, Allison Norton, and Jeff Norton for their friendships, insights, and encouragement. Thanks to the Vanderbilt English Department, to my colleagues Kate Daniels, Mark Jarman, Lorraine Lopez, Tony Earley, Justin Quarry, Janis May, Margaret Quigley, Jen Holt, Mark Schoenfield, and Vereen Bell, whose kindness and support have made all the difference; and to Vanderbilt's MFA and undergraduate writers, whose openness, inventiveness, and generosity continue to teach me.

I wrote *Trompe l'Oeil* over time with the great good luck of residencies at the American Academy in Rome, Blue Mountain Center, the Brecht House, the MacDowell Colony, the Ragdale Foundation, Virginia Center for the Creative Arts, and The Corporation of Yaddo; and with support from the Tennessee Commission for the Arts and from Vanderbilt University. Many thanks to all. Abiding gratitude, always, to my husband Rick Hilles, and to my Buffalo family: David Reisman, Sofia Reisman, and Betsy Abramson, Linda Reisman and Jack Reisman, Jeanne Reisman, Len Goldschmidt, and Deborah Goldschmidt, Janet Gross, Lo Wunder, and Sue Cooperman, Judy and Len Katz, Mort and Natalie Abramson, Jill Polk, Isabella Polk, Lorinda Tennyson, and Wendy Teplitsky. My gratitude beyond words to Rena and Robert Reisman.